U0092781

實用商業美語
——實況模擬
Vol. I. —基礎篇—

杉田敏　著　　張錦源　校譯

三民書局　印行

國家圖書館出版品預行編目資料

實用商業美語 I ——實況模擬／杉田敏著，張錦源校譯．--初版．--臺北市：三民，民86

面；　公分

ISBN 957-14-2580-X（平裝）

1.英國語言-讀本

805.18　　　86003301

網際網路位址　http://www.sanmin.com.tw

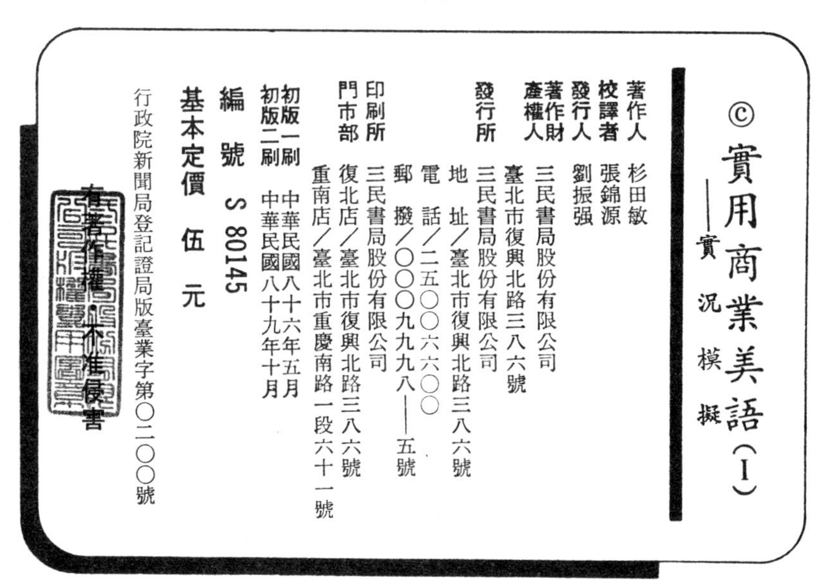

© 實用商業美語（I）——實況模擬

著作人　杉田敏
校譯者　張錦源
發行人　劉振强
著作財產權人　三民書局股份有限公司
臺北市復興北路三八六號
發行所　三民書局股份有限公司
地址／臺北市復興北路三八六號
電話／二五〇〇六六〇〇
郵撥／〇〇九九九八——五號
印刷所　三民書局股份有限公司
門市部　復北店／臺北市復興北路三八六號
重南店／臺北市重慶南路一段六十一號
初版一刷　中華民國八十六年五月
初版二刷　中華民國八十九年十月
編號　S 80145
基本定價　伍　元
行政院新聞局登記證局版臺業字第〇二〇〇號

ISBN 957-14-2580-X（第一册：平裝）

Original Japanese language edition published by NHK Publishing (Japan Broadcast Publishing Co.,Ltd.), Tokyo

序

學習語言固然會有個人適應上的問題，但可以斷言的是，若沒有學習動機，是絕對學不好的。

1987年4月，NHK電臺第二廣播網的「簡易商用英語」節目開播時，我曾引用過George Bernard Shaw所說的一句話，“If you teach a man anything, he will never learn.”意思就是說，學習的過程是積極自主的，別人勉強不來，也強教不來，大半要靠自我努力。

英文若學習到某一個程度，就不再往前了，那麼以後很有可能會再回到原來的程度。所以，雖然好不容易才有了些進步，但若不能持之以恆，繼續求進步的話，那也是枉然。

在戲劇界也有人說，有些演員會在某一天突然變得很會演戲。這是由於他日復一日地努力，加上某天受到了一些衝擊，因而大大地得到啟發，瞭解箇中三昧。然而有許多人雖然也是孜孜不倦地在做事，但在這些衝擊尚未臨到之前，就舉手投降了，這實在是很可惜。

「學好英文的訣竅在於努力」，像這類的話聽起來雖然有老生常談之嫌，但也請各位記住，語言的學習是沒有「捷徑」的；而首要問題就是要產生興趣、激發動機。其次，就是要能大膽地使用英語，不要怕丟臉。依我的經驗，丟臉的次數與進步曲線之間是大有關聯的。

從1987年4月起，至1991年9月止，在「簡易商用英語」節目中播出的「澤崎昭一系列」可說是頗受好評。本系列書籍的一至三冊即是從這一百集的課程中挑選出四十五個故事，再加以潤飾而成。若能對諸位在學習上造成若干衝擊，實屬萬幸。

杉田　敏

本書的使用方法

要想用英語跟老外「暢所欲言」並不容易。即使你買了幾本會話書籍，且一字不漏地背誦下來，但你接下來卻會面臨到無法「照本宣科」的問題，因你無法掌握實際談話內容。在本書中，會有各種狀況的模擬，告訴你要如何在不同的情境中與人展開對話。本書更以商場上的實際對話為例，引導讀者去思索學習會話之道。

預習

先仔細閱讀「課文內容」，並將概要記住。若要使用另售的錄音帶，則一開始盡量不要看課本，試著用耳朵專注地聽。Sentences 是故事中所使用句子的採樣，這也是大腦的暖身操。

課文・翻譯

試著於閱讀完「狀況」之後，在心中描摹該場景。若是配合錄音帶使用，則先不要看劇情內容。嘗試用耳朵聽。如果覺得會話速度太快而無法理解，千萬不要立刻放棄，可以多聽幾次。

字彙

基本上，只要有初步的字彙能力，便足以應付大部分的商務英語會話了。但若自己需要遊走多國，則應該要背誦基本商務用語的廣義解釋及其正確發音。在 Vocabulary Building 中則藉由例句來學習活用法。並請讀者參考本書末了的單字表。

習題

在不改變句子原意的前提下，使用括弧中的字加以改寫，練習另造新句。

簡短對話

與內文的說法和談話進行方向不同的對話。

重點文法・語法

研討口語中的文法和語法，以及一些學校不太教授的會話說法。

總結

會話應盡量具有實用性，且能反映國際商業環境。所以每一課在總結的地方都會有異國文化的應對之道、社會語言學知識以及各種重要的商業情報。

CONTENTS

《實用商業美語》Vol.II，III的內容

Vol. II

Vol. III

PROFILE

～故事中出現的主要人物～

●Shoichi Sawasaki／澤崎昭一（36歲）

由日系的食品公司轉任外商 ABC 食品公司的行銷經理。他是本書的主角，以天生的積極與幽默，適應新的企業環境。

●Tom Noonan／湯姆·諾南（55歲）

昭一的直屬上司，營業部門的常務董事，因接受公司方面提出希望其提早退休的條件而決定提前退休。

●Nancy Yamamoto／南西·山本（25歲）

昭一的祕書。在美國出生受教育的第三代日裔女性，在公司內亦頗獲信賴。

●Makato(Mike) Yamaguchi／山口誠（通稱麥可）（38歲）

ABC 食品公司營業部的經理，在公司已有十五年的資歷。雖很能幹，但總給人狡猾的感覺。

●Juergen Schumann／優根·舒曼（40歲）

從法蘭克福到東京上任的財務部經理。德國人，具有耿直、踏實的性格。

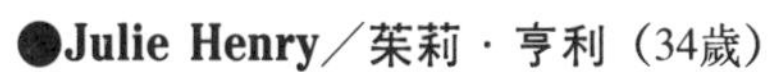

●Julie Henry／茱莉·亨利（34歲）

湯姆·諾南的接替者，昭一的新上司。她擁有日本現代史的博士學位，是個才貌兼備的現代女性。性格外向，善於交際。

Lesson 1

First Day on the Job

（上班的第一天）

Lesson 1 的內容

今天是澤崎到新職場工作的第一天。到新公司上班的第一天、第一個禮拜，總是不安和期待參半，而且也會緊張個不停。雖然澤崎對行銷很有自信，但是面對新公司、新同事、新責任，這是一項很大的精神負擔，使人覺得喘不過氣來。這時候，對新進人員而言，最高興的莫過於受到親切的「照顧」。而諾南則希望能讓有前途的新進人員感覺到「受照顧」。現在就讓我們來讀一讀諾南和澤崎的對話吧！

Lesson 1

First Day on the Job (1) （上班的第一天）

預習—*Sentences*

· I'm delighted to be working here.
· We're so happy to have you with us.
· Call me Tom, will you?
· Don't worry.
· You seem nervous.

Vignette

Noonan: Welcome aboard, Shoichi.

Sawasaki: Thank you. I'm delighted to be working here, Mr. Noonan.

Noonan: You were the perfect man for the job and we're so happy to have you with us. By the way, call me Tom, will you?

Sawasaki: I feel a bit awkward calling you by your first name. It sounds, what shall I say, disrespectful.

Noonan: Don't worry. Everybody in this company all the way up and down the line is called by their first name. OK?

Sawasaki: I'll try.

Noonan: Good. Oh, but in the presence of outsiders in formal business situations, it may be good manners to address your higher-ups as Mr., Ms., or whatever is appropriate. Understand?

Sawasaki: Yes, sir.

Noonan: [*Laughing*] And don't "sir" me either. You seem nervous.

Sawasaki: Well, I do have butterflies.

Noonan: Everybody's like that on their first day. You'll get over it soon. Now I'll show you your office.

Sawasaki: It's such a nice office.

Noonan: This is your secretary, Nancy Yamamoto. She's a sansei, but she's completely bilingual.

狀況

澤崎到新職場上班的第一天開始於諾南的歡迎詞 “Welcome aboard, Shoichi.” Welcome aboard 原本是服務員對搭船或搭機旅客的問候語:「歡迎搭乘」。在此也用來表示對搭乘「公司號」者的歡迎。澤崎看起來很緊張，因此諾南跟他說了一句:「每個人的第一天都是如此」。

諾南: 昭一，歡迎加入。

澤崎: 謝謝您。諾南先生，我很高興能來這裡工作。

諾南: 你是這個職位的最佳人選，很高興你能加入我們。還有，叫我湯姆就可以了，好嗎?

澤崎: 這樣直呼您的名字我覺得有一點不太妥當。聽起來…怎麼說呢? 有些不敬吧?

諾南: 別擔心，公司上上下下的員工都是以名字相稱，可以嗎?

澤崎: 我盡量。

諾南: 很好。噢，可是如果在正式商務場合，有外人在場的時候，還是要以先生，女士或任何適當的方式來稱呼你的上司，這樣會比較得體，瞭解嗎?

澤崎: 是的，先生。

諾南: [笑著說] 也別叫我「先生」。你好像很緊張。

澤崎: 嗯，我的確是忐忑不安。

諾南: 第一天上班的人都會這樣，你很快就能適應的。我現在帶你去看你的辦公室。

澤崎: 這辦公室真漂亮。

諾南: 這位是你的祕書，南西・山本。她是第三代美籍日裔，不過她是道地的雙聲帶。

Words and Phrases

by the way　順帶一提
awkward [`ɔkwɚd]　笨拙的；不雅的
what shall I say　該怎麼說呢
disrespectful　無禮的；失禮的
good manners *pl.*　良好的行為
address　*v.*　稱呼
Ms. [mɪz]　女士（用於稱呼未婚或已婚女性）
sir　*v.*　以 sir 稱呼…
have butterflies　感到興奮或緊張
secretary　祕書
bilingual [baɪ`lɪŋgwəl]　會說兩國語言的；雙聲帶的

Vocabulary Building

● **perfect**　完美的；熟練的

Hiroshi's English is perfect. I thought he was a sansei.

（浩志的英文好得不得了，我原以為他是第三代美籍日裔。）

● **outsider**　局外人；非公司的人

Outsiders often have difficulty understanding our paternalistic corporate environment.

（非本公司的人通常很難理解我們溫情主義式的企業環境。）

● **higher-up**〔口語〕上司；在上位的人

cf. Talk to your superior immediately if you make a major error on the job. Don't just try to solve it by yourself.

（你若在工作上犯了嚴重的錯誤，即刻找你的上司談，別想一味地靠自己解決。）

重點文法・語法

Everybody is called by their first name.

everybody 後面通常接單數動詞。但特別是在口語裡，後面會接複數代名詞 they，因此對應的動詞也變成複數。

也就是說，在正式的文體中，要用 Everybody is called by his〔或 his or her〕first name，可是，用 his 來表示「每個人」，會產生「性別歧視」的問題，但如果每次都一直反覆 "his or her" 也很麻煩。因此在現代英語中，Everybody is called by their first name. 慢慢地變成了一般的說法。

▶*Exercises*

請利用括弧內的詞語改寫下列例句，並盡量保持原來的語意。

（解答見247頁）

1. You were the perfect man for the job.
   (more qualified, to get, than)

2. I feel awkward calling you by your first name.
   (embarrassed, as Tom, addressing)

3. You'll get over it soon.
   (before long, return to normal)

◆◆◆◆◆◆◆◆◆◆◆◆◆◆ 簡短對話 ◆◆◆◆◆◆◆◆◆◆◆◆◆◆

Noonan: Good to have you aboard.
Sawasaki: Thank you very much. I'm happy to be here.
Noonan: Excited?
Sawasaki: Very.
Noonan: Relax.

* * *

Noonan: Even though everybody's quite friendly here, it's not good to be too familiar with your superiors. Does that make sense to you?
Sawasaki: Yes, it does. Thanks for your advice.
Noonan: Not at all. I'll take you to your office.

---

have someone aboard 有某人加入 **be too familiar with** 和…交往過密；沒有保持適當距離 **superior** 上司 **make sense** 有道理；合理

Lesson 1

First Day on the Job (2)（上班的第一天）

預習—*Sentences*

· Let me know if you have any questions.
· Nancy's been here eight years.
· She knows the company inside and out.
· I'll show you your way around.
· Let's have lunch together.

Vignette

Yamamoto: Hello. How do you do, Mr. Sawasaki?
Sawasaki: How do you do?
Noonan: Nancy, tell Shoichi how to fill out the expense sheets after I've taken him around.
Yamamoto: Certainly. Let me know if you have any questions.
Noonan: Nancy's been here eight years. Knows the company inside and out. Now I'll show you your way around and let you get your bearings.
Sawasaki: My bearings?
Noonan: Oh, that's just a colloquial expression. It means knowing which way is which.
Sawasaki: Oh, I see.
Noonan: Here. This is your program for the week.
Sawasaki: My program?
Noonan: Yes, you'll spend most of this week talking to different line managers, learning about their functions in the organization.
Sawasaki: Great!
Noonan: Before I forget, let's have lunch together today. I can tell you about good eating places in the neighborhood. Now I'll give you a quick tour of the offices. This is our company cafeteria. I'll show you the ropes . . .

* * *

■狀況

對新進人員而言，有一件事很重要，就是早一點熟悉公司內的組織，知道哪裡有什麼。諾南忙著替澤崎介紹公司，介紹新同事，我們可以看得出他希望讓澤崎早點熟悉公司的用心。而能夠有一位熟悉公司事務，又有能力的日裔美籍祕書，對澤崎來說也是很幸運的事。第一天中午，諾南邀他一道去吃飯。

山本：嗨！你好，澤崎先生。

澤崎：你好。

諾南：南西，我先帶昭一四處看看，之後，請你告訴他如何填寫費用傳票。

山本：沒問題。如果你有任何疑問就告訴我。

諾南：南西在公司已經八年了。公司裡裡外外的事她都知道。我現在帶你去四處看看，讓你知道你的方位。

澤崎：我的方位？

諾南：哦，那只是一種口語，意思是讓你熟悉公司的內部環境。

澤崎：哦，我懂了。

諾南：這個，是你這一週的計畫表。

澤崎：我的計畫表？

諾南：對，這個星期你大部份的時間要花在和其他部門的經理會談，以瞭解他們在公司扮演的角色。

澤崎：太好了！

諾南：趁我還沒忘記，記得今天中午一起用餐。我可以告訴你這附近有什麼好吃的餐館。現在我很快地帶你看一下各個部門。這是我們公司的員工餐廳，我會告訴你如何使用…

＊　＊　＊

Words and Phrases

fill out 填寫
get one's bearings 熟悉環境
colloquial [kə`lokwɪəl] 口語的；會話用語的
line manager 部門經理
before I forget 趁我還沒忘記
eating place 餐館；飯館
cafeteria [,kæfə`tɪrɪə] 員工餐廳
show the ropes 示範使用方式

Vocabulary Building

- **expense sheet** 費用傳票

  Be sure to turn in your weekly expense sheet by Tuesday morning of the following week.

  (記得在星期二早上之前繳交你上週的費用傳票。)

- **inside and out** 裡裡外外；整個…上下

  Dave knows Ethiopia inside and out. He was born there and spent most of his boyhood days in Addis Ababa.

  (戴維對伊索比亞瞭若指掌。他在那裡出生，而且他大部分的童年時光都是在阿迪斯阿貝巴度過的。)

- **function** 職責；集會；招待會

  cf. Top corporate executives should attend all the press functions on behalf of the company.

  (高層企業主管應代表公司參加所有的媒體招待會。)

重點文法・語法

Let's have lunch together.

let's是let us的縮寫，否定的正式寫法為let us not，let's not，此外，在美口語也使用don't let's 或 let's don't 。再者，以 Let's 開頭的句子，其附加問句為shall we?

Let us not have lunch together.
Let's not have lunch together.
Don't let's have lunch together.
Let's don't have lunch together.〔美口〕

▶ *Exercises*

請利用括弧內的詞語改寫下列例句，並盡量保持原來的語意。

(解答見247頁)

1. Tell Shoichi how to fill out the expense sheets.
   (show, do his)

2. Nancy knows the company inside and out.
   (Nancy doesn't know, nothing)

3. I can tell you about good eating places in the neighborhood.
   (give you some tips, fine restaurants, near here)

◆◆◆◆◆◆◆◆◆◆◆◆◆◆◆ 簡短對話 ◆◆◆◆◆◆◆◆◆◆◆◆◆◆◆

Noonan: Meet your secretary, Mrs. Nancy Yamamoto.
Yamamoto: Hi. I'm happy to meet you.
Sawasaki: Same here.
Noonan: She's been here a long time and knows everything about the company.
Yamamoto: Well, not quite everything but I can tell you the shortest route from the subway station to the office.
Sawasaki: Super. I'll see you later.

* * *

Sawasaki: Beg your pardon. I'm not familiar with that phrase.
Noonan: To get your bearings simply means to find out where you are. Sorry if you thought I meant stocking up on little metal balls.

Same here. 我也是。 **route** 路線；程序 **I'll see you later.** 待會兒見。 **Beg your pardon.** 抱歉；對不起。 **get one's bearings** 知道某人的所在位置及四周環境 **stock up** 貯存 **little metal balls** 小鋼珠〈意指軸承裡的小鋼珠〉

Lesson 1

First Day on the Job (3)（上班的第一天）

預習—*Sentences*

- I'd like you to meet Mike Yamaguchi.
- It's good to have you aboard.
- That's an excellent company.
- We're more aggressive than they are.
- I'm sure you'll like it here.

Vignette

Noonan: I'd like you to meet Mike Yamaguchi, manager of sales. Mike, this is Shoichi Sawasaki, our new marketing manager.

Yamaguchi: Hi. It's good to have you aboard.

Sawasaki: I'm very pleased to meet you.

Yamaguchi: You've come from International Foods, I believe.

Sawasaki: That's right. I was with them six years.

Yamaguchi: That's an excellent company. The two organizations are now about the same size but you may find our corporate culture quite different.

Sawasaki: In what way, if I may ask?

Yamaguchi: Well, I'd say that you'll find our management team members extremely down-to-earth and open with employees.

Noonan: I agree. Also we're more aggressive than they are. And our growth record attests to that. What we have here is a more competitive work environment and more entrepreneurial spirit.

Yamaguchi: It won't take you long to get oriented to our corporate style. To say the least, you won't get bored. I'm sure you'll like it here.

Sawasaki: Thanks. I look forward to working with you.

■狀況

接下來介紹的是山口誠。在 ABC食品公司，若有新進人員到職，則此人的經歷等會藉著便條在公司內傳閱，因此山口也早就知道澤崎先前是在國際食品公司。對澤崎而言，儘早掌握公司的企業形態，並努力與之同化是很重要的一件事。

諾南：我為你介紹一下，這位是營業部經理，山口誠。

山口：嗨！你能加入真是太好了。

澤崎：很高興認識你。

山口：你一定是從國際食品公司轉過來的吧！

澤崎：沒錯，我在那裡待了六年。

山口：那個公司十分出色。我們兩家公司現在的規模差不多，但你會發現我們公司的企業文化十分不同。

澤崎：在哪一方面？我可以知道嗎？

山口：嗯，我想你會發覺我們管理階層的成員十分地踏實，並且對員工總是敞開心胸來溝通。

諾南：我同意。而且我們比他們要積極得多。我們的業績成長可以證明。而且我們這裡擁有較具競爭性的工作環境，並更富企業家精神。

山口：不用多久你便可以融入我們的企業風格了。最起碼，你不會感到乏味。我相信你會喜歡上這裡的。

澤崎：謝謝。我期待能和你們一起共事。

Words and Phrases

excellent 優秀的
extremely 極度的；極端的
down-to-earth 實際的；現實的
open 敞開心胸的；沒有隱瞞的；率直的
competitive work environment 具競爭性的工作環境
entrepreneurial spirit 企業家精神
orient 使適應環境；使熟悉狀況
to say the least 最起碼
get bored 感到厭煩
look forward to 期待著…

Vocabulary Building

● **corporate culture** 企業文化；公司的風氣

"Honesty" is emphasized in our corporate culture.

（在我們的企業文化中，「誠實」十分重要。）

● **aggressive** 積極進取的；有侵略性的

Wanted: Aggressive self-starter for the position of sales manager.

（徵人啟事：積極、主動，擔任業務經理一職。）

● **attest** 為…作證；證明

The fact that Susan got her MBA by attending a night course attests to her diligence.

（蘇珊能靠著參加夜間課程而取得企管碩士的學位，足以證明她的勤奮有加。）

重點文法・語法

I was with them six years.

在這個句子當中，省略掉 six years 前面的介系詞 for。for 有「…期間」之意，但若接在動詞之後，常會被省略。

The war lasted (for) four years.
We've been studying English (for) more than ten years.
Tom waited (for) hours and hours for Mary to come.
I've been with the company (for) six years.

▶*Exercises*

請利用括弧內的詞語改寫下列例句，並盡量保持原來的語意。

(解答見247頁)

1. You've come from International Foods, I believe.
   (with, you were, I understand)

2. Also we're more aggressive than they are.
   (less aggressive, we are)

3. It won't take you long to get oriented to our corporate style.
   (get used to, you'll soon)

◆◆◆◆◆◆◆◆◆◆◆◆◆◆◆ 簡短對話 ◆◆◆◆◆◆◆◆◆◆◆◆◆◆

Sawasaki: I worked at International Foods for six years.

Yamaguchi: They're real pros in the food business. We have something to learn from their marketing strategies too.

Sawasaki: I'm glad you feel that way.

Yamaguchi: Do you know anything about the frozen food market?

Sawasaki: Not enough, I'm afraid. But I know the basics and I'm a quick study.

* * *

Yamamoto: We have an "open door" policy. Any time you have a question or grievance, you can go into any executive's office.

Noonan: Our management team is a bunch of top-flight people. You'll enjoy talking to them later.

---

pro (<professional) 專家 **marketing strategy** 行銷策略 **basics** 原理 **quick study** 學習能力強的人 **"open door policy"** 門戶開放政策〈上級主管保持辦公室的門敞開，使員工隨時能和其接觸的管理方式〉 **grievance** 抱怨 **bunch of** 成群的；一群的 **top-flight** 一流的；最高的

Lesson 1 First Day on the Job — 總結

美國的企業並非錄用「人」，他們的出發點是某個「職位」有空缺時，要把它填補起來。而且他們是採取中途雇用 (mid-career hiring) 的方式。每一次有新人進來，都要帶領著認識公司環境。在大企業裡，人事或總務的負責人員在為新進職員解說過公司的歷史、規定等之後，會帶他們認識一下公司內部、介紹新同事、並發給他們公司手冊。

即使公司沒有那麼完整的新人訓練，上司或同事也會為新進人員介紹公司內部情形，以及工作上必須注意的重要事項。澤崎也是依程序在規定的時間內與各式各樣的人會面、知道那些人在公司裡所扮演的角色。在某些公司裡，傳統上新人第一天上班時，上司會帶他同去用餐。

在外商公司中，同公司的人多以 first name 互稱。而在一些中小企業或設計、廣告等較自由的行業中，上至董事長，下至 mail boy，大家也常以 first name 互稱。

但在外人面前，對上司要加上 Mr. 或 Miss 等敬稱會比較妥當。有的公司只習慣在稱呼直屬上司、年長同事或幹部時加上敬稱。

無論如何，重要的是要有分寸，不要一開始就太隨便 (familiar)，而失去了該有的禮貌。

Lesson 2

Company Rules and Regulations

（公司規章）

Lesson 2 的內容

對一個新進人員來說，初到一家公司，最重要的事莫過於早日熟悉該公司的環境。為達此一目的，事先瞭解公司規章是不可少的動作。公司規章一般稱 manual 或 handbook。另外值得注意的是一些所謂的「不成文」規定。這些東西有的是公司傳統的一部分，有的則是一些經營者個人的「喜好」，通常不會在規章中明列條款，且不同的公司會有相當大的差異，有時，一些在 A 公司是「正當」的事，到了 B 公司也許會成為碰不得的禁忌。

Lesson 2

Company Rules and Regulations (1)

（公司規章）

預習—*Sentences*

- I appreciate that very much.
- Please have a seat.
- I'd like to be of assistance to you.
- Here's my first question.
- I've quit smoking.

Vignette

Kim: Good morning. I'm Ingrid Kim from General Affairs. Tom Noonan has asked me to come and explain the company rules and regulations to you

Sawasaki: I appreciate that very much, Ingrid. Please have a seat. I really need your help to learn how this company runs.

Kim: I'd like to be of as much assistance to you as possible. If you have any questions, just ask.

Sawasaki: Here's my first question. Can I smoke?

Kim: Yes, you can, provided you always ask permission of the others in the room.

Sawasaki: May I offer you a cigarette?

Kim: No, thank you. I've quit smoking.

Sawasaki: I believe that each organization has its own set of unwritten rules about behavior. What may be considered "good" manners at another company could be totally unacceptable here. At my old job, they were fairly strict about requiring employees to be punctual at the beginning of the working day no matter how late they might have stayed the night before.

■狀況

京來向澤崎說明公司的規章了。這對於想早一點熟悉公司環境的澤崎來說，簡直是求之不得的事。對於澤崎所提出的問題，京並沒有因為老是要回答新人這些問題而露出不耐，反而還親切地一一說明。於是澤崎便能較無顧忌地問及公司的「不成文規定」。

京：早。我是總務部的英格・京，湯姆・諾南要我來向你說明公司的規章。

澤崎：非常感激，英格。我真的需要你協助我瞭解公司是如何運作的。

京：我會盡可能幫助你。如果你有任何問題，儘管問我。

澤崎：第一個問題，我可以抽菸嗎?

京：可以，只要你在抽菸之前都能徵求辦公室裡其他人的同意。

澤崎：你要不要來一根?

京：不，謝謝。我已經戒菸了。

澤崎：我相信每一個機構對於員工的行為，都有其不成文的規定。在其他公司被認為「好」的舉止，在這兒可能完全不被接受。在我以前的公司，不管前一天可能加班到多晚，他們仍嚴格要求員工要準時上班。

Words and Phrases

appreciate 感激	behavior 行為
Have a seat. 請坐。	unacceptable 無法接受的
be of assistance to 有助於…	strict 嚴格的
as much as possible 盡可能地多…	punctual 守時的
provided 假使	

Vocabulary Building

- **General Affairs** 總務（課、部）

  George wanted to transfer from General Affairs to Human Resources.

  （喬治想從總務部調到人力資源部。）
- **rules and regulations** *pl.* 規章

  cf. Rules are made to be broken.

  （規章是訂來被破壞的；有規章的制定，才有違規的情事。）
- **quit** 辭職

  I quit. I can't stand my boss anymore.

  （我辭職了。因為我再也無法忍受我的老闆。）

重點文法・語法

Can I smoke?

想吸菸時，若要徵求別人同意，一般而言，較委婉的說法是 "May I smoke?" 而在一些英美家庭，若孩子說出 "Can I have butter, please?" 的句子，父母會予以糾正為 "May I . . . ?"

類似的委婉說法如下：

Could I smoke, please?	OK if I light up?
Do you mind [Mind] if I smoke?	Would you object if I smoked?
I wonder if I could smoke.	Will it bother you if I smoke?

▶Exercises

請利用括弧內的詞語改寫下列例句，並盡量保持原來的語意。

(解答見247頁)

1. I really need your help to learn how this company runs.
   (to help me, I'd like, figure out)

2. I'd like to be of as much assistance to you as possible.
   (offer, as much help, need)

3. If you have any questions, just ask.
   (let me know, unclear to you, there's anything)

◆◆◆◆◆◆◆◆◆◆◆◆◆◆ 簡短對話 ◆◆◆◆◆◆◆◆◆◆◆◆◆◆

Kim: Tom Noonan asked me to give you a brief rundown about company policy.

Sawasaki: I'm grateful for that. I've read the policy manual but it seemed to be written in legalese.

Kim: It certainly reads like that, I'm afraid. Did you have any questions?

Sawasaki: Yes, I have some outside business interests. Do I have to report them to the management?

Kim: No, not unless you have a sizable holding in an entity that does business with the company.

---

rundown 口頭簡報 **legalese** 法律術語 **business interest** 商業股權 **report** *v.* 報告 **sizable** 相當大的 **holding** 持有 **entity** 實體 **do business with** 與…做買賣（交易）

Lesson 2

Company Rules and Regulations (2)

（公司規章）

預習—*Sentences*

- I suspect that's not the same here.
- I'm glad you raised that issue.
- The answer is yes.
- Salaries are adjusted once a year.
- The office is closed on Christmas Day.

Vignette

Sawasaki: I suspect that's not the same here, is it?

Kim: I'm glad you raised that issue, because we've adopted the flex-time system here. It means that you can choose what time you are going to start and finish.

Sawasaki: Oh? I thought the office hours were 9 to 5:30.

Kim: Yes, but managerial people can set their own work schedules. You don't have to start each day at the same time, but you must be here for core time, which is from 10 to 3. Also, you're expected to put in at least 37½ hours a week.

Sawasaki: I see. Not that it matters, but do I get a yearly salary increase? I'm just curious.

Kim: The answer is yes. Our work rules say salaries are adjusted once a year. Your immediate supervisor will review your compensation against your performance and recommend an increase. This year the average hike is three percent.

Sawasaki: How many days vacation can I take in the first year?

Kim: You're entitled to ten days of vacation for the balance of this year. In addition, you'll get special days off on your anniversary day and birthday. The whole company is closed for two days in mid-August for summer holidays. Besides traditional Japanese holidays, the office is closed on Christmas Day.

■狀況

澤崎問到一些細節，像是前一天如果工作太晚，次日是否允許晚到、以及「調薪」與「年假」的算法等。京還告訴澤崎，公司採取的是彈性工時制，員工可以自由調整上下班時間，而且在自己服務滿週年和過生日時，都有特休。澤崎在得知這些之後，真是又驚又喜。

澤崎：我猜這兒並不是這樣規定的，對吧?

京：很高興你提起這個問題，因為在這兒我們採行彈性工時制度。你可以選擇你的上下班時間。

澤崎：真的?我以為上班時間是早上九點到下午五點半。

京：沒錯，但是管理級人員可以自行訂定上班時間。你不用每天在相同的時間上班，但是核心時間你必須在辦公室，也就是早上十點到下午三點。還有，你每週至少要工作三十七又二分之一個小時。

澤崎：原來是這樣。有一件事，也不是甚麼要緊的，我們的薪水年年都會調嗎?我只是好奇。

京：會的。公司的工作章程訂明薪資一年調整一次。你的頂頭上司會看看目前公司給你的報酬，再看看你的工作表現，然後建議公司該給你加多少。今年的平均調升幅度是百分之三。

澤崎：第一年我會有幾天的休假?

京：今年你有權休假十天。除此之外，在服務滿週年及過生日時，你還會有特別假日。在八月中旬，整個公司會休業兩個星期，算是暑假。另外，除了傳統的日本節日之外，我們在聖誕節也不上班。

Words and Phrases

suspect 猜想；猜疑
core 核心
not that it matters 也不是甚麼要緊的事
curious *adj.* 好奇的；想要知道的
adjust 調整
be entitled to 有權利享有
in addition 除此之外；此外

Vocabulary Building

- **flextime** (flexitime) 彈性工時〈員工可以彈性調整上下班時間，只要上班時數達到公司要求即可〉
  In the flextime work system, you can basically decide when to report for work and when to quit.
  (在彈性工時的制度裡，基本上，上下班時間由你決定。)
- **compensation** 報酬；薪資
  The total cash compensation for the new employee was set at $65,000.
  (公司對新進員工的現金報酬訂為六萬五千美元。)
- **performance** 工作表現；業績
  Mark was terminated for performance reasons.
  (馬克因工作表現欠佳而被辭退。)

重點文法・語法

The office hours are 9 to 5:30.
You're expected to put in at least 37½ hours a week.
This year the average hike is three percent.

以上是數字的寫法。一般英文報紙上，數字中只有 1~10 (或 9) 會 spell out(拼出來)，其他便用阿拉伯數字表示。但若是學術論文等的，則 1~99 的數字通常都會 spell out。

但也有幾種例外情形。如第一句中，在時間的說法上，即使 10 以下也習慣用數字表達。(另外，此句原本在 9 之前的 from 已被省略。) 至於「百分比」也是 spell out 較多，但在商業雜誌等，則使用%的符號及數字，如 35%。

▶Exercises

請利用括弧內的詞語改寫下列例句，並盡量保持原來的語意。

(解答見247頁)

1. I thought the office hours were 9 to 5:30.
   (was open, I was told, from)

2. Managerial people can set their own work schedules.
   (are allowed to choose, managers)

3. You're expected to put in at least 37½ hours a week.
   (minimum of, work, supposed to)

◆◆◆◆◆◆◆◆◆◆◆◆◆◆ 簡短對話 ◆◆◆◆◆◆◆◆◆◆◆◆◆◆

Sawasaki: What about things like clean desks?

Kim: There are no written rules about them, but you're expected not to leave anything on your desk when you leave the office for the day.

Sawasaki: You mean not even a calculator or a pencil case?

Kim: You really should put them in your drawers. The desk top is supposed to be bare except for the telephone.

Sawasaki: Is that fairly well observed?

Kim: Yes. Our management believes that a cluttered desk is a sign of a cluttered mind.

---

written rules 成文規定 **leave for the day** 下班 **be supposed to** 應該 **bare** 空的 **except for** 除了…之外 **well observed** 被好好地遵守 **sign of** …的象徵 **cluttered** 淩亂的

Lesson 2

Company Rules and Regulations (3)

（公司規章）

預習—*Sentences*

- You'll find out who keeps long lunch hours.
- Can I eat in?
- You're not supposed to have noodles catered in.
- The cafeteria is open from 11 to 2 o'clock.
- You should watch out.

Vignette

Sawasaki: That sounds quite generous. What's the office regulation about lunch hours?

Kim: It's supposed to be from 12 noon to 1, but people are somewhat flexible.You'll soon find out who keeps long lunch hours. But it's difficult to control the time precisely, especially if you're with a customer.

Sawasaki: Can I eat in?

Kim: If you prefer to brown-bag it, you can eat in the cafeteria or the employees' lounge. Employees aren't allowed to use the conference room for eating. And you're not supposed to have noodles and things like that catered in. The cafeteria is open from 11 to 2 o'clock, and you can buy lunch tickets at Finance.

Sawasaki: I'll take the time to read the company rules and guidelines. But is there anything in particular I should pay attention to?

Kim: As a marketing manager, you may be in a position to be entertained or receive gifts from suppliers. We have strict regulations about excessive entertainment or presents. Customary seasonal gifts and occasional meal invitations are usually no problem, but you should watch out. There's no such thing as a free lunch, as they say.

Sawasaki: I know.

■狀況

看來這家公司有不少細節該注意，像是不可以叫外食進來吃，下班時須將桌面收拾整齊後方可離去等的。此外，還有極其嚴格的 code of ethics（道德規範）。他們就和大多數的國際企業一樣，禁止收受不正當的金錢、禮物，即使是中元、歲末的往來贈禮，也有違反規定之嫌。

澤崎：聽起來相當不錯。午餐時間是幾點呢？

京：應該是十二點到一點，但這是有點彈性的。你很快就會發現哪些人的午餐時間比別人長。不過，要分秒不差地掌握用餐時間是很難的，特別是在你跟客戶一道用餐的時候。

澤崎：我可以把東西帶到辦公室來吃嗎？

京：如果你要自己帶便當，你可以在餐廳或員工休息室進餐。可是，員工不可以跑到會議室吃東西，你也不可以從外面叫麵或類似的外食進來吃。餐廳從十一點開到二點，你可以在財務部買到餐券。

澤崎：我會花點時間研讀公司的章程。不過，有沒有甚麼要特別注意的事情？

京：身為一個行銷經理，可能常會有人請你吃飯，或是會有廠商送禮物給你。但是公司對於過多的交際和禮物的收受是有嚴格規定的。習俗上的季節性禮品和偶爾請請吃飯通常不會有問題，但你要注意，就像人們常說的，天下沒有白吃的午餐。

澤崎：我知道。

Words and Phrases

generous 寬大的
somewhat 有點；稍微
flexible 有彈性的
eat in 在裡面用飯〈eat out: 在外面餐館用餐〉
prefer 偏好
brown-bag it *v.* 自己帶便當（或自製的餐點）到辦公室等
cater in 外燴；叫外食進來吃
excessive 過度的；過量的
seasonal gift （值中秋(中元)或年終之際所饋送的）季節性禮品〈註：日本習慣在中元節送禮，其習俗上的重要性同於國人所過的中秋節〉
watch out 注意；小心

Vocabulary Building

● **entertain** 招待；宴請

I'd like you to entertain an important customer this evening.

（我希望你在今晚招待一位重要的客戶。）

● **supplier** （上游的）業者；供應商

You should not squeeze suppliers just to get more profit.

（你不應該為了得到較多的利潤而剝削供應商。）

● **free lunch** 白吃的午餐

Don't let the contractors wine and dine you. Remember there's no such thing as a free lunch.

（不要讓承包商請你喝酒吃飯。要記得，天下沒有白吃的午餐。）

重點文法・語法

What's the office regulation about lunch hours?
It's supposed to be from 12 noon to 1.

it's supposed to be 的 it 指前述的 lunch hours，而lunch hours 為複數，原本應該寫成 they're，但口語上並不完全照著文法來講。口語中像這類和文法不一致的情形是常有的。

▶*Exercises*

請利用括弧內的詞語改寫下列例句，並盡量保持原來的語意。

（解答見247頁）

1. Employees aren't allowed to use the conference room for eating.
   (to eat in, employee rules, it's against)

2. You may be in a position to receive gifts from suppliers.
   (vendors, presents, it's possible)

3. Seasonal gifts and occasional meal invitations are no problem.
   (semi-yearly, dinner, all right)

◆◆◆◆◆◆◆◆◆◆◆◆◆◆◆◆ 簡短對話 ◆◆◆◆◆◆◆◆◆◆◆◆◆◆◆◆

Sawasaki: If I had a business lunch with a customer, how should I charge that to the company?

Kim: Put it on your expense account sheet. You should describe where the business entertainment took place, who you entertained, what business relationship you have with the person, and what the purpose was.

Sawasaki: Do I get a per diem for business trips?

Kim: As a matter of policy, you can opt either for a per diem or to get reimbursed for actual expenses incurred.

---

charge 將某項開支記在某人帳上 **expense account sheet** （公務交際費的）公關費用傳票 **describe** 說明 **take place** 發生 **per diem** 每日零用金 **as a matter of policy** 政策上 **opt for** 選擇 **get reimbursed for** 得到…的償還 **incur** 招致

Lesson 2 Company Rules and Regulations —總結

一個公司本身會有很多規定，從工作規則 (work rules)、「員工守則」到公平交易法，以及關於不正當的金錢或禮物收受等內部規章，形式可說是五花八門。但最令新進人員感到頭痛的，還是 unwritten rules（不成文規定）。

有些公司會要求全體員工一律身著西裝，而男性為了遮住腿毛，即使夏天也須穿長統襪，還有辦公室內禁止開 praty 等。至於辦公室內吸菸、進食等的規定，美國大部分的企業不是全面禁止，就是局部禁止。要想熟悉這些「遊戲規則」，除了請教周遭的人外，祇有靠自己多觀察了。

澤崎用一副 not that it matters （沒甚麼要緊的）的態度，淡淡地問了有關調薪的事，這是任何上班族都想了解的問題。

以往，管理階層一年半或二年調薪一次的並不在少數，而這種傾向正慢慢延伸到勞動階級。最近流行所謂的 lump-sum payment，就是將調薪部分的金額，在退休時一併給付，而基本薪資維持不變的一種給薪方式。調薪部分一般由直屬上司 recommend，再經其上司 approve 後決定。

美國大企業中，對於賄賂等有嚴格的管制，有些公司甚至要求員工定期提出切結書。此外，與有違反公平交易法之虞的同業進行交涉、或在公司關係企業中有個人投資行為，都是不被允許的。

Lesson 3

Talking on the Phone

（電話交談）

Lesson 3 的內容

在辦公室裡會接到各式各樣的電話，有國際電話，國內電話，公司內部電話，還有重要電話，瑣事電話，私人電話，以及推銷員的推銷電話，打錯的電話，和抱怨的電話等等。

諾南的祕書後藤，不管接到任何電話都能當機立斷，處理得乾淨俐落。像後藤這種處理方式，不但能教來電者安心，同時還會讓人覺得這是個講究效率，成長快速的企業。

今天，後藤依然以她甜美的聲音接聽電話。

Lesson 3

Talking on the Phone (1)（電話交談）

預習—*Sentences*

- Calling for Tom Noonan, please.
- May I ask who's calling?
- Which company are you with, Mr. Little?
- I work for Carpets International.
- I wish to speak with Mr. Noonan.

Vignette

Goto: Good morning, ABC Foods. Mr. Noonan's office.
Heinrichs: Calling for Tom Noonan, please. My name is Heinrichs.
Goto: Sorry. I didn't catch your name.
Heinrichs: Heinrichs. Richard Heinrichs.
Goto: Would you spell that for me, sir?
Heinrichs: Sure. H-E-I-N-R-I-C-H-S. Heinrichs.
Goto: H-E-I-N-R-I-C-H-S?
Heinrichs: That's correct.
Goto: Will Mr. Noonan know what this is in reference to?
Heinrichs: He should remember me from last week's food symposium we attended together.

* * *

Goto: Mr. Noonan's office.
Riddle: Is he in?
Goto: May I ask who's calling?
Riddle: I'm Jack Riddle.
Goto: Which company are you with, Mr. Little?
Riddle: No, my name is Riddle. R-I-double D-L-E. I work for Carpets International. I wish to speak with Mr. Noonan.
Goto: One moment, please.

■狀況

時間是早上九點，公司才開始上班，後藤正在接聽電話。雖然後藤已經是老資格的祕書了，但她在確認來電者姓名時仍然小心翼翼。如果是第一次聽到的名字，後藤除了要確認名字的拼法外，她也必須禮貌地詢問來電者有甚麼事情。

後藤：ABC食品公司，早安！這裡是諾南先生辦公室。

漢尼詩：麻煩妳請湯姆・諾南聽電話。我是漢尼詩。

後藤：抱歉，我沒聽清楚您的大名。

漢尼詩：漢尼詩。理察・漢尼詩。

後藤：先生，可以告訴我您的大名怎麼拼嗎？

漢尼詩：當然可以。H-E-I-N-R-I-C-H-S。漢尼詩。

後藤：H-E-I-N-R-I-C-H-S？

漢尼詩：對了。

後藤：諾南先生知道是關於哪方面的事嗎？

漢尼詩：他應該記得我。我們上星期一起出席一場食品研討會。

* * *

後藤：諾南先生辦公室。

律德：他在嗎？

後藤：請問是哪位？

律德：我是傑克・律德。

後藤：利多先生，請問您在哪服務？

律德：不，我的名字是律德。R-I兩個D-L-E。我服務於國際地毯公司。我想和諾南先生說話。

後藤：請稍等。

Words and Phrases

catch 聽清楚；了解
remember 記得
symposium [sɪm`pozɪəm] 研討會
attend 出席；參加

Vocabulary Building

- **Mr. Noonan's office.** 諾南先生辦公室。〈祕書在接到打給老闆的外線電話時，除了先報上老闆的姓名之外，有時還會接著告訴對方自己的姓名，如"Mr. Noonan's office. Miss Goto speaking."〉
  cf. Mary Jones speaking. How may I help you?
  (我是瑪莉・瓊斯。有甚麼可以效勞的嗎?)
- **in reference to** 有關…；關於…
  In reference to your inquiry, we've suspended the production of the motor.
  (關於你所問到的事，我們已經停止該馬達的生產了。)
- **One moment, please.** 請稍等。
  cf. Please hold the line.
  (請先別掛斷。)

重點文法・語法

Good morning.

「早安」是用於早上碰到人或是接電話時的問候語。但在英國，也有人在道別時說"Good morning"。"Good morning"，"Good afternoon"，和"Good evening"有時也作「再見」之意。在電話中與人道別時，亦可用 cheers 作為結尾。

在美國，一般用 Have a nice day. 作為道別時的說法。但現在也有人指其為陳腔濫調。話雖如此，可以取而代之的說法仍付之闕如。

勉強的替代方案可以用Take care.或 Enjoy your day. 此外，偶爾也會聽到類似 Have a good one. Make it a good one. Talk to you soon. See you soon. Catch you soon. 或 I'll be in touch. 等的說法。

▶Exercises

請利用括弧內的詞語改寫下列例句，並盡量保持原來的語意。

(解答見247頁)

1. Sorry. I didn't catch your name.
   (recognize, pardon, me)

2. Would you spell that for me, sir?
   (spelling, do you mind, your name)

3. Will Mr. Noonan know what this is in reference to?
   (is all about, does, understand)

◆◆◆◆◆◆◆◆◆◆◆◆◆◆ 簡短對話 ◆◆◆◆◆◆◆◆◆◆◆◆◆◆

Muir: This is Frank Muir. Is Sawasaki in?
Yamamoto: What did you say your name was?
Muir: Frank Muir.
Yamamoto: How do you spell it?
Muir: M-U-I-R. May I talk to Mr. Sawasaki?
Yamamoto: What company are you with, Mr. Muir?
Muir: Muir, Koonce & Godown Associates.
Yamamoto: Is that a law firm?
Muir: Yes. Now, is he in today?

What did you say your name was? (=What was your name?) 你剛剛說你叫甚麼名字來著? **be with** 服務於… **law firm** 法律事務所

Lesson 3

Talking on the Phone (2) (電話交談)

預習—*Sentences*

· Mr. Noonan is not available right now.
· Would you mind calling back?
· What can I do for you?
· It just arrived this morning.
· That's all I wanted to know.

Vignette

Goto: [*Using an extension*] Mr. Noonan, Mr. Riddle of Carpets International is on the line.

Noonan: Oh, he's bugging me again. Tell him I'm not interested to see him, not after he sold me that junk. Tell him to get lost!

Goto: I'm sorry, Mr. Riddle, Mr. Noonan is not available right now. Would you mind calling back?

Riddle: What's the best time to call him?

Goto: I'm afraid he'll be completely tied up with overseas visitors this week.

Riddle: All right. I'll try again.

Goto: Thank you.

* * *

Noonan: Mike? This is a quickie since I have a department meeting starting in just a minute.

Yamaguchi: What can I do for you, Tom?

Noonan: A question: Have you received the latest lab analysis of the new food additives from the London office?

Yamaguchi: Yes, it just arrived this morning. You need a copy?

Noonan: No, that's all I wanted to know. Thanks.

■狀況

聽到「律德」這個名子，諾南立刻火冒三丈。因為諾南上過他的當。律德曾把所謂的「高級波斯地毯」賣給他。諾南後來才發現那原來是便宜的冒牌貨。諾南要律德滾蛋。後藤當然不會一五一十地轉述諾南的話。她知道該怎麼做，畢竟，「婉拒推銷員」也是她份內的工作。

後藤：[使用分機] 諾南先生，國際地毯公司的律德先生在線上。

諾南：哦，他又來煩我了。告訴他我沒興趣見他，尤其在他把那種垃圾賣給我以後。叫他滾蛋！

後藤：抱歉，律德先生。諾南先生現在沒空。請您再打來好嗎？

律德：甚麼時候打給他最合適呢？

後藤：恐怕他這星期都要接見國外訪客而分不開身。

律德：好吧。那我會再打打看。

後藤：謝謝您。

* * *

諾南：麥可嗎？馬上有個部門會議要開，所以我得長話短說。

山口：湯姆，我可以幫甚麼忙嗎？

諾南：我有一個問題：你有沒有接到倫敦辦事處有關新食品添加物的最新化驗報告？

山口：有，今天早上剛到。要影印一份給你嗎？

諾南：不用，我只想知道它到了沒。謝了。

Words and Phrases

on the line 在線上
bug 煩擾
junk 垃圾；品質不好的東西
Get lost. 滾開！
available 有空暇的
right now 現在
call back 再打電話來
food additive 食品添加物

Vocabulary Building

- **be tied up** 分不開身
  I'm going to be tied up in meetings all day today.
  (我今天一整天都要開會，分不開身。)
- **quickie** 倉促解決的事物；倉促的行為
  We don't have much time for lunch. Let's have a quickie.
  (我們沒多少時間吃午餐了，隨便吃吃就好了。)
- **analysis** 分析
  What is your expert analysis of the situation on Korean Peninsula?
  (關於朝鮮半島的情勢，你們專家的分析如何?)

重點文法・語法

I'm not interested to see him.

在學校所教的文法中，動詞 interest 的用法通常是 be interested in V-ing；但在實際用法中，接不定詞 to V 卻是相當普遍的。

▶Exercises

請利用括弧內的詞語改寫下列例句，並盡量保持原來的語意。

(解答見247頁)

1. I'm sorry, Mr. Noonan is not available right now.
   (is occupied, I'm afraid, at the moment)

2. What's the best time to call him?
   (the most convenient, of the day, when's)

3. He'll be completely tied up with overseas visitors this week.
   (out-of-town, he's busy)

◆◆◆◆◆◆◆◆◆◆◆◆◆◆◆ 簡短對話 ◆◆◆◆◆◆◆◆◆◆◆◆◆◆◆

Yamamoto: Mr. Sawasaki has someone with him. May I tell him what this is about?

Muir: Will you just have him call me back, please?

Yamamoto: Does he have your number, Mr. Muir?

Muir: Yes, he does.

Yamamoto: May I have it just in case?

Muir: It's (202) 923-4011.

* * *

Goto: Mr. Noonan is speaking to someone on another line. Can you hold on for just a second, please? [*Pause*] Mr. Noonan's line is now open. Thank you for waiting.

May I tell him what this is about? 可以讓我轉告他是甚麼事嗎? **just in case** 以防萬一 **on another line** 在講另外一通電話 **hold on** 稍等 **for just a second** 一下子

Lesson 3

Talking on the Phone (3)（電話交談）

預習—*Sentences*

- This is a surprise.
- Can you hear me clearly?
- The morning seems pretty full.
- I have a lunch engagement on that day.
- Have a good trip over.

Vignette

Rawe: Hello. This is Dick Rawe of Giant Plastics. How are you, Tom?

Noonan: Hello, Dick. Well, well, this is a surprise. I haven't heard from you for ages. How have you been?

Rawe: Oh, there have been ups and downs, but things are not too bad lately. Can you hear me clearly?

Noonan: Barely. You sound as though you're speaking from the other side of the moon. Where are you calling from?

Rawe: I'm in Hong Kong now but I'll visit Tokyo next week. Can we get together and catch up on each other and possibly do some business talk?

Noonan: Of course. I never turn away an old friend. Let's see, I'll be out of town on Monday and Tuesday. Would Wednesday be all right?

Rawe: That'd be super. What time would you say?

Noonan: Well, the morning seems pretty full. How about 4:30? Or we could have lunch together.

Rawe: I already have a lunch engagement on that day, so let's make it 4:30. I'll come to your office.

Noonan: Good. I look forward to seeing you then. Have a good trip over.

Rawe: Fine. Thank you. See you soon.

Noonan: Take care of yourself.

Rawe: You too, Tom.

■狀況

諾南上一次見到老同事狄克・羅已經是五、六年前的事了。羅應該已從ABC食品公司轉到某塑膠公司去了。多年不見，聲音還是很耳熟。如果他來到東京，可以相約吃頓中飯，知道一下彼此的近況。

羅：喂，我是狄克・羅，巨人塑膠公司。湯姆，你好嗎？

諾南：嗨，狄克！這，這真是太意外了。好久沒有你的消息了。你過得怎樣？

羅：嗯，有好有壞啦。不過最近還不算太糟。你聽得清楚我的聲音嗎？

南：很勉強。你聽起來好像是在月球的另一端。你是在哪裡打的電話？

羅：我現在人在香港，但我下星期要到東京出差，到時我們可以聚一聚嗎？我們可以瞭解一下彼此的近況，可能的話，也談點生意上的事。

諾南：哦，這是當然。我絕不會甩掉老朋友的。我想想看，週一和週二我有事，不會在東京，週三可以嗎？

羅：那再好也沒有了。幾點呢？

諾南：嗯，那天早上行程都排滿了。下午四點半好不好？或者，我們可以一起吃午飯。

羅：我那天中午已經有約了。所以，還是四點半吧！我到你辦公室去。

諾南：好。我期待著到時與你見面。祝你旅途愉快。

羅：謝謝。到時見了。

諾南：保重。

羅：你也一樣，湯姆。

Words and Phrases

things *pl.* 事情；事態	turn away 不理睬
barely 幾乎不	how about …如何
as though 好像；似乎	lunch engagement 午餐約會
get together 聚在一起	take care of 照顧
catch up on 趕上	

Vocabulary Building

- **ups and downs** 起起落落；時好時壞；變動
  There are frequent ups and downs in this business.
  (這個行業的起起落落十分頻繁。)
- **business talk** 公事上的談話；談生意；談正事
  cf. Don't talk business over dinner with me at home.
  (在家裡吃晚飯的時候不要跟我談公事。)
- **be out of town** 因出差到外地而不在〈out-of-town是形容詞，表示從其他城市來的人〉
  cf. We have a few out-of-town visitors this week.
  (這個禮拜我們有一些從外地來的訪客。)

重點文法・語法

I haven't heard from you for ages.

age 的意思是「一輩子」或「時代」。在口語會說 for [in] ages，這是一種誇飾法 (hyperbole)，表示「長年累月」或是「很長的一段時間」。

此外，英語中類似的誇張說法還有 I'm starved.(我餓死了)和 My back is killing me.(我的背疼死了)等。

▶*Exercises*

請利用括弧內的詞語改寫下列例句，並盡量保持原來的語意。

(解答見248頁)

1. I haven't heard from you for ages.
   (last, a long time, it's)

2. You sound as though you're speaking from the moon.
   (it sounds, calling, a far-off country)

3. I'm in Hong Kong now but I'll visit Tokyo next week.
   (I'll leave, to visit Tokyo)

◆◆◆◆◆◆◆◆◆◆◆◆◆◆◆◆◆ 簡短對話 ◆◆◆◆◆◆◆◆◆◆◆◆◆◆◆◆◆

Goto: Mr. Noonan is in a meeting just now. I'll be glad to give him your message when he's free. What would you like me to tell him?

Rawe: Please tell him that Dick Rawe called. My lunch appointment on Wednesday has been canceled. So I could have lunch with Tom if he's still available. Did you get that?

Goto: Yes, I did. I'll see if Mr. Noonan could lunch with you on Wednesday. Where can I reach you, Mr. Rawe?

Rawe: I'm staying at the Grand Kanto Hotel. Room 3434.

Goto: Thank you. I'll talk to Mr. Noonan later and leave a message for you at the hotel this afternoon. Is that all right?

Rawe: Yes, that'd be excellent.

---

lunch appointment 午餐約會 **available** 有空的 **lunch with** 與…吃午餐 **excellent** 很好；很棒

Lesson 3 Talking on the Phone — 總結

在電話交談中，第一步通常是要確認對方的名字。而對方的名字不可能一直都像 Smith 或 Jones 這麼簡單。所以，在碰到比較特殊的名字時，最好還是確定一下正確的拼法。否則，在不熟悉的情況下，很容易出錯。看來，要想既順利又確實地取得對方名字和電話號碼，還得費些工夫學習呢！

對於第一次打電話來的人，祕書有時會詢問其公司名稱，並瞭解他來電的目的。但在某些場合中，問人家有甚麼事情是很不禮貌的。有些美商公司甚至還規定祕書不可以詢問對方來電的目的。

雖然諾南以「不想見他」和「叫他滾」回絕了律德。但後藤還是用「他忙得無法分身」為由，婉拒了律德。像這種委婉的拒絕，對方可能不會死心。所以不妨在適當時機，明白地告訴對方，Mr. Noonan has asked me to tell you he's not interested to talk to you.

諾南先告訴山口，「會議要開始了，我長話短說」，然後，他馬上說明為何事去電。就算事實上並沒有會議要開，但如果你趕時間，或者對方正好是個喜歡東拉西扯的人，這句話會十分好用（但切忌重複使用）。

在國外的企業中，老闆若要請祕書代為撥通電話，他常會要求祕書讓他在對方接電話之前，先在線上等著，尤其在對方是長輩時，若不這樣，會顯得十分無禮。如果因對方不在，而必須請祕書留話的時候，也一定要確定接聽者已確實做好留言。必要時，甚至還可以要求對方複述一遍。

國外的商人在處理商務時，除非是十分緊急的事，否則不會隨便打電話到別人家裡去。因為將商務與私人時間混淆是很令人反感的。

此外，若對方來電時，自己正在與重要人士會晤，為避免談話中斷，最好是請對方再打電話來，或由自己回電，這也是很重要的商業禮儀。

Lesson 4

Visitors

（訪客）

Lesson 4 的內容

一個公司給人的企業形象，會受到諸多因素的影響。對於一個初次到訪的人而言，他首先見到的公司員工通常會決定他對這家公司的印象。而這個員工通常是公司的櫃臺人員。這也意味著，總機小姐代表公司的門面，也是公司宣傳的showcase。

在本課，上次從香港來電的羅先生來到了東京。還有，我們也會看到弗肯先生。他突然打電話給諾南，希望能「明早碰面」。請特別注意祕書在應答時「正」「反」兩面的說法。此外，本課也會有行銷顧問公司所做的市場調查簡報。

Lesson 4

Visitors (1)（訪客）

預習—*Sentences*

· I'm here to see Mr. Thomas Noonan, please.
· Is he expecting you?
· Someone will be with you shortly.
· I'm on a house-hunting trip.
· I'm a bit uneasy about apartment costs here.

Vignette

Rawe: Good morning. My name is Dick Rawe. I'm here to see Mr. Thomas Noonan, please.

Receptionist: Good morning, Mr. Rawe. Is he expecting you?

Rawe: I have a lunch date with him.

Receptionist: [*On the phone*] Miss Goto, this is the receptionist. I have a Mr. Rawe here ... Yes, I understand. Mr. Rawe, please have a seat. Someone will be with you shortly.

Rawe: Thanks.

Noonan: Hello, Dick. It's so nice to see you again. You look very fit.

Rawe: Nice to see you, Tom. You look pretty healthy and prosperous yourself.

Noonan: Tell me what brings you to Tokyo this time.

Rawe: I'll tell you what. The company is reassigning me here next month and I'm on a house-hunting trip.

Noonan: That's marvelous news.

Rawe: Yes, but I'm a bit uneasy about apartment costs here. They're just out of this world.

Noonan: You're right, but I'm sure your company will help you find a nice place. Let's go have a bite and hear the rest of your story.

* * *

■狀況

上禮拜從香港來電的狄克 · 羅來到了公司。由於是過去的同事，諾南親自到櫃臺迎接他。羅很久沒到 ABC 食品公司了。他看來似乎很懷念這裏。接著兩個人大概有意邊吃中飯邊聊一些過去的事情吧！

羅：早安，我是狄克・羅。我是來找湯瑪士・諾南先生的。

櫃臺小姐：羅先生，您早。他知道您要來嗎?

羅：我跟他約好吃午餐。

櫃臺小姐：[電話中] 後藤小姐，我這邊是櫃臺。有位羅先生在這兒 … 是的，我知道了。羅先生請坐。一會兒就會有人來見你的。

羅：謝謝。

諾南：嗨，狄克。真高興又看到你，你看來氣色不錯。

羅：湯姆，真高興看到你。你看來也不錯，事事順心的樣子。

諾南：這次是甚麼風把你吹到東京來的。

羅：是這樣子的。下個月公司重新派遣我到東京，我這次是來找房子的。

諾南：這真是個好消息。

羅：是啊，不過這裡的房價讓我有點吃不消。實在貴得不像話。

諾南：你說的沒錯，不過我相信你的公司會幫你找個好地方的。我們去吃個飯，再聽你說說其他的事。

* * *

Words and Phrases

expect 預期；期待
shortly 不久
fit 強健的；身體狀況佳的
healthy 健康的
prosperous 成功的；諸事順遂的
house-hunting 找房子
marvelous 奇妙的；難以置信的
uneasy 不安的
have a bite 〔俗〕吃東西；用餐

Vocabulary Building

- **date** *n.* 約會 *v.* 日期為…

  cf. I've just received your letter dated May 1.
  (我剛收到你五月一日寫的信。)

- **reassign** 重新分派

  You'll soon be reassigned to handle China trade.
  (你很快便會被重新任命處理對中國的貿易。)

- **out of this world** 極好的；不同凡響的；不像是世上該有的

  The food your wife cooks is just out of this world.
  (你太太煮的菜真是美味極了。)

重點文法・語法

I have a Mr. Rawe here.

專有名詞之前加上 a 時，其意義即變為「一位叫做…的人」。在此即表示「有一位姓羅的先生在這兒」之意。

就普通名詞而言，亦可解釋做「像…這樣的人」或是「…家的成員」這種意思。譬如說，I'd rather be an Edison than a Shakespeare.（比起莎士比亞，我倒是希望成為像愛迪生這樣的人物)，或是He's a Carter.（他是卡特家族的一員)，諸如此類。

▶*Exercises*

請利用括弧內的詞語改寫下列例句，並盡量保持原來的語意。 (解答見248頁)

1. Tell me what brings you to Tokyo this time.
   (what business, you have in, I'd like to know)

2. The company is reassigning me here next month.
   (transferred to Tokyo, being, shortly)

3. I'm sure your company will help you find a nice place.
   (positive, employer, locate)

簡短對話

Noonan: How's the family doing?
Rawe: They're doing just fine, thanks. How's yours?
Noonan: My son is going off to college in the States this year. He hasn't decided which one, though. How's your business these days?
Rawe: You know, I've been heavily involved with the manufacture of plastic food containers and I want to strengthen that business in Tokyo.
Noonan: Uh-huh. Maybe we can do business together.
Rawe: Is there anyone at ABC Foods that I can talk to ?
Noonan: Yeah, I'll introduce him to you after lunch.

How's the family doing? 你的家人好嗎？ **How's yours?** 你的家人呢？ **be involved with** 與…有牽連；專心於… **food container** 食品容器 **Uh-huh.** 嗯哼。〈在聽別人講話時表示附和之意的發語詞〉

Lesson 4

Visitors (2)（訪客）

預習—*Sentences*

· I can't imagine what he wants out of me.
· Maybe I could take him around for you.
· I never drop in without an appointment.
· I do have a message from Mr. Noonan's office.
· His secretary will be here soon.

Vignette

Goto: I just finished speaking with Mr. Doug Falcon of Crockett Corp. He's been referred to us by Mel Wakita of Hawaiian Pineapple Co. Mr. Falcon said he's only staying in Tokyo for a few days and he wanted to have an appointment to see you.

Noonan: Crockett is a pet food company. I can't imagine what he wants out of me.

Goto: He said he'd like to see you tomorrow morning and visit our plant.

Noonan: Tomorrow? I have a feeling it'll be a waste of time.

Goto: Since he's got Mr. Wakita's introduction, maybe I could take him around for you.

Noonan: Good idea. Why don't you give him a tour first and then bring him in? But be sure to interrupt us after 15 minutes and remind me that I've got another meeting starting shortly.

Goto: Yes, Mr. Noonan.

* * *

Falcon: May I see Mr. Noonan, please.

Receptionist: Do you have an appointment with him?

Falcon: Of course, I do. I never drop in without an appointment.

Receptionist: I beg your pardon. You must be Mr. Falcon. I do have a message from Mr. Noonan's office to notify him as soon as you've arrived. His secretary will be here soon.

Goto: Good morning, Mr. Falcon. My name is Miss Goto. I'm Mr. Noonan's secretary. I'm sorry but Mr. Noonan was called by the chairman about ten minutes ago. He should be back any minute now, but may I take you around the plant first?

* * *

■狀況

經由在夏威夷經營鳳梨工廠的日裔美國人河木田的介紹，弗肯突然打電話給諾南。由於他要求碰面，並且希望時間是明天早上，所以諾南感到非常地困擾。他大概是認為，「河木田那邊甚麼也沒聽說，若只是來看看工廠消磨時間的話，就沒必要見面」吧。

後藤：我剛和克洛基公司的道・弗肯先生談過話，他是夏威夷鳳梨公司的梅爾・河木田介紹的。弗肯先生說他只在東京停留幾天，想跟你約個時間見見面。

諾南：克洛基是個寵物食品公司。我無法想像他想從我身上得到些甚麼。

後藤：他說他想明天早上來找你，並參觀我們的工廠。

諾南：明天？我覺得那會是浪費時間。

後藤：不過，他是河木田先生介紹的，也許我可以替你帶他參觀一下。

諾南：好主意。妳何不先帶他參觀，再帶他來見我？可是，記得一定要在十五分鐘後進來打斷我們的談話，提醒我稍後有個會議要開。

後藤：好的，諾南先生。

* * *

弗肯：我想見諾南先生，謝謝。

櫃臺小姐：你跟他有約時間嗎？

弗肯：當然有。我都會事先約好時間再來造訪的。

櫃臺小姐：非常抱歉。你一定是弗肯先生。諾南先生的辦公室留話說你一來就通知他。他的祕書很快就會過來。

後藤：早安，弗肯先生。我是後藤，諾南先生的祕書。很抱歉，諾南先生大概十分鐘前被董事長叫去。他應該很快就會回來，可否先由我帶您參觀工廠？

* * *

Words and Phrases

imagine 想像
waste of time 浪費時間
tour （工廠等的）參觀；巡禮
interrupt 打斷
drop in 不期然的造訪
any minute 隨時都有可能

Vocabulary Building

- **refer** 介紹；稱…為…

  cf. The new detergent is what's generally referred to as a "me-too product."
  (這種新的清潔劑被稱為是「具同樣效果的產品（相仿產品）」。)

- **appointment** 約會

  I'd like to have an appointment with your chairman for at least 20 minutes.
  (我想和你們董事長約個時間見面，至少要個二十分鐘。)

- **introduction** 介紹

  By way of introduction, I'm forwarding a sample product for your personal use.
  (為了介紹產品，我寄上樣品供你個人使用看看。)

重點文法・語法

May I see Mr. Noonan, please.

此文以 May I 開始，結構上雖屬疑問句，但就其意義而言，應為直述句（「我想見諾南先生」）。一般在此情形下，可以不用問號 (?)。

▶*Exercises* 請利用括弧內的詞語改寫下列例句，並盡量保持原來的語意。

（解答見248頁）

1. I have a feeling it'll be a waste of time.
   (can't help but feel, unproductive, meeting)

2. Why don't you give him a tour first and then bring him in?
   (would you like to, before, bringing)

3. Do you have an appointment with him?
   (expecting, is he)

◆◆◆◆◆◆◆◆◆◆◆◆◆◆◆ 簡短對話 ◆◆◆◆◆◆◆◆◆◆◆◆◆◆◆

Goto: Mr. Falcon, would you like to take a look around our plant first until Mr. Noonan is available.
Falcon: I sure would.
Goto: Come this way, please. Watch your step.
Falcon: What are these cartons?
Goto: I believe they're canned pineapples waiting for shipment.
Falcon: Where do you get your pineapples?
Goto: Mostly from the Philippines and Hawaii. Let me take you to the production area.

---

take a look around 四處看看… **Watch your step.** 小心腳下；走路小心。
carton 紙箱 **canned** 罐裝的 **shipment** 發貨；裝運

Lesson 4

Visitors (3) (訪客)

預習—*Sentences*

· What's your projection for our market share?
· It'll exceed 20 percent in the Kanto area.
· Is it still a good strategy to focus on Kanto?
· This discussion has been very helpful.
· We'll get to work on this right away.

Vignette

Miki: In conclusion, you may be pleased to know that the results of the market research by our firm are quite encouraging. Prospects are bright for the new yogurt to garner a substantial share of the market in a relatively short span of time.

Noonan: Excellent. What's your projection for our market share a year after its launch?

Miki: If supported by a well-prepared advertising program, it's quite possible to exceed 20 percent in the Kanto area. You'll find our detailed quantitative study in this report, which I'll leave with you.

Noonan: That's very good, Mr. Miki. Any questions, Shoichi?

Sawasaki: You still think it's a good strategy to focus on Kanto?

Miki: Initially, yes. Our research shows that ABC Foods has a strong quality image in the Kanto area and the up-market yogurt will capitalize on that.

Noonan: This discussion has been very helpful and has cleared up most of our questions. We'll get to work on this right away.

■狀況

行銷顧問公司的三木發表了計畫研究成果。雖然結果顯示前途一片光明，但卻令人感到有些過度樂觀。不過，整個新產品的行銷計畫看來沒甚麼問題。接下來，為著新產品的上市，他們可有得忙了。

三木：總歸來說，看到我們公司做出來的市場調查報告，你們會很滿意的，因為結果顯示，這個市場的前景相當看好。新種優酪乳很有希望在相當短的時間內就占有市場的大部分。

諾南：好極了。那你預測我們的新產品在上市一年後，市場占有率會有多少?

三木：如果有妥善的廣告計畫配合的話，在關東地區的占有率可能會超過百分之二十。在這份要給你的報告中，你可以找到有關產品市場定量分析的詳盡資料。

諾南：非常好，三木先生。昭一，有沒有甚麼問題?

澤崎：你還是認為，將重心放在關東區是個好策略嗎?

三木：初步來看，我是這麼想。我們的研究顯示，ABC 食品公司在關東區的產品品質形象很好。而採高檔市場取向的優酪乳就是要利用這既有的品質形象。

諾南：這次的討論很有助益，幫我們澄清了大部分的疑點。我們立刻開始著手進行吧!

Words and Phrases

in conclusion 歸結來說
research 調查
encouraging 振奮人心的；令人覺得充滿希望的
yogurt [`jogɚt] 養樂多；優酪乳
garner 獲得
substantial 相當的；重大的
span of time 時間的長度
projection 預測
launch 開始發售
quality image （產品的）品質形象
capitalize on 利用…

Vocabulary Building

● **share of the market** 市場占有率

cf. The beer has a 50 percent market share in Japan.

（這種啤酒在日本有百分之五十的市場占有率。）

● **quantitative study** 定量分析

I know that public relations is good for our corporate image, but I want a quantitative study about its effect on sales.

（我了解宣傳活動有助於提升我們公司的形象，但我想要一份它如何影響銷售的定量研究。）

● **up-market** 高檔市場的

The shoddy ornament destroys our up-market image.

（這假飾品破壞了我們高檔市場的形象。）

重點文法・語法

ABC Foods has a strong quality image.

在美國，公司名稱以單數處理。但是在英國，由於一般都視為複數，所以是ABC Foods have . . . 。至於 company 或 government 之類的集合名詞，在英國通常以複數來處理。

▶Exercises

請利用括弧內的詞語改寫下列例句，並盡量保持原來的語意。

(解答見248頁)

1. The results of the market research are quite encouraging.
   (findings, reassuring)

2. You'll find our detailed quantitative study in this report.
   (take a look at, presented in)

3. Our research shows that ABC Foods has a strong quality image.
   (your company, according to)

◆◆◆◆◆◆◆◆◆◆◆◆◆◆ 簡短對話 ◆◆◆◆◆◆◆◆◆◆◆◆◆◆

Noonan: Mr. Miki, other than advertising what do you recommend we do for the launch?

Miki: You may want to consider a kick-off press conference. You could also do a reception for representatives of major supermarket chains.

Noonan: I like the press conference idea but I'm afraid we don't have much experience in that area.

Miki: I'll be happy to get you in contact with a couple of public relations firms that can organize a press conference for you.

Noonan: Would they have a bikini-clad girl jumping out of our yogurt?

---

other than 除了…以外 **launch** *n.* 發售；發表 **kick-off** 開始的 **press conference** 記者招待會 **get someone in contact with** 使某人與…取得聯絡 **bikini-clad** 身著比基尼泳裝的

Lesson 4 Visitors — 總結

公司的櫃臺人員由於會接觸許多訪客，所以一定得確認來訪者的姓名、所屬單位及其是否事先約好等事情。櫃臺人員對羅先生的應對方法應該是標準的。就說法而言，比起 What is your name? Do you have an appointment with him? 來說， May I have your name, please? 和 Is he expecting you? 都顯得有禮貌得多。

但是，也有像弗肯這樣的情形，他不喜歡別人問他有沒有事先約好。他會覺得說，「我並非那麼不懂禮貌的人」。實際上，對外國人而言，事先排定約會是一般的常識。「碰巧來這邊，順道過來看看」的情形是絕對沒有的。

跟在上位的人見面時，一般是先在櫃臺連絡，然後由祕書出來引導至辦公室。但是，來訪者若是像羅先生這種好朋友或是重要人物，有時本人也會親自出來迎接。

在弗肯的情形，如果河木田的介紹信能早他一步到，也許就不會有太大的問題了。像他這樣突然打電話要求見面，是否安排 appointment，就看祕書後藤如何決定。而後藤大概也是自行研判而予以接受的。諾南囑咐說，「過十五分鐘，就使它結束」。

但即使沒有這個暗示，細心的祕書在客人待得很久時，也會觀察老闆的臉色，就算接下來沒有任何約會，也會過來說「下個會議馬上要開始」，或是「某某人從剛才就一直在等」，再不然，就塞張便條進來。

跟忙碌的人約會碰面時，在去之前通常會先說，I know you're a busy person, so I won't take much of your time. 而對於撥空會見的對方，致上感謝之詞亦是一種禮貌的表示。

在最後的部分中，諾南所說的 This disussion has been very helpful and has cleared up most of our questions. 也表示了「我們這邊想要結束」的意思。

Lesson 5

Getting Ready for a Business Trip

（出差在即）

Lesson 5 的內容

出差之前必須把事情都交待清楚，免得因為人不在公司而使業務停擺。此外，還得將工作處理妥當，並為出差時的工作先有準備。一旦遇上國外出差，像護照、機票等種種煩人的瑣事便接踵而至，令人手忙腳亂。澤崎是第一次奉命到美國總公司出差。行程從紐約的簡報開始，相當緊湊。

不過他預備在最後一週的週末到夏威夷朋友那兒，好好逍遙一下。

Lesson 5

Getting Ready for a Business Trip (1)

（出差在即）

預習—*Sentences*

· Getting ready for a vacation in the States?
· I've been to New York but never to Cincinnati.
· You're a worrier, aren't you?
· Give my regards to everybody.
· You deserve a vacation.

Vignette

Noonan: Hi, Shoichi. Getting ready for a vacation in the States?

Sawasaki: Hello, Tom. It's no vacation. I've got to make a pitch to the Management Council in New York and visit the computer center in Cincinnati. And then ...

Noonan: I know, I know. I was only kidding. Are you excited?

Sawasaki: I guess you could say so. I've been to New York but never to Cincinnati.

Noonan: The computer center operation in Cincinnati is so brand new I haven't seen it either. I understand it's got all the leading-edge technologies. You'll also visit the main plant in New Jersey?

Sawasaki: Yes, I'll spend a couple of days there too. But what worries me is this presentation I have to give to the top management at headquarters.

Noonan: You're a worrier, aren't you? I'm positive that you'll come out of that meeting with flying colors. Give my regards to everybody. When will you be back?

Sawasaki: Two weeks from Monday. I'll spend the last weekend in Hawaii on the way back. I have some good nisei friends on Kauai I haven't seen for a while.

Noonan: Good. You deserve a vacation. Have a ball.

* * *

■狀況

當澤崎正在為他第一次的赴美出差做行前準備時，諾南也來了。諾南一直想藉著開玩笑來減輕澤崎的緊張情緒，可是澤崎似乎滿腦子只想著他在紐約要作的那場簡報。

諾南：嗨，昭一。準備好到美國度假了嗎？

澤崎：哈囉，湯姆。我不是去度假。我得出席紐約的經營管理會議，並在會中作發表，之後要到辛辛那提參觀那裡的電腦中心，然後…

諾南：我知道，我知道。只是開個玩笑而已。你會不會很興奮？

澤崎：我想應該會吧！我是去過紐約，但沒去過辛辛那提。

諾南：辛辛那提電腦中心的運作相當新穎，連我都還沒看過呢。就我所知，所有那些尖端科技它全都有了。你也要參觀公司在紐澤西的總廠嗎？

澤崎：沒錯，我會在那兒待幾天。但我擔心的是在紐約總公司時，我要對著那些最高管理階層所作的那場簡報。

諾南：你真是個緊張大師耶，對不對？我相信你一定會凱旋著步出會場的。記得替我向大家問好。你甚麼時候會回來？

澤崎：下週一出發，兩個禮拜後回來。回程時，我會在夏威夷度過最後的週末。我在考愛島有些日裔第二代的好朋友，我們有陣子沒見面了。

諾南：你是該度個假了。祝你玩的愉快。

＊ ＊ ＊

Words and Phrases

Management Council 經營管理會議
kid *v.* 開玩笑
excited 興奮的
brand new 嶄新的
worrier 愛尋煩惱的人
positive 確信的
give one's regards to 替某人問候…
deserve 配得…
have a ball 有個美好時光

Vocabulary Building

- **pitch** 〔俗〕發表；宣傳

  Jay made a good sales pitch on the new product.
  (傑對於這個新商品做了相當好的銷售宣傳。)

- **leading-edge technology** 尖端科技

  Our accountant still prefers to use an abacus. He just doesn't understand leading-edge technology.
  (我們的會計仍然偏愛使用算盤，他就是不瞭解所謂的尖端科技。)

- **with flying colors** 獲得極大的成功；凱旋

  Michael passed the in-house advancement test with flying colors.
  (麥可很成功地通過了公司內部的升等考試。)

重點文法・語法

It's no vacation.

用 no 來修飾作補語的名詞比用 not 來否定動詞（即 It's not a vacation.）更強調否定的意味。表示「才不是去度假」之意。

▶Exercises

請利用括弧內的詞語改寫下列例句，並盡量保持原來的語意。

(解答見248頁)

1. The computer center is so brand new I haven't seen it either.
   (just opened, so, visited)

2. What worries me is this presentation I have to give at headquarters.
   (I'm worried about, in New York)

3. I'll spend the last weekend in Hawaii on the way back.
   (en route to Tokyo, intend to)

◆◆◆◆◆◆◆◆◆◆◆◆◆◆ 簡短對話 ◆◆◆◆◆◆◆◆◆◆◆◆◆◆

Noonan: Have you put together the business presentation?

Sawasaki: Yes, and I'll be using a dozen overhead slides too. But frankly I feel a bit edgy about it. Am I supposed to tell a joke before I start?

Noonan: No, don't do that if you're not comfortable with it. Just rehearse well and be prepared to field some tough questions. I know you've put a lot of hours into it. You'll come out all right.

Sawasaki: I certainly hope so.

---

put together 放在一起 **a dozen** 一打 **overhead slide** 幻燈片 **edgy** 焦躁的 **be supposed to** 應該要… **rehearse** 排練 **field** *v.* 有技巧地處理〔問題〕 **tough** 難辦的；難以解決的 **put a lot of hours into** 花費很長的時間在… **come out** 結果

Lesson 5

Getting Ready for a Business Trip (2)

（出差在即）

預習—*Sentences*

· I'll pick up my traveler's checks after lunch.
· I have a notice here from the seminars committee.
· Here's your memo on competitors' moves in Japan.
· I don't know what I'd do without you.
· That's what I really want.

Vignette

Sawasaki: I'll pick up my traveler's checks after lunch and go straight to the ad agency to look at the final proof of the new ad series. I'll be back around 4, but I'm going to be tied up for the rest of the day. Say, Nancy, who am I having lunch with today?

Yamamoto: Mr. Suzuki of the marketing association.

Sawasaki: Oh, that's right. By the way, I have a notice here from the seminars committee about next week's meeting. Could you call the chamber of commerce and say I won't be able to make it?

Yamamoto: Yes, I will. There are a couple of phone messages, none urgent. And here's your memo on competitors' moves in Japan that I've prepared in rough draft.

Sawasaki: This looks great. You know something, Nancy? You are a fantastic secretary. As always, you've caught my spelling and grammatical errors and corrected them. I don't know what I'd do without you.

Yamamoto: Thanks. That's what I really want—compliments rather than a raise.

Sawasaki: You bet.

■狀況

出差的前一天，澤崎為各種大小事情忙亂不已。幸好，祕書山本是個勤快可靠的好幫手，讓澤崎省事不少。澤崎還拜託她看一看自己要在紐約作簡報的稿子，而山本連那些文法和拼字上的錯誤都替他糾正過來了。

澤崎：午餐後，我得去拿我的旅行支票，再直接到廣告公司那兒看看我們新系列廣告的最後校樣。我大約會在四點左右回來，但其他時間也全都排滿了。嘿，南西，我今天中午要和誰吃飯呀?

山本：行銷協會的鈴木先生。

澤崎：哦，是他沒錯。對了，我這裡有個研討委員會的通知，上面說下星期有個會議要開，妳能不能幫我打個電話給商會，告訴他們我沒辦法出席?

山本：好的。你有兩三通電話留言，但都不是緊急的。還有，這是你簡報中，關於日本同業動向的備忘錄，我已經擬好草稿了。

澤崎：這看來好極了！南西，妳知道嗎? 妳是個很了不起的祕書。妳總是能挑出我在文法和拼字上的錯誤，並予以改正。我真不知道，沒有了妳我該怎麼辦！

山本：謝謝，這就是我所想要的——讚賞而非加薪。

澤崎：那當然了。

Words and Phrases

ad (<advertising) agency 廣告代理商；廣告公司	competitor 競爭對手
proof 校樣	draft 草稿
make it 〔口語〕趕上；成功；做到	fantastic 極好的
urgent 緊急的	as always 一如以往
	You bet. 〔口語〕當然；的確。

Vocabulary Building

● **traveler's check** 旅行支票

You should sign your traveler's checks as soon as you get them but never countersign until you actually use them.

(你一拿到旅行支票，要先在上面簽名，之後，除非是你要用它來付帳了，否則不要副簽確認。)

● **chamber of commerce** 商會〈也可略作 chamber〉

cf. I have to go to the chamber to attend the meeting of the employment practices committee.

(我必須到商會去參加勞工雇用會議。)

● **You know something?** 你知道嗎?〈也可用You know what?〉

cf. "You know what?" — "Tell me." — "There's something on your hair."

(「你知道嗎?」「甚麼事?」「你頭髮上面有東西。」)

重點文法・語法

traveler's check

在英國，traveler 拼成 traveller，要 double l，而 check 則拼作 cheque。

▶*Exercises*

請利用括弧內的詞語改寫下列例句，並盡量保持原來的語意。

(解答見248頁)

1. Could you call them and say I won't be able to make it?
   (will be absent, give them a ring, advise)

2. You've caught my grammatical errors and corrected them.
   (were good enough to, mistakes, correct)

3. I don't know what I'd do without you.
   (be helpless, your assistance)

◆◆◆◆◆◆◆◆◆◆◆◆◆◆ 簡短對話 ◆◆◆◆◆◆◆◆◆◆◆◆◆◆

Yamamoto: Shoichi, I've listed on this sheet your passport number and the numbers on your credit cards and traveler's checks.

Sawasaki: What would I need that for?

Yamamoto: In case you lose your cards or passport, the list should come in handy.

Sawasaki: Well, I hope that won't happen but thanks all the same.

Yamamoto: You should watch out in New York. I've heard so many horror stories.

Sawasaki: Those stories tend to be exaggerated. Don't worry.

---

in case 如果；倘若 **come in handy** 派上用場 **all the same** 照樣；仍然 **watch out** 留心 **horror story** 恐怖的事 **exaggerate** 誇張；渲染

Lesson 5

Getting Ready for a Business Trip (3)

（出差在即）

預習—*Sentences*

· Do you have a copy of my itinerary?
· You know where to get in contact with me.
· I'll initial these interoffice memos.
· I wonder if you can do a small favor for me.
· My brother works there.

Vignette

Sawasaki: Now do you have a copy of my itinerary?

Yamamoto: Yes.

Sawasaki: You know where to get in contact with me. I'll leave the address of my friends on Kauai in case you have to reach me there. You can open all my letters, except for the ones marked "Personal." All invoices can wait till I come back, I think. I'll initial these interoffice memos now. Incidentally, is there anything you want me to get for you in the States?

Yamamoto: That's very kind of you, Shoichi. But no thanks. Instead, I wonder if you can do a small favor for me while you're in the New York area.

Sawasaki: What is it?

Yamamoto: My brother works there. Would you be good enough to give him a ring and tell him I'm doing all right? Here's his number.

Sawasaki: I'll be delighted to. I'll tell him how well you're doing and all the rest of it. Anything you want me to take to him? No? Now can you do me a small favor in return while I'm away?

Yamamoto: Of course.

Sawasaki: Can you water my plants and take good care of them?

Yamamoto: Sure. I'll even talk to them every morning like you do.

■狀況

澤崎將行程表交給山本，並告訴她自己在美國的緊急聯絡處。雖然山本說她沒有甚麼特別想要的東西，但澤崎心想，若有空的話，要買些裝飾品之類的禮物送給她。因為他不在公司的時候，擺在辦公室裡的盆栽還得託她照料呢！

澤崎：你有我行程表的複本了嗎？

山本：是的。

澤崎：你知道哪裏可以聯絡得上我。我會把我朋友在考愛島上的地址留給妳，這樣的話，萬一臨時有事，妳也可以找得到我。我所有的信件，妳都可以拆開來看，除非上面寫著要本人親啟。發票的話，我想都可以等到我回來再說。我現在先在公司內部的通報字條上簽上我的姓名縮寫。對了，妳有沒有甚麼東西要我幫妳從美國帶回來的？

山本：昭一，你人真好。不過，謝了，沒甚麼需要的。只是我在想，不知你在紐約時，能否幫我個小忙？

澤崎：甚麼事？

山本：我哥哥在那兒做事。你能不能行行好幫我打個電話給他，並告訴他我在這兒一切都好。這是他的電話號碼。

澤崎：我很樂意替你打這個電話。我會告訴他妳現在過得有多好，以及所有其他的事。還有東西要我帶給他的嗎？沒有啦？那換我要請妳在我離開時幫我個小忙了。

山本：那當然。

澤崎：你能幫我替我的盆栽澆水並妥善照顧它們嗎？

南西：當然，我甚至還會像你一樣，每天早上跟它們說說話。

Words and Phrases

get in contact with 與…連絡
initial *v.* 簽姓名的第一個字母於…
incidentally 順便一提
instead 作為代替
give someone a ring 給某人打通電話
do someone a favor 幫某人一點忙
in return 作為回報；作為替換
water *v.* 澆水

Vocabulary Building

● **itinerary** 行程表

Your itinerary shows you'll spend a whole week in Las Vegas for just a two-day meeting. Why?
(你在拉斯維加斯的會議只有兩天，可是你的行程表上卻寫著你要在那裡待上一個禮拜，這是甚麼原因?)

● **personal** 親啟〈也可作 Personal and Confidential〉

Please stamp the letter "Personal and Confidential."
(請在這封信上蓋上「私人郵件」的戳記。)

● **interoffice memo** 公司內部的通報字條

Keep your interoffice memos to one page. Be concise.
(你在寫辦公室內通報字條時，內容不要超過一頁。務必簡潔。)

重點文法・語法

Is there anything you want me to get for you in the States?
Anything you want me to take to him?

基本單字 take, get, bring 的用法千萬不要混淆。從這裡「帶去」用 take，從那裡「帶來」用 get，bring 則有把東西或人「帶來」之意。

▶Exercises 請利用括弧內的詞語改寫下列例句，並盡量保持原來的語意。 (解答見248頁)

1. You know where to get in contact with me.
   (reach, how to)

2. All invoices can wait till I come back, I think.
   (guess you can, hold, until)

3. That's very kind of you, Shoichi. But no thanks.
   (a sweet person, that's all right)

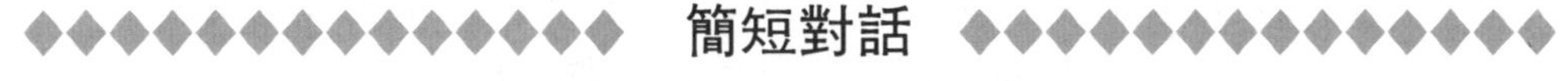

簡短對話

Sawasaki: Are the airline tickets here too?

Yamamoto: No, the travel agency said they'll send them to us this afternoon by messenger. They'll also bring your travel insurance cards.

Sawasaki: Good. Have you been able to confirm my hotel for one night in Waikiki?

Yamamoto: Not yet, but I'll fax the name of the hotel via the New York office as soon as confirmation is received.

---

travel insurance 旅行保險 **confirm** 確認 **via** 經由… **confirmation** 確認

Lesson 5 Getting Ready for a Business Trip — 總結

當你告訴別人說，「我一年要到國外出差好幾次」時，對方可能會回答，「真好」。在本課故事開頭，諾南就是這樣子地調侃昭一，「準備好到美國度假了嗎?」

一提起國外出差，或許有人會認為那跟去觀光旅遊沒甚麼兩樣。但事實上，出差通常都會有許多預定的商務活動。在出差期間，不論清晨或深夜，都要與本國的公司以電話聯繫。出差回來後，則得面對堆積如山的文件。而出差時除了週末可以喘口氣之外，根本沒有時間觀光。聽說最近還有人前往美西做當天來回的出差。這是由於時差的關係，所以根本沒在當地過夜便搭機返國。這也太辛苦了。

話雖如此，一年到國外出差數次也不是甚麼壞事。因為這畢竟可以增廣見聞，開拓視野。同時，也可以舒解一下平日僵化的上班生活。而且，相信在一路的行程中，都能使人獲益良多。

到國外出差時，記得要攜帶幾張信用卡、一千美元左右的旅行支票、和少許的本國貨幣（回家時的交通費）。至於美鈔現金，則只要夠付計程車費和請人搬運行李時的小費（餐廳的小費可以用信用卡付）就可以了。

這樣，就大致可以安心出門了。不過，如果你到的是治安不佳的城市，最好把護照、信用卡、旅行支票等的號碼都記在備忘錄上以防萬一。

Lesson 6

Small Talk

（閒聊）

Lesson 6 的內容

即使在商業界裡，有時候如果能先以愉快的閒聊緩和對方的情緒，然後再切入主題，也是會很有助益的。這種閒聊，英文稱為small talk。西方人在研討會或餐會上，只要與不認識的人目光接觸，會先微笑示意，再報上姓名，並上前握手，然後就會有些 small talk。和上司在同一輛車中，也可以用small talk來打破沈默，突破窘境。在本課，我們將做這方面的練習。

到紐約總公司訪問的澤崎，立刻就能將前一天在機場發生的事巧妙應用到small talk 裡面。

Lesson 6

Small Talk (1)（閒聊）

預習—*Sentences*

· How was your flight?
· I went to a newsstand to buy a newspaper.
· I'm very sorry to hear that.
· I should have been more careful.
· What was in the bag?

Vignette

Turner: Welcome to the Big Apple. How was your flight?
Sawasaki: The flight was very smooth but I received a most unusual welcome yesterday.
Turner: What happened?
Sawasaki: I'd just arrived at JFK. I went to a newsstand to buy a newspaper and put down my shoulder bag to pay for it. I counted the change and looked at where I'd put the bag. It was gone. It was just a matter of a few seconds.
Turner: Oh, it sounds like you were ripped off. Real pros need only that much time to do the job. But I'm very sorry to hear that.
Sawasaki: I should have been more careful. I felt bad.
Turner: Did you contact the police?
Sawasaki: Yes. I was told that I was the sixth Japanese to report trouble at the airport yesterday. New York thieves had a field day.
Turner: What was in the bag ?
Sawasaki: Traveler's checks for $1,000, some credit cards, and my return airplane ticket. Luckily, I carried about $200 in my hip pocket, so that was safe at least.
Turner: It's ironic, because that's usually the most dangerous spot to carry cash.

* * *

■狀況

在總公司，由行銷部門的艾瑞克 · 透納接待澤崎。澤崎對前一天在紐約機場遭竊的事仍耿耿於懷。他萬萬沒有想到會受到那樣子的「歡迎」。那天發生的事立刻成為他倆的話題。

透納：歡迎到紐約來。一路上還順利吧？

澤崎：飛行是很平順，不過昨天我所受到的歡迎可就不怎麼樣了。

透納：怎麼啦？

澤崎：剛到達甘迺迪機場，我就去報攤買報紙，為了付錢，我放下肩包。數零錢時，我看了一下放肩包的地方，它卻不見了。前後不過幾秒鐘而已。

透納：看來你被偷了。高手只要那幾秒鐘就到手了。我很遺憾發生這種事。

澤崎：我應該再小心點才是。我覺得好嘔。

透納：你向警察報案了嗎？

澤崎：報了。他們說我是昨天第六個在機場報案的日本人。看來昨天紐約的竊賊都出籠了。

透納：你包包裡有些甚麼東西？

澤崎：總值一千美元的旅行支票，幾張信用卡，還有我的回程機票。還好我在褲子後面的口袋放了兩百元美金。那至少是個安全的地方。

透納：真夠諷刺了。那裡通常是錢最容易被偷的地方。

* * *

Words and Phrases

Big Apple (the ~) 紐約市的別稱
flight 航空旅行
newsstand 書報攤
rip off 偷竊
pro (<professional) 專家；熟諳此道者
ironic 諷刺的

Vocabulary Building

- **change** 零錢

  Can you spare some change?

  (能不能施捨我一點零錢?)

- **have a field day** 有重大事件的日子；特別活躍的日子（field day 是「運動會」之意）

  cf. We've invited athletes from local schools for our field day.

  (我們已邀請了當地學校的運動員來參加我們的運動會。)

- **credit card** 信用卡

  cf. Cash or credit?

  (付現或刷卡?)

重點文法・語法

I felt bad.

也可寫成 I felt badly. 但一般而言，這視為錯誤用法。fell, look, smell, taste, prove等動詞當作不及物動詞使用時，其後接形容詞。例如：

You look happy to meet me.（你好像很高興見到我。）

Your voice sounds sweet.（你的聲音聽起來很甜美。）

The milk smells sour.（這牛奶聞起來好像酸掉了。）

The beer tastes bitter.（這啤酒喝起來很苦。）

The new secretary proved incompetent.（這位新來的祕書被發現沒有能力。）

▶*Exercises*

請利用括弧內的詞語改寫下列例句，並盡量保持原來的語意。 (解答見249頁)

1. The flight was very smooth but I received a most unusual welcome.
   (bizarre, encounter, pleasant)

2. Real pros need only that much time to do the job.
   (professional thieves, just a few seconds)

3. I was told that I was the sixth Japanese to report trouble.
   (police said, get into, visitor from Japan)

◆◆◆◆◆◆◆◆◆◆◆◆◆◆◆ 簡短對話 ◆◆◆◆◆◆◆◆◆◆◆◆◆◆◆

Turner: It must have been a professional thief to do such a quick job.
Sawasaki: That's what the police told me too.
Turner: Were they helpful to you?
Sawasaki: Not really. They just had me file a report. I guess they're too busy with more serious crimes.
Turner: I understand that the Japanese travelers are often victimized abroad, because they believe in carrying cash around, don't they?
Sawasaki: That's true. But I've learned my lesson now.

---

quick job （偷竊）手腳俐落的工作；敏捷的勾當 **file a report** 提出報告 **be victimized** 犧牲；受害 **learn one's lesson** 得到教訓

Lesson 6

Small Talk (2) (閒聊)

預習—*Sentences*

· It's a bit cold in here, isn't it?
· It's absolutely freezing.
· Do you come to these conventions often?
· I'm with a meat-packing company in Missouri.
· What do you do in Tokyo?

Vignette

Sawasaki: It's a bit cold in here, isn't it?
Fox: You can say that again. It's absolutely freezing. The air conditioning isn't working properly.
Sawasaki: Do you come to these conventions often?
Fox: No, but I was interested in this year's theme—how to manage change. Some speakers bored me to sleep but there were a couple of good presentations that gave me fresh insights.
Sawasaki: I was impressed with this morning's speaker. He knew exactly what he was talking about. My name is Shoichi Sawasaki. I'm from Tokyo.
Fox: Hi. I'm Henry Fox. I'm with a meat-packing company in Missouri.
Sawasaki: I'll give you my business card.
Fox: Thank you. I don't have mine with me. I see you're from ABC Foods. What do you do in Tokyo?
Sawasaki: I'm a marketing manager in charge of frozen foods.
Fox: I hear that the cost of beef is exorbitant in Japan. Why is that?
Sawasaki: Raising cattle is quite expensive. It takes sizable pasture for grazing and farmers depend to a large extent on imported feed grains.

* * *

■狀況

隔日，澤崎出席由全美食品產業協會在紐約所主辦的研討會。中場喝咖啡休息時間，澤崎和鄰座的與會者交談了起來。雙方都作了自我介紹，而日本牛肉則成為兩人的話題。

澤崎：這裡有點冷，不是嗎？

福斯：對啊！實在冷透了。空調並沒調好。

澤崎：你常來參加這些會議嗎？

福斯：不常，不過我對今年的議題很感興趣——如何駕馭轉變。有些演講人無聊到令人打瞌睡，不過有幾場倒是叫人耳目一新。

澤崎：今天早上那位演講人就令我印象非常深刻，他對所講的主題很在行。我是東京來的澤崎昭一。

福斯：嗨，我是亨利・福斯，我在密蘇里的一家精肉業公司工作。

澤崎：這是我的名片。

福斯：謝謝。不過我身上沒帶名片。你名片上寫你在 ABC 食品公司做事，你在東京負責甚麼？

澤崎：我是冷凍食品的行銷經理。

福斯：聽說日本的牛肉非常昂貴，是甚麼原因呢？

澤崎：飼養牛隻很昂貴，要有可供放牧的大型牧場，而且農場經營者大部分都得倚賴進口的穀物飼料。

* * *

Words and Phrases

You can say that again.
〔口語〕我完全同意。
freezing 極冷的
bore someone to sleep 無趣到令某人想睡覺
meat-packing 〔美〕精肉業的
exorbitant [ɪgˋzɔrbətənt] （價格、要求等）過高的
sizable 相當大的；可觀的
pasture 牧場
grazing 放牧
feed grains 穀物飼料

Vocabulary Building

● **convention** 會議
The convention business plays an important role in shaping the economy of many American cities.
(在決定美國多數城市的經濟發展方向上，商業會議扮演著重要的角色。)

● **insight** 洞察（力）
The study tour gave me a good insight into the life of average Americans.
(遊學讓我對一般美國人的生活有了一番認識。)

● **business card** 名片
It's embarrassing to have run out of business cards when you are introduced to someone.
(引見於他方時發現自己的名片用完是很尷尬的。)

重點文法・語法

I'm with a meat-packing company in Missouri.

be with是表示「在 … 工作」的一般說法。若要詢問對方的工作單位，較正式的說法是 What's the name of the company you work for? 而口語中更簡單的說法為 Who are you with? 或 Who do you work for? 對應的回答則為 I'm with ABC Foods. 或 I work for ABC Foods.

Who. . .? 是在詢問企業（組織）的名字時使用，但若用在已經知道企業（組織）的名稱，或者是對同公司的人，則變成表示詢問「上司」的名字。

▶*Exercises*

請利用括弧內的詞語改寫下列例句，並盡量保持原來的語意。

（解答見249頁）

1. Some speakers bored me to sleep.
   (were so boring, put me)

2. I see you're from ABC Foods.
   (with, your card says)

3. farmers depend to a large extent on imported feed grains.
   (greatly dependent on, from overseas)

◆◆◆◆◆◆◆◆◆◆◆◆◆◆◆◆◆ 簡短對話 ◆◆◆◆◆◆◆◆◆◆◆◆◆◆◆◆◆

Fox: You folks massage your cattle and feed beer to them, don't you? What's that for?

Sawasaki: I guess that's intended to make the meat tender. You're talking about what's known as Kobe beef. It has a reputation for its marbled and tender texture—and high price.

Fox: I know I can't afford to eat beefsteaks in Japan. But I'd like to visit Tokyo again. I made a quick stopover there during the Vietnam war.

Sawasaki: If you do come, I'll be happy to take you around.

Fox: Thank you.

---

cattle 〔集合〕牛 **tender** 柔嫩的 **marbled** 夾有脂肪的 **texture** 肉的肌理 **stopover** （旅途中的）中途下車（稍作停留） **take someone around** 帶某人四處參觀

Lesson 6

Small Talk (3) (閒聊)

預習—*Sentences*

- Look at this bumper-to-bumper traffic.
- Our mass transit systems are well developed.
- I heard you bought a new house.
- You've got to be kidding.
- "Astronomical" is the word.

Vignette

Sawasaki: Look at this bumper-to-bumper traffic. Reminds me of Tokyo.

Turner: Do you commute by car, Shoichi?

Sawasaki: No, there's too much traffic in Tokyo. Besides, our mass transit systems are very well developed. But because of soaring land costs, people are commuting to work over longer and longer distances.

Turner: Are the commuter trains crowded?

Sawasaki: Terribly. You spend a great deal of energy even before getting to the office. I change trains at Shinjuku Station, where over a million passengers get on and off trains each day.

Turner: That's more than the entire population of Cincinnati. What about housing? I heard you bought a new house.

Sawasaki: Yes, but it's very small. In fact, it's so small we have to use condensed milk and concentrated juice.

Turner: [*Laughs*] You've got to be kidding! Is housing expensive in Japan?

Sawasaki: "Astronomical" is the word. I live about an hour away from downtown Tokyo. Even there a piece of land about the size of my handkerchief costs more than a couple of thousand dollars.

■狀況

澤崎坐上透納的車子，要去紐澤西州的工廠。路上車潮不斷，嚴重的大塞車使他們的心情也開始浮躁起來。兩人間的對話一時中斷，於是澤崎聊起了東京的通勤和居住情況。

澤崎：看到這車水馬龍的交通讓我想起了東京。

透納：昭一，你開車上班嗎？

澤崎：沒有，東京的交通太繁忙了。此外，我們的大眾運輸系統發展得非常完備。不過因為地價高漲，人們住得越來越遠，而通勤的路程也就越來越遠了。

透納：那通勤電車擁擠嗎？

澤崎：非常擠。還沒到辦公室你氣力就花掉了一大半。我在新宿車站換車，那裡每天有超過一百萬以上的人次上下車。

透納：那可比辛辛那提的總人口還多。住的方面怎麼樣？聽說你買了新房子。

澤崎：沒錯，不過房子很小。老實說，因房子太小，我們不得不使用煉乳和濃縮果汁。

透納：[笑] 你一定在開玩笑！日本的房子很貴嗎？

澤崎：只能用「天價」兩個字來形容。我住在離東京市區大約一小時車程遠的地方。在那裡，連我手帕一般大小的地都值兩千元美金以上。

Words and Phrases

bumper-to-bumper 車水馬龍（保險槓幾乎相碰，形容交通之繁忙）	soaring （價格）高漲的
remind 令…想起	commuter train 通勤電車
commute 通勤	condensed milk 煉乳
	concentrated juice 濃縮果汁

Vocabulary Building

● **mass transit system** 大眾運輸系統

The nationwide transportation strike crippled the mass transit system.

（全國性交通運輸機構的罷工使得大眾運輸系統陷於癱瘓。）

● **housing** 住屋；住宅

Housing and education are the two main headaches for many Japanese.

（住屋及教育是最令日本人頭痛的兩大問題。）

● **astronomical** 天文學（上）的；龐大的

Astronomical sums of money have been spent to develop the new supersonic jet.

（巨額的經費花在發展新式的超音速噴射機上。）

重點文法・語法

I live about an hour away from downtown Tokyo.

downtown Tokyo 指的並不是東京日本橋、淺草等「商人或工人居住的地方」。英語的 downtown 是指「都市的中心」或「商業街」。（在英國則稱為 city centre, business centre等）與之相對的 uptown 通常是指「住宅區」。

▶Exercises

請利用括弧內的詞語改寫下列例句，並盡量保持原來的語意。

（解答見249頁）

1. Because of soaring land costs, people are commuting to work over longer and longer distances.
   (increasingly long, are forcing people to)

2. You spend a great deal of energy even before getting to the office.
   (by the time you get to, already spent)

3. Is housing expensive in Japan?
   (housing costs, high)

◆◆◆◆◆◆◆◆◆◆◆◆◆◆◆ 簡短對話 ◆◆◆◆◆◆◆◆◆◆◆◆◆◆◆

Turner: Why is housing so expensive?

Sawasaki: The supply of land for residential use is very scarce. And there's a tremendous concentration of population around major cities.

Turner: What's homeownership like?

Sawasaki: It's around 60 percent.

Turner: That's not too bad, is it?

Sawasaki: No, the only thing is that Japanese homes are so much smaller. The average new house built in Japan is only half the size of a new American home.

---

residential use 住宅用（地） **concentration** 集中 **homeownership** 房屋擁有率

Lesson 6 Small Talk — 總結

對澤崎而言，他遭遇了較之 small talk 更令人意想不到的「異鄉記聞」。還好他的祕書山本事先把信用卡和旅行支票的號碼記下來，所以之後的手續大概可以順利進行了。

通常，只要能清楚地告知失竊的事實，並出示本人的身分證明，過不了幾天，當地的辦事處便會補發信用卡和旅行支票。而機票如果被變賣成現金或遭不正當使用的話，以後還是會退還。就算信用卡被不正當使用，因為有保險，所以也不需要擔心。也就是說，澤崎所失去的只有錢包和肩包而已。

但不管怎麼說，就如眾所周知的，日本人最常把現金帶在身上去旅行，所以出國時就得隨時注意防竊。為顧及便利性和安全性，到外國出差時最好還是使用信用卡。

與初次見面的人開始會話 (strike up a conversation) 時，最常使用的話題是「天氣」(weather)。因為它最 harmless (無害),而且不會引起對方警戒而能自然地對話。在本課當中，澤崎就是以「這裡有點冷!」而開始和鄰座的人交談起來。

在研討會和餐會中，對於底下的與會者而言，一些關於主講人或是議題的小小評論，都會是些令人感興趣的共通話題。但如果發表太深入、太具體的感想，或是胡亂地挑毛病，則會引起對方的反感。澤崎和透納在車中所談關於日本的情況，也是一個容易帶動氣氛的話題。

要記得的是，先用深呼吸來緩和剛開始的緊張感，之後便能輕鬆地繼續談下去。早日習得這種how to break the ice（打破僵局）的技巧是非常重要的。

Lesson 7

Money Talks

（金錢萬能）

Lesson 7 的內容

在紐約停留的最後一晚，澤崎受到艾瑞克・透納的招待，在一間高級餐廳進晚餐。結束之後，話題移轉到「小費」上面。對澤崎來說，每回在海外出差時最感麻煩的就是給小費這件事了。

Lesson 7

Money Talks (1)（金錢萬能）

預習—*Sentences*

· You'll have to let me reciprocate.
· Just excuse me for a second.
· What do you do about tipping in Japan?
· You just pay what it says on the meter.
· You'd have a revolution on your hands.

Vignette

Sawasaki: Thank you, Eric. That was the most magnificent meal I've had in years. You'll have to let me reciprocate the next time you're in Tokyo.

Turner: Don't worry about it, Shoichi. That's not a bad deal, though, because I know that a steak dinner would cost at least three times as much in Tokyo. Anyway, just excuse me for a second while I check the numbers here and figure out how much to give the waiter. [*Examines bill*] Hmm, by the way, what do you do about tipping in Japan?

Sawasaki: We don't.

Turner: No tipping? Now that's what I'd call a civilized system.

Sawasaki: At hotels and some restaurants they add a service charge to the bill, but other than that, tipping isn't customary.

Turner: What about cab drivers and porters?

Sawasaki: In a cab you just pay what it says on the meter. I generally tip hotel porters ¥ 100 per bag, but in first-class hotels they're instructed not to accept gratuities.

Turner: You'd have a revolution on your hands if you tried to introduce that sort of system here.

Sawasaki: It's a big difference betweeen Japanese and American customs. It's created complications, I've noticed, at Japanese restaurants here in the States. A sushi bar I went to the last time I was here had a big sign in Japanese saying, "You are requested to tip here." I guess people feel so at home that they tend to leave without tipping.

■狀況

透納戴上眼鏡，開始查看帳單上的數字。他是要看看他們有沒有算錯，並計算小費要給多少。透納聽澤崎說日本不用給小費，便有感而發地說，「那才是所謂的文明社會嘛！」雖說美國人已經很習慣付小費了，但感到麻煩的人似乎也很多。

澤崎：艾瑞克，謝謝。這是我近幾年來吃過最棒的一頓飯了。下次你到東京來，一定得讓我回請你。

透納：這你可別擔心，昭一，搞不好，還是我賺到了呢，因為就我所知，東京的一頓牛排大餐，至少比這裡貴上三倍。不管怎樣，先讓我看一下他們有沒有算錯錢，再看看該給服務生多少小費。[查看帳單] 嗯，對了，在日本你們都怎麼給小費？

澤崎：我們不給小費。

透納：不給小費？對嘛，那才是所謂的文明社會。

澤崎：在飯店和一些餐廳中，他們會在帳單內加上服務費，除此之外，我們沒有給小費的習慣。

透納：那計程車司機和行李搬運工呢？

澤崎：計程車只要照表付費。至於旅館的行李搬運工，我通常是一件行李給他們一百日圓。不過，如果是在五星級飯店，他們也會被告知不能收小費。

透納：如果你想把那套制度引進到這裡的話，那可是會鬧革命的。

澤崎：日本和美國的習慣是差很多。我注意到，因著這種習慣的不同，所以對於開在美國的日本料理店而言，情況就變得有些複雜了。我上次到這裡時，去過一家壽司店，我看到裡頭有張大大的告示，上頭用日文寫著，「此地須付小費」。我猜想這可能是因為日本人來到這種店就像回到家一樣，所以他們也像在日本一樣不付小費就走了。

Words and Phrases

magnificent [mæg`nɪfəsənt] 棒極了；絕佳的
Don't worry about it. 別擔心。
That's not a bad deal. 這個交易不壞。
civilized 文明的；開化的
customary 習慣上的；一般的
cab 計程車
porter 腳夫；行李搬運工
gratuity [grə`tjuətɪ] 小費；賞錢
introduce 引入
complication 複雜的事態
feel at home 感覺像在自己本國內
tend to 傾向…

Vocabulary Building

● **reciprocate** 回禮

cf. Let me return the favor when you came to Japan.
(你到日本時得讓我回請你。)

● **for a second** 一下子；瞬間〈口語中也可將second 縮寫為sec〉

cf. Just a sec. I have to answer a call on another line.
(你先稍等，我得接一下另外一條線上的電話。)

● **revolution** 革命

cf. The company introduced a revolutionary concept in inventory control.
(那家公司引進了一套存貨管制的革命性觀念。)

重點文法・語法

... figure out how much to give the waiter

若想減低言語中帶有性別歧視的成分，可以將後面接man或woman的詞改成～person，或是換個說法來表示。比如：newsman改成reporter, policeman改成police officer, stewardess 改成 flight attendant；或是把 chairman 改成 chairperson, salesman 改成 salesperson 等。

waiter 是男性名詞，waitress 是女性名詞，所以雖然有wait person 這樣的詞，但就像 houseperson (<house wife) 一樣，在英語中尚未成為固定用法。

▶Exercises

請利用括弧內的詞語改寫下列例句，並盡量保持原來的語意。

(解答見249頁)

1. That was the most magnificent meal I've had in years.
   (splendid dinner, enjoyed, in many)

2. A steak dinner would cost at least three times as much in Tokyo.
   (200 percent more, the least expensive)

3. Now that's what I'd call a civilized system.
   (institution, strikes me as, decent)

◆◆◆◆◆◆◆◆◆◆◆◆◆◆◆ 簡短對話 ◆◆◆◆◆◆◆◆◆◆◆◆◆◆◆

Waiter: Would you care for some dessert?

Turner: How about you, Shoichi?

Sawasaki: Thanks, but I couldn't eat another bite. Maybe just a cup of coffee.

Turner: [*To waiter*] OK. I guess we'll just have two coffees, then. Oh, and I'd like the check now, please.

Waiter: Just a moment, sir.

---

care for 喜歡… **couldn't eat another bite** 再也吃不下了 **check** 帳單

Lesson 7

Money Talks (2)（金錢萬能）

預習—*Sentences*

· They don't do that with their local customers.
· I don't care for that kind of pushy style.
· He was holding out a fistful of dollar bills.
· How did this all get started?
· I don't want to sound too inquisitive.

Vignette

Sawasaki: At another Japanese restaurant I went to, the waiter brought me a bill that already included a 15 percent tip. Later I found out that they don't do that with their local customers, but with their Japanese clientele they're taking no chances.

Turner: Is that a fact? Sometimes I get tired of the whole business, though. I rode in a limo once with a sign prominently displayed behind the driver's seat saying, "Gratuity not included in fare." Had to stare at it the whole way to JFK. I don't care for that kind of pushy style.

Sawasaki: It's so cumbersome for us to figure out how much to tip. I saw one Japanese tourist who had given up. He was holding out a fistful of dollar bills to a taxi driver and letting him take what he wanted. But that's hardly an ideal solution either. Anyway, how did this all get started, do you know?

Turner: I understand it's an old English custom. There are a number of stories about the origin of the word "tip," but the one I like best is that it's an acronym standing for "to insure promptness."

Sawasaki: Hmm, does that make sense? After all, you usually tip after you receive a service, not before, right?

Turner: Actually, that's true, of course, and I admit the theory I gave you is probably nothing more than a folk etymology.

Sawasaki: Uh, I don't want to sound too inquisitive, but how much do you tip in a place like this?

Turner: In a regular restaurant I'd give the waiter 15 percent of the total bill. Here I leave 20 percent.

■狀況

小費是日本和歐美差異甚大的習慣之一,因為在日本沒有給小費的習慣。澤崎舉例說明了關於日本遊客到國外的日本料理店時產生的混亂情形 。但是“ tip”的真正語源是什麼呢?

澤崎：我去過另外一家日本餐館，服務生給我的帳單就已包括了百分之十五的小費。之後，我發現他們對當地顧客並不那樣做；就只有對日本顧客，他們是絲毫不敢大意。

透納：真有這回事？其實我自己有時候對這一切也很厭煩。有一次我搭了輛小型巴士要到機場，司機座椅後面掛了一塊很顯眼的牌子，上面寫著：「小費另賞」。我必須一路盯著這些字眼到甘迺迪國際機場。我不喜歡這種湊著臉向人要錢的方式。

澤崎：對我們來說，要計算該給多少小費還挺累人的。我見過一個日本遊客，他根本就不算了，他掏出一大把一元美鈔，讓計程車司機自取。但這種辦法實在也算不得高明。到底，這一切是怎麼開始的？你知道嗎？

透納：就我瞭解，這是一種舊式英國習俗。至於“tip”這個字的來源，則有數種不同的說法。但我最喜歡的一種是，t.i.p. “ To Insure Promptness”，「保證服務迅速」之意。

澤崎：嗯，這樣說合理嗎？畢竟，大家總是在得到服務之後才給小費，而非事先付費，不是嗎？

透納：實際上，你這樣說當然也沒錯。而且，我得說，我告訴你的這種理論或許不過是某種民間語源罷了。

澤崎：呃，希望你不會覺得我問題太多。我想知道，像在這種地方，你會給多少小費？

透納：在一般餐廳，我會給服務生總消費額的百分之十五作小費。在這裡，我會給百分之二十。

Words and Phrases

clientele [ˌklaɪən`tɛl] 顧客
take no chances 不冒險；謹慎其事
limo (<limousine) 〔口語〕往返於機場和市區之間載送旅客的小型巴士
prominently 突出的；醒目的
fare 費用
cumbersome 不方便的
fistful 一把之量的
acronym [`ækrənɪm] 頭字語
insure 保證
promptness 迅速；敏捷
theory 理論；學理
folk etymology 通俗語源〈像是把 tulip 解釋作從 two lips 演變而來的說法〉
inquisitive [ɪn`kwɪzətɪv] 好追根究底的

Vocabulary Building

● **(the) whole business** 〔口語〕整件事
The whole business of filling out tax returns is such a pain in the neck.
(填寫退稅申報表這件事實在令人痛苦。)

● **pushy** 〔口語〕太積極或太堅持己見而令人生厭的
There's a difference between aggressive selling and a pushy style.
(在所謂的積極推銷和強迫推銷兩者之間是有所不同的。)

● **make sense** 有道理
No explanation is adequate if it doesn't make sense.
(任何解釋，只要在道理上說不通，就是不充分。)

重點文法・語法

But with their Japanese clientele they're taking no chances.

clientele 是表示「(商店、餐廳等的) 顧客」、「(醫生的) 病人」、「常客」等的集合名詞。也就是將複數的人集合為整體，用一單位來表示，通常沒有複數形。

表示「員工」、「職員」的集合名詞，還有staff, personnel, workforce 等。

▶Exercises

請利用括弧內的詞語改寫下列例句，並盡量保持原來的語意。

(解答見249頁)

1. I don't care for that kind of pushy style.
   (aggressive, object to)

2. It's so cumbersome for us to figure out how much to tip.
   (calculate, give the waiter, troublesome)

3. That's hardly an ideal solution.
   (not a good answer, to my dilemma)

◆◆◆◆◆◆◆◆◆◆◆◆◆◆◆◆ 簡短對話 ◆◆◆◆◆◆◆◆◆◆◆◆◆◆◆◆

Turner:[*Puts on glasses*] Excuse me, I've now reached the age where I can't read without these things.

Sawasaki: Do you always check the bill before you pay?

Turner: It's a good idea. Sometimes they've added it up wrong, and a couple of times I've been given the bill for another party.

Sawasaki: But at a fancy place like this . . .

Turner: Makes no difference. You still have to be careful.

---

add it up wrong 加錯了 **party** 一夥人 **fancy** 高級的 **make no difference** 並無差別

Lesson 7

Money Talks (3)（金錢萬能）

預習—*Sentences*

· How about if the service wasn't good?
· I wouldn't advise going back to that restaurant again.
· You should always leave something.
· I've written a polite letter to the management.
· You can't get out the door without tipping.

Vignette

Turner: Today I'm also giving $5 to the sommelier—the wine steward, that is—for his suggestion of a wine, which I thought was excellent. Oh, and it's customary to tip the coatroom attendant a dollar per coat and to give the doorman a dollar if he catches you a taxi.

Sawasaki: How about if the service wasn't good? Can you leave without tipping?

Turner: [*Laughs*]You could try it, but I wouldn't advise going back to that restaurant again. The way I see it, you should always leave something, because the tips are often an essential part of the employees' wages. If the service is lousy or nonexistent, you can always choose to go somewhere else next time. Also, on occasion I've written a polite letter to the management suggesting that the food or the service wasn't up to par.

Sawasaki: That seems like a lot of trouble to go to.

Turner: If you can't be bothered to write a letter, I understand there's an organization that gives out preprinted complaint cards to its members. You can check off the items corresponding to your grievance and leave the card either in lieu of a tip or to explain why you left so little. In this particular restaurant, however, you really can't get out the door without tipping. It's called the Palms, you see.

Sawasaki: I don't understand.

Turner: Wait, I'll explain it to you once we're outside.

■狀況

小費若是賞錢，那服務不好的時候可以不給嗎？透納回答說，這麼做雖然可以，但那家餐廳以後最好不要再去了。然而，據說在這家餐廳，「你不付小費的話，休想走出大門。」這是什麼意思呢？

透納：我今天也給sommelier——就是那個酒保——五塊錢美金作小費，謝謝他對酒的建議，我認為他建議的酒棒極了。對了，我們也習慣要給衣帽間的服務生小費，一件外衣一塊錢。如果門僮替你叫了計程車，你也要給他一元小費。

澤崎：如果服務不周到呢？可以不給小費嗎？

透納：[笑著] 你可以試試看，不過我會勸你下次別再到那家餐廳去了。依我來看，你每次都應該多少留點小費，因為有很多員工的薪水大半來自顧客留給他們的這些錢。如果服務很差，或是根本沒有服務，你總是可以選擇下次換一家。此外，有時候我會寫封客氣的信給他們的管理部門，表示他們提供的食物或服務夠不上標準。

澤崎：那好像很麻煩。

透納：如果你不想寫信的話，我知道有個機構，他們提供事先印好的抱怨卡給他們的會員。你自己看看有甚麼不滿，再逐項圈選，最後，留下這張卡當作小費，或是將此卡連同些微小費留下，以資說明。不過，在這家特別的餐廳裡，你別想不給小費就走出大門。你瞧，這家店叫做 Palms。

澤崎：我不明白。

透納：等會兒，我們到外面之後，我再跟你解釋。

Words and Phrases

advise *v.* 勸告；忠告
(the) way I see it 依我所見
lousy 〔口語〕差勁的
nonexistent 不存在的
on occasion 有時；偶爾
up to par 達到標準
preprinted 事先印好的
check off 查驗是否符合或滿意而予以畫記
in lieu [lu] of 代替…

Vocabulary Building

● **sommelier** [ˌsʌməˋlje] （餐廳中）專門負責酒類的侍者；酒保
I hate it when people use French words like "sommelier." Why don't they just say "wine steward"?
(我討厭人們用像"sommelier"之類的法文，為甚麼他們不能就說「酒保」呢?)

● **can't be bothered to** 不願意去做…
I can't be bothered to read all the junk mail I get.
(我不可能費心去看所有我收到的垃圾信函。)

● **grievance** [ˋgrivəns] 抱怨；不滿
The company set up a grievance board to handle employees' complaints.
(公司設立一申訴部門來處理員工的不滿投訴。)

重點文法・語法

The tips are often an essential part of the employees' wages.

wage是「工資」、「薪水」的意思，但以複數形 wages 表示已成慣例。

同樣的，表示「遺蹟」、「遺骨」等意義的remains，或表示「感謝」之意的 thanks 等詞，也常用複數形，而不用單數形。

▶*Exercises*

請利用括弧內的詞語改寫下列例句，並盡量保持原來的語意。

(解答見249頁)

1. How about if the service wasn't good?
   (what if, was below par)

2. The way I see it, you should always leave something.
   (in my opinion, all the time, you'd better)

3. You can always choose to go somewhere else next time.
   (the same place, not to, return)

◆◆◆◆◆◆◆◆◆◆◆◆◆◆◆◆ 簡短對話 ◆◆◆◆◆◆◆◆◆◆◆◆◆◆◆◆

Sawasaki: I always find it a little awkward to pull out my wallet to tip people like bellhops in hotels.

Turner: My system there is to take the money out of my billfold in advance and have it ready in my pocket.

Sawasaki: But what if you don't have the right amount?

Turner: That can be a problem. I try to keep a good supply of singles on hand, especially when I'm traveling.

---

awkward 困窘的 **pull out** 掏出 **bellhop** 服務生 **billfold** 皮夾 **in advance** 事先 **single** 〔美俗〕一美元紙幣

Lesson 7 Money Talks — 總結

西方給小費的習慣對東方人而言實在是件麻煩的事。但在國外，無論是到哪裡，做甚麼，都離不開小費。原本，給小費的用意是為自己受到的服務 (service performed) 表示感謝 (thanks)。但實際上，小費在餐廳等地方已成為他們員工收入的重要部分了。

一般而言，小費大致是總消費額的一成，但這又依國家和餐廳格調的不同而有差異。若要到一個陌生的環境，最好事先向旅行社請教，或是詢問當地的人。如果正好沒有零錢可以給小費，也可以向收小費的對方要求找零。

在美國，計程車司機的小費最少要50 cent，通常會付到費用的百分之十五。而行李搬運員（在機場稱skycap，車站稱redcap，飯店稱 bellhop）的小費，一件行李約 1 dollar；但如果行李較重或搬運距離較長，則要再多付一些。

在餐廳中，就像本課故事裡頭一樣，給 waiter 的小費約為百分之十五 (高級餐廳則要百分之二十)，wine steward 則是每一瓶酒三到 五元（都是以加算稅金前的數目計算即可）。而付給 checkroom（可以寄放衣物、行李的地方）人員的小費是一次 1 dollar，而付給飯店門僮幫忙叫計程車的小費也是1 dollar。

另外，西方人會當著客人的面，很自然地檢查帳單上面的數目，而不以此為失禮。

在最後的場景中，透納說了一句話，「因為店名是Palms」。這其實是雙關語。既然名字是 palms，店門前可能會有棕櫚或椰子樹等的裝飾。但這個字還有另一個意思，就是「手掌」。也就是說，透納真正的意思是，「如果不給小費就想從這兒走出去的話，服務生就會張著手掌準備打你了。」

Lesson 8

Business Entertainment

（招待）

Lesson 8 的內容

澤崎將招待常年走訪日本的史本塞。史本塞是一家大規模連鎖餐廳的資深副總(senior vice president)。該餐廳的總公司在亞特蘭大。史本塞是澤崎的客戶，為業務來日本購買冰淇淋和奶油。他們兩人來到澤崎常去的北海道鄉村料理店。雖說史本塞對日本料理頗為內行，他甚至常以壽司當午餐，但澤崎點的菜似乎也太像「山珍海味」了。

Lesson 8

Business Entertainment (1)（招待）

預習—*Sentences*

· Is there anything you'd like to see or do?
· That's very thoughtful of you.
· Let's just go to some quaint little restaurant.
· I'm an adventurous eater.
· What time shall we go?

Vignette

Sawasaki: I'd like to take you out tonight. Is there anything you'd especially like to see or do— or any restaurant you're particularly interested in having dinner at?

Spencer: Thank you, Shoichi. That's very thoughtful of you. When I was here last time three years ago, someone took me to Kabuki. I was grateful for his kindness, but that wasn't my <u>cup of tea</u>. Let's just go to some quaint little restaurant where not many foreign tourists go.

Sawasaki: Do you care for Japanese food?

Spencer: Oh, I love it.

Sawasaki: You have no problem with raw fish?

Spencer: No problem at all. I'm an adventurous eater.

Sawasaki: And you don't mind squatting on the floor? All right, I'll take you to a nice Japanese restaurant that features country-style <u>cuisine</u> from Hokkaido. Is that all right?

Spencer: Sure. That sounds very <u>intriguing</u>.

Sawasaki: What time shall we go?

Spencer: Whenever. Shall we say 6 or 6:30?

Sawasaki: OK, I'll meet you in the main lobby of the hotel at 6:30.

Spencer: Super. See you then.

* * *

狀況

澤崎將招待 ABC 食品公司的重要客戶史本塞。在確定史本塞喜歡日本料理之後，澤崎決定帶他到自己常去的北海道鄉村料理店。他們約在飯店的大廳碰面。

澤崎：今晚我想帶你出去。你有沒有甚麼特別想看或特別想做的事？或者，你有沒有對哪家餐廳特別感興趣，想去吃頓晚飯甚麼的？

史本塞：謝謝你，昭一，你想得真周到。我三年前到這裡來時，有人帶我去看歌舞伎。我是很感激他的好意，只是，那實在不對我的味。我們就去些沒有太多外國觀光客駐足的店吧，就是那種有點古老又不太大的店。

澤崎：你喜歡日本料理嗎？

史本塞：哦，我很喜歡。

澤崎：那生魚片怎麼樣？

史本塞：沒問題。我是個勇於嘗試的饕客。

澤崎：這麼說你也不介意跪坐在地板上囉？那好，我就帶你去一家很好的日式餐廳，它的特色是北海道鄉村風味的料理。這樣好嗎？

史本塞：那當然。聽起來相當誘人。

澤崎：我們甚麼時候走呢？

史本塞：甚麼時候都可以。我看就六點或六點半怎麼樣？

澤崎：沒問題，我六點半在旅館大廳跟你碰頭。

史本塞：太棒了。到時見。

* * *

Words and Phrases

especially 特別地
thoughtful 體貼的；設想周到的
grateful 感激的
quaint 饒富古風的
care for 喜歡
raw fish 生魚片
adventurous [əd`vɛntʃərəs] 喜歡冒險的；大膽的
squat 盤坐
country-style 田園風味的
whenever 任何時候

Vocabulary Building

- **cup of tea** 口味；愛好〈通常用於否定句〉
  I don't know why Annette's so popular in the office. She just isn't my cup of tea.
  (我不懂為甚麼安妮特在辦公室會那麼受歡迎。她實在不是我喜歡的那一型。)
- **cuisine** [kwɪ`zin] 料理；烹飪法
  Do you have a preference for any particular type of cuisine?
  (你有沒有甚麼特別喜歡的料理呢?)
- **intriguing** 有趣的；吸引人的
  cf. I was quite intrigued by the police detective dressed in an old trench coat.
  (那個身穿老舊防水大衣的警探令我相當感興趣。)

重點文法・語法

That sounds very intriguing.

動詞 intrigue [in`trig] 本來的意思是「耍陰謀」、「施詭計」，但由於法語腔調深受喜愛，而開始以「引起興趣」之意流行開來。有些語言學家認為後者是unneeded French substitute (多餘的法語代用詞)，可用英語 interest, fascinate, puzzle 等表達，而不太接受。但現今後者使用的普遍已遠超過前者。該字在語感上有「(因珍貴、魅力等而) 引起興趣、激發好奇心」的味道。

▶ *Exercises*

請利用括弧内的詞語改寫下列例句，並盡量保持原來的語意。

（解答見249頁）

1. I'd like to take you out tonight.
   (have dinner, I wish to, with)

2. I was grateful for his kindness, but that wasn't my cup of tea.
   (appreciated, thoughtfulness, like the place)

3. You have no problem with raw fish?
   (is there, any)

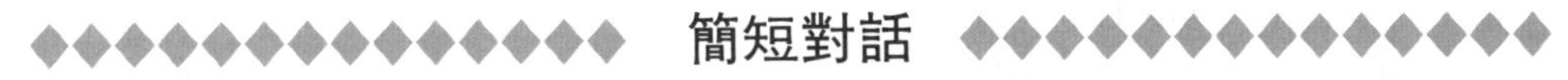

簡短對話

Sawasaki: May I take you out to dinner tonight, if you're free?
Spencer: Thank you. That's very kind of you.
Sawasaki: Do you have a preference as to the kind of restaurant we go to?
Spencer: I like Japanese food but I'll leave it up to you. I do have one slight problem though. I'm allergic to eggs.
Sawasaki: All right. Do you like raw fish and stuff like that?
Spencer: Yes. I often have sushi for lunch.

---

take someone out 帶某人出去（吃飯） **preference** 喜好 **leave something up to** 把某事留給…來決定 **allergic to** 對…過敏 **stuff** 東西

Lesson 8

Business Entertainment (2)（招待）

預習—*Sentences*

- This is just the kind of place I had in mind.
- Perhaps not *that* adventurous.
- Do you prefer it cold?
- I like it just the way it is.
- I didn't quite understand what was going on.

Vignette

Spencer: This is just the kind of place I had in mind for a relaxed evening. But I never could have found a place like this without a local guide. A good choice, Shoichi.

Sawasaki: I'm glad you like it, John.

Spencer: Now what are these?

Sawasaki: This is sea slug and this is wasp larva. They're my favorites. You did say you were adventurous, didn't you?

Spencer: Perhaps not *that* adventurous. [*Eats them*] Hmm, this is not bad. I wouldn't have them for breakfast, though. Tell me, how was your first visit to headquarters?

Sawasaki: I thought it was very worthwhile for me to see the operations over there and get to know my counterparts.

Spencer: Oh, yes, it's very important to know the key people on the other end. Now, is this sake?

Sawasaki: Yes. It's been warmed. Do you prefer it cold?

Spencer: No, I like it just the way it is. By the way, perhaps you could help me with a question I had. At my office today, my associates were talking about having to accept promissory notes. I didn't quite understand what was going on.

■狀況

史本塞似乎很喜歡這家北海道料理店。剛開始時雖然有點舉箸不定，但每盤菜最後還是被一掃而空。並且他還喜歡喝溫酒。史本塞想起今天在辦公室的事，於是問到關於「期票」的問題。

史本塞：這就是我心中所想要的地方，一個可以輕鬆一晚的地方。不過，如果沒有當地嚮導，我是絕對找不到這種地方的。選得好，昭一。

澤崎：約翰，很高興你喜歡這裡。

史本塞：這些是甚麼東西？

澤崎：這是海蛞蝓，而這是黃蜂的幼蟲。這是我最喜歡的兩道菜。你不是說你勇於嘗試嗎？

史本塞：也許不是「那麼地」勇於嘗試。[吃了] 嗯，還不錯嘛！不過，我是不會拿它們當早餐的。告訴我，你第一次去參觀你們總公司，感覺怎樣？

澤崎：我想，對我而言，去看看那裡的運作情形，並認識一下和我職務相當的人，是十分值得的。

史本塞：哦，是啊，認識一下另外一邊的重要人物是很重要的。這是清酒嗎？

澤崎：是的，它已經溫過了。或是你喜歡涼一點的？

史本塞：不，我就喜歡它這個溫度。對了，有一個問題，也許你可以幫我解答。今天在我辦公室裡，同事們在講關於必須接受期票付款的事。我不太瞭解這是怎麼一回事。

Words and Phrases

relaxed 輕鬆的
choice 選擇
sea slug 海蛞蝓
wasp larva 黃蜂的幼蟲
favorite 最喜歡的人或物
worthwhile 有價值的
by the way 順帶一提

Vocabulary Building

- **counterpart** 對等的人物
  Frank Johnson is my counterpart in the London office.
  (法蘭克・強森是我們公司在倫敦辦事處跟我職務相當的人。)
- **key** 主要的
  Please tell me about the key projects you've handled in the past five years.
  (請告訴我你在過去這五年來經手過哪些主要計畫。)
- **promissory note** 本票；期票
  Our corporate policy is never to accept promissory notes. All transactions should be made in cash.
  (我們公司的政策是絕不接受期票付款；所有買賣都要用現金交易。)

重點文法・語法

I wouldn't have them for breakfast, though.

這裡的 though 是口語用法，表示「還是」、「不過」、「可是」、「然而」，屬於副詞。其用法與當連接詞的 though 略有不同，多置於句尾或插入句中，請參考下列例句：

I can't buy it. It's so cheap, though.（我不能買那個東西，不過，它真的很便宜。）
Your father, though, will miss you.（可是，你的父親會很想你的。）
I get paid well. My work is not challenging, though.（我的薪水是不錯，可是，工作卻沒有甚麼挑戰性。）

▶*Exercises*

請利用括弧內的詞語改寫下列例句，並盡量保持原來的語意。

（解答見250頁）

1. I never could have found a place like this without a local guide.
   (you need a native, a restaurant, hit)

2. Tell me, how was your first visit to headquarters?
   (how, went, I wonder)

3. It's very important to know the key people on the other end.
   (knowing, a necessity, is)

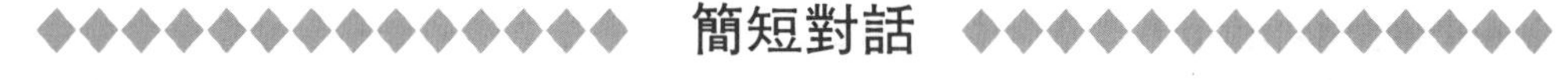

簡短對話

Spencer: Do you see a lot of night life?

Sawasaki: I'm not really the "night on the town" type. I very seldom go barhopping, if that's what you mean.

Spencer: There seem to be millions of drinking establishments in major night spots in Japan. Do they mostly cater to customers doing business entertaining?

Sawasaki: Oh, yes. Business entertainment is big business in Japan. But now golf is used quite frequently to entertain customers too.

---

night life 夜生活；夜遊 **night on the town** 晚上在街上閒蕩 **go barhopping** 到酒吧喝酒 **drinking establishment** 供人飲酒的店；酒館 **cater to** 備辦食物或提供娛樂 **business entertaining** 商務上的招待應酬

Lesson 8

Business Entertainment (3) (招待)

預習—*Sentences*

- What's a promissory note?
- Some notes aren't payable for 9 to 12 months.
- Don't they realize that you're not a bank?
- This is what we call squid noodles.
- Actually they're real delicacies.

Vignette

Spencer: What's a promissory note?

Sawasaki: It's a written promise to pay a designated amount at a certain future time— usually three to six months.

Spencer: Six months! At no interest?

Sawasaki: No interest. Some notes aren't payable for 9 to 12 months.

Spencer: We can't afford to work like that. It'd have a terrible effect on our cash flow.

Sawasaki: Japanese companies sometimes pay their suppliers in promissory notes. Once a hotel chain offered to pay us half in promissory notes and half in accommodation coupons. We declined.

Spencer: Don't they realize that you're not a bank? What are we getting now?

Sawasaki: This is what we call squid noodles. And these are sea toad liver and sea urchin. They may not sound very good, but actually they're real delicacies.

Spencer: Do you often go out drinking with your colleagues after work?

Sawasaki: Yes. I'm a great believer in *nomunication*.

Spencer: What's that supposed to mean?

Sawasaki: It's a combination of the Japanese word *nomu*, which means to drink, and communication. It means you can communicate better through drinking.

■狀況

澤崎正在說明期票。在歐美也有期票，但在使用上並不像日本那麼普遍。史本塞甚至沒聽過這個用詞。當他得知有些期票可以六個月後才兌現，而不必付利息時，他真是驚訝不已。

史本塞：期票是甚麼？

澤崎：那是一種書面承諾，應允在未來某一時期支付一筆款項，而這個期間通常是三到六個月左右。

史本塞：六個月！不必付利息？

澤崎：沒有利息。有些期票甚至長到九至十二個月。

史本塞：我們實在無法那樣運作，因為我們的現金流量可能會大受影響。

澤崎：日本公司有時候會用期票來支付他們向廠商購買的東西。有一次，一家旅館連鎖店向我們提出要用一半期票、一半住宿券的方式來付款。我們拒絕了。

史本塞：難道他們以為你在開銀行啊？現在上的又是甚麼菜？

澤崎：這個我們叫做烏賊麵，而這些是鮟鱇魚的肝還有海膽。聽起來可能不怎麼好聽，不過他們真的是美味佳餚。

史本塞：你下班後常跟你公司的同事出來喝酒嗎？

澤崎：是啊，我可是絕對相信“nomunication”的。

史本塞：那個字是甚麼意思？

澤崎：那是個複合字。就是把日文中意指喝酒的“nomu”加上英文的“communication”（溝通）。合起來就是說，一道喝酒，溝通會更順暢。

Words and Phrases

payable 到期應付的
supplier （上游的）業者；供應商
accommodation coupon 住宿券
decline 拒絕
squid 烏賊
sea toad 鮟鱇魚
sea urchin 海膽
delicacy 佳餚；美味
combination 組合；結合在一起的人或物

Vocabulary Building

- **designated** 指定的；指派的
  You will receive job instructions from your direct supervisor or his designated representative.
  (你將會從你的直屬上司或其指定代理人那兒得到工作指示。)
- **interest** 利息
  The public is now more interested in stocks because of the low interest on regular savings.
  (因為現在普通存款的利率低，所以民眾對股市更有興趣了。)
- **cash flow** 現金流量
  Even though our books show a profit, our cash flow situation is critical this month.
  (雖然我們帳面上顯示的是盈餘，但本月的現金流量情形卻是岌岌可危。)

重點文法・語法

We can't afford to work like that.

afford 一字通常與 can 或 be able to 連用。它有一個特殊的地方，就是主要用於否定句和疑問句，表示「在資金或時間上有餘裕可以做某事」。

▶Exercises

請利用括弧內的詞語改寫下列例句，並盡量保持原來的語意。

（解答見250頁）

1. It'd have a terrible effect on our cash flow.
   (adversely affect)

2. Japanese companies sometimes pay their suppliers in promissory notes.
   (use, in paying, corporations)

3. Don't they realize that you're not a bank?
   (provide, banking services, understand)

◆◆◆◆◆◆◆◆◆◆◆◆◆◆◆ 簡短對話 ◆◆◆◆◆◆◆◆◆◆◆◆◆◆◆

Sawasaki: There's a notion in Japan that unless you drink together, you can't form close human ties.

Spencer: Here's to our close human ties. Cheers.

Sawasaki: Cheers.

Spencer: Drinking places seem to be crowded with businessmen after office hours.

Sawasaki: Yes, it's a good way for them to unwind. Alcohol also loosens the tongue and lets people speak their minds. You can get their honest sentiments, which are otherwise often covered behind the Japanese poker face.

---

notion 概念；想法 **close** *adj.* 親密的 **human ties** 人際關係 **Cheers.** 乾杯！ **unwind** 鬆弛 **alcohol** 酒類 **loosen the tongue** 使人暢所欲言 **speak one's mind** 說出心中的話 **sentiment** 感情 **be covered behind** 被隱藏在…之後 **poker face** 撲克臉〈形容人的表情嚴肅；缺乏感情〉

Lesson 8 Business Entertainment—總結

常聽人說，跟老外吃飯時，要一面吃，一面在腦子裡組織英文句子，結果一頓飯下來，有吃跟沒吃簡直沒甚麼兩樣。

但是這樣子的「招待」場合，不但能藉著緩和的氣氛使彼此更為熟識，而且還能為未來的商業往來舖路。優點不可謂不多。

business entertainment 是一種概括的說法。其實它的形式五花八門，有以business talk為主的breakfast meeting，公司會議室裡的deli lunch（三明治或沙拉之類的簡單午餐），邀請到家中作客，打高爾夫球，觀看運動比賽，或開車到郊外兜風等等，可說是不一而足。

至於如何招待，那就要視預算、時間、以及對方在商務上的份量如何而定了。不過，為了要成功，一定要事先確定客戶的興趣所在。在本次的故事中，澤崎就是這樣先問好了客戶的興趣。

由於這正好是難得的休假，所以澤崎想吃頓日本料理甚麼的。但他還是得先問一下對方吃不吃生魚片，能不能接受跪坐在地板上的用餐方式，然後再據此考量是要吃外國人口味的日式牛排，還是純粹的日本料理。

一般而言，老外用餐並不講求速戰速決的吃法，所以享受美食時千萬不要慌慌張張的。而各個國家用晚餐的時間也不盡相同。像在拉丁國家，晚上九、十點才用餐也是常有的。

在business dinner中，要避開嚴肅的公事話題。與客戶聊些輕鬆的事，並好好享受美食，才是待客之道。像澤崎這樣，邊解說菜色，邊聊日本人的生活百態，以及日本人的商務習慣，可說是善盡了地主之誼。

Lesson 9

Expense Report

（費用報銷報告）

Lesson 9 的內容

剛出差回來的澤崎，馬上就被財務部「傳喚」。原來是他的報銷報告出了問題。澤崎犯了點小錯。舒曼對他說：「因有出差規定，所以不能自己隨意判斷。」雖然他的語氣並不嚴厲，但這對難得出錯的澤崎而言，已有點受不了了。

Lesson 9

Expense Report (1)（費用報銷報告）

預習—*Sentences*

· He said it was urgent.
· Were you looking for me?
· Sorry to take your time now.
· What can I do for you?
· I'm sure we can clear it right up.

Vignette

Yamamoto: Oh, Shoichi, Juergen Schumann of Financial Operations just called. He said it was urgent. Do you suppose there's some problem?

Sawasaki: Well, those bean counters always want something done yesterday. They also tend to have an inflated view of their own importance, I've found, as if the future of the company rested entirely in their hands. Wait a minute. Maybe he wants to talk to me about the expense report I submitted the other day.

* * *

Sawasaki: Were you looking for me, Juergen?

Schumann: Oh, Shoichi. Please come in. How are you today?

Sawasaki: Keeping alive. And you?

Schumann: Fine, thanks. Sorry to take your time now. I know you're quite busy on that strategic alliance project.

Sawasaki: It's all right. What can I do for you, chief?

Schumann: Well, it's about the statement you submitted for your trip to New York. I think there may be some slight misunderstandings on your part about corporate policy on travel expenses. It's no big problem and I'm sure we can clear it right up if you'll just allow me to ask a few questions. All right?

Sawasaki: Fair enough.

Schumann: Very well. You indicate on your expense sheet that you stayed at a hotel for five nights and that it cost you $90 a night. But you attach no receipt. Now I know how expensive decent hotels are in New York and for safety considerations I would not advise any of our employees to stay in a $90-a-night place.

■狀況

新任的財務部經理優根 · 舒曼是剛從法蘭克福調來的。雖然他對澤崎說話很客氣，但他確實是指出澤崎不少錯誤。首先發生問題的是紐約之行的「住宿費」，澤崎並沒有附上收據。

山本：噢，昭一，財務部的舒曼剛打電話來。他說有急事。你想，會不會有甚麼問題？

澤崎：唉，那些專門算小錢的財務人員總是把每件事都看作最急件來處理。而且我發現，他們似乎過於膨脹自我的重要性，好像公司的未來完全掌握在他們的手裡。等一下！也許他是要找我談有關我前幾天交出去的報銷報告。

* * *

澤崎：優根，你找我嗎？

舒曼：哦，昭一，請進。你今天好嗎？

澤崎：想辦法活下去啊！你呢？

舒曼：謝謝，我很好。抱歉現在佔用你的時間。我知道你最近在忙著那個策略聯盟計畫。

澤崎：沒有關係。有甚麼需要我幫忙的嗎，老大？

舒曼：嗯，是關於你這次到紐出差所交來的這分報銷報表。我想你對公司的出差旅費政策有些許誤解。這不是甚麼大問題。而且我想只要你回答我幾個問題，我們就可以把事情搞清楚了。可以嗎？

澤崎：可以啊！

舒曼：很好。你的報銷單中表明，你在飯店住了五個晚上，而且一個晚上要九十塊美金。可是你並沒有附上收據。現在我才了解，在紐約的高級飯店原來要這麼貴。而基於安全的考量，我會建議員工不要去住超過一晚九十美元的地方。

Words and Phrases

urgent 緊急的	chief 老闆；上司
inflated 自我膨脹的	misunderstanding 誤解
expense report 費用報銷報告	clear *v.* 解決；澄清
keeping alive 設法活下去	receipt 收據
strategic alliane 戰略聯盟	

Vocabulary Building

● **bean counter** 財務部門的人〈帶有輕蔑意味〉

Don't call accounting people "bean counters" to their faces.

(別當著財務人員的面說他們是專門算小錢的人。)

● **want something done yesterday** 很急地要某件事儘速完成〈今天告訴人，卻希望早在昨天就做好了〉

If you want everything done yesterday, what will you do tomorrow?

(如果你要所有的事都在昨天完成，那你明天要做甚麼?)

● **Fair enough.** 好吧；可以啊!〈消極地同意對方所說的事〉

"That's all I can give you for a raise this year. OK?" — "Fair enough."

(「今年的調薪，我只能給你加這麼多了，可以嗎?」「好吧。」)

重點文法・語法

Keeping alive.

對於How are you?簡略地回答I've been keeping alive.是說「我正想辦法活下去!」這是一種籠統的回答。類似的回答還有:

I've been [Been] getting by.

I've been [Been] keeping (myself) busy.

I've been [Been] keeping out of trouble. 等等。

▶*Exercises*

請利用括弧內的詞語改寫下列例句，並盡量保持原來的語意。

(解答見250頁)

1. Those bean counters always want something done yesterday.
   (accountants, in a hurry, to get something done)

2. It's about the statement you submitted for your trip to New York.
   (turned in, I want to talk to you, the New York visit)

3. There may be some slight misunderstandings on your part.
   (perhaps, a few things, you misunderstand)

◆◆◆◆◆◆◆◆◆◆◆◆◆◆◆ 簡短對話 ◆◆◆◆◆◆◆◆◆◆◆◆◆◆◆

Sawasaki: The last thing I need today is to get stuck in a session with our esteemed accountant. I have to visit two customers this afternoon and New York is on my back for my quarterly sales projections. Could you ask Juergen if it can wait?

Yamamoto: Certainly, but don't you think it might be more effective if you called him yourself? He may prefer telling you what it's about personally.

Sawasaki: OK. I'll give him a call and see if I can get a reprieve.

---

get stuck in 陷入…而無法動彈 **esteemed** 受尊敬的；可敬的 **accountant** 會計員；會計師 **be on someone's back** 催促某人 **sales projections** 銷售計畫 **get a reprieve** 獲得暫緩

Lesson 9

Expense Report (2)（費用報銷報告）

預習—*Sentences*

- Did you actually stay in a hotel?
- I bought a gift to bring to my host.
- You should charge it under "other expenses."
- Did you keep the receipts?
- Isn't that the standard amount?

Vignette

Schumann: What I want to ask you, Shoichi, is did you actually stay in a hotel?

Sawasaki: Er, actually I didn't. To be honest with you, I stayed at a friend's house in New Jersey.

Schumann: Then you can't claim hotel expenses.

Sawasaki: But I bought a gift to bring to my host and I also took him and his wife out for a night on the town to thank them for putting me up. So I thought I'd bill the company half of what a hotel would've cost me so as to cover my expenses.

Schumann: I'm sorry, Shoichi, but you may not exercise that kind of arbitrary judgment. If you spent money in lieu of hotel expenses, you should charge it under "other expenses" with an itemization of the gift and entertainment. Did you keep the receipts?

Sawasaki: I guess so.

Schumann: Good. Now, I see you're requesting a per diem of $50 for six days.

Sawasaki: Isn't that the standard amount to cover the cost of meals?

Schumann: Yes, it is. But I presume that you had breakfast and perhaps some other meals at your friend's place. And I imagine your contact people at the head office took you out for lunch or dinner, at least once. Am I wrong?

Sawasaki: No, but—

Schumann: Technically the cost of those meals should be deducted from the per diem. In your case, it's probably better to enter the actual out-of-pocket expenses that you personally paid for, along with verification.

狀況

實際上澤崎在紐約並沒有住飯店，但他也就此提出辯解。在財務上，雖然也認可所謂「替代旅館費」的情事，但一定要有可資證明的收據明細才行。此外，澤崎對「每日津貼」的想法也有錯誤之處。

舒曼：昭一，我想問你的是，你真的住有進飯店嗎?

澤崎：呃，其實是沒有。坦白跟你說，我住在紐澤西州的一個朋友家裡。

舒曼：那你就不能要求支領飯店住宿費用。

澤崎：可是我買了一份禮物送給我朋友，而且我還帶他們夫婦倆到城裡玩了一個晚上，以酬謝他們提供我住宿。所以我才會想把住飯店應花費用的一半記在公司帳上，以彌補我的開支。

舒曼：很抱歉，昭一，你不能任意作這樣的判斷。如果你的開支不是用在飯店的住宿，你就應該把它記在「其他」這一欄，並附上禮物和招待費用的明細，你的收據還留著嗎?

澤崎：我想有吧。

舒曼：很好。還有，我看到你要求支領為期六天，每天五十美元的每日津貼。

澤崎：公司規定的伙食費不就是這個數目嗎?

舒曼：是這樣沒錯。不過，我猜想你是在朋友家中吃的早餐，或許還有幾頓中餐或晚餐。然後，我想你在總公司的聯絡人至少請你到外面吃了一頓午餐或晚餐。我沒猜錯吧?

澤崎：沒錯，可是——

舒曼：照規定來講，這幾餐的費用都應從每日津貼中扣除。不過，以你的情況來看，比較好的方式，可能還是報上你個人實際支出的費用，並且附上證明。

Words and Phrases

to be honest with you 坦白跟你說
night on the town 晚上去城裡玩
put someone up 留…住宿
exercise 行使
arbitrary 憑自己決斷的；隨意的
judgment 判斷
itemization 明細
entertainment 招待
per diem 每日的零用金
presume 認為；推想
contact people 聯絡人
deduct 扣除
verification 證明

Vocabulary Building

- **claim** 要求
  Tom tried to claim a deduction for his ex-wife on his tax return.
  (在退稅單上，湯姆要求減免他付給前妻的那筆錢。)
- **in lieu of** 代替…
  George submitted a credit card slip in lieu of a receipt.
  (喬治繳交一張信用卡的帳單代替收據。)
- **out-of-pocket expenses** 實付的費用；付現的費用
  cf. I paid for the meal out of my own pocket.
  (我自己掏腰包吃飯。)

重點文法・語法

I see you're requesting a per diem of $50 for six days.

per diem [pɚˋdiəm] 是表示 per day 的拉丁語。當名詞時作「出差的生活費」、「(旅費) 每日津貼」之意。

per之後所接的詞，在英語中有固定用法，如：per annum (每一年)、per capita (每一人)、percent (百分比)、perse (本身、本質上) 等。

▶Exercises

請利用括弧內的詞語改寫下列例句，並盡量保持原來的語意。

(解答見250頁)

1. To be honest with you, I stayed at a friend's house in New Jersey.
   (my friend, honestly speaking, put me up)

2. Then you can't claim hotel expenses.
   (charge the company, in that case, accommodations)

3. I presume that you had breakfast and some other meals at your friend's place.
   (house, ate, take it)

◆◆◆◆◆◆◆◆◆◆◆◆◆◆◆ 簡短對話 ◆◆◆◆◆◆◆◆◆◆◆◆◆◆◆

Schumann: Tell me, Shoichi, what was the name of this budget-priced hotel?

Sawasaki: Er, it was called the . . .

Schumann: Let's stop playing games with each other. You didn't stay in any hotel, did you?

Sawasaki: [*Hesitates*] No.

Schumann: Shoichi, I hope you realize that a falsified expense report is no laughing matter.

Sawasaki: I know, but can I explain?

---

budget-priced 便宜的 **play games** 玩把戲 **falsified** 假造的 **no laughing matter** 不是開玩笑的事

Lesson 9

Expense Report (3)（費用報銷報告）

預習—*Sentences*

- Put it down under "entertainment."
- You have to opt for one or the other.
- No need to apologize.
- I didn't mean to be too hard on you.
- Will that be all?

Vignette

Schumann: If it was a business meal, put it down under "entertainment,"and be sure to include the name of the other party and your business relationship with them. Incidentally, company policy is that the per diem and actual costs may not be mixed during the same trip. You have to opt for one or the other.

Sawasaki: Oh, I didn't know that. Anyway, I'm sorry. I'll be more careful with my expense reports in the future.

Schumann: No need to apologize. I'm sure there'll be no further problems once you understand the proper procedures. I think I'll send out a general memorandum just to be sure everybody understands our expense account policy. Oh, one more thing, Shoichi. You've put down several "miscellaneous." What are they?

Sawasaki: Let's see, that refers to money for the porters at the airport, a shoeshine, a haircut and some newspapers.

Schumann: In that case, you can charge for porterage but not the other expenses, since they're of a personal nature. As a matter of principle, an expense report should not include the term miscellaneous. Specify the actual item.

Sawasaki: Yes, sir.

Schumann: Sorry, Shoichi, I didn't mean to be too hard on you. Please don't take it personally. And I want to commend you on the promptness of your report.

Sawasaki: Thank you. Will that be all?

■狀況

ABC食品公司似乎有相當嚴格的費用報銷規定。財務部方面原則上不承認「雜費」這個項目，所以下次澤崎出差時就得多注意些了。

舒曼：如果是業務上的用餐，就把費用記在「招待」的項目下，並且記得要註明跟你用餐的是誰，以及他們跟你在業務上的關係。附帶一提，公司的政策是，在同一趟行程裡，不可以又要每日津貼，又報實際開支。你只能選一種，要不就只領每日津貼，要不就實報實銷。

澤崎：噢，這點我並不曉得。無論如何，我很抱歉。以後在處理費用報銷報告的時候，我會小心一點。

舒曼：不必道歉，我相信只要你弄清楚了正確的作法之後，一定不會再有任何問題了。我想我會發出一份一般性備忘錄，以確保每個人都瞭解我們的交際費報銷政策。哦，還有一件事，昭一，你記了好幾筆「雜費」是什麼東西?

澤崎：我看一下，那是在機場付給行李搬運工的小費，我又擦了個皮鞋，剪個頭髮，還買了幾份報紙。

舒曼：那樣的話，你可以記作運費；但其他的費用就不能報銷，因為這屬於私人消費性質。原則上，費用報銷報告裡不可以有「雜費」這種東西。只要是開支，一定要寫明確實原因。

澤崎：我都瞭解了。

舒曼：抱歉，昭一，我並非故意要對你嚴厲，請不要認為我是在找碴。而且我要稱讚你交報告的速度很快。

澤崎：謝謝。這樣就可以了嗎?

Words and Phrases

incidentally 順便一提	公關費帳目
one or the other 兩者其中之一	miscellaneous [ˌmɪsə`leniəs] 雜費
apologize 道歉	porterage 運費
procedure 程序；作法	be hard on someone 對某人嚴厲
expense account 交際費帳目；	commend 稱讚

Vocabulary Building

● **opt for** 選擇

cf. One of our options is to sell the headquarters building and rent it back from the new owner.

（我們可以走的一條路是，把總部大樓賣掉，然後再向新所有人承租下來。）

● **as a matter of principle** 原則上

This firm does not represent competing clients as a matter of principle.

（原則上，這家事務所不將競爭對手做為顧客對象。）

● **take something personally** 把…當作人身攻擊；找碴

I didn't mean to be too harsh to you in my criticism. Please don't take it personally.

（我並非故意嚴厲地批評你，請別把這件事當作是在找碴。）

重點文法・語法

I'll send out a general memorandum.

memorandum [ˌmɛmə`rændəm]也是拉丁文，簡寫成memo，複數形有memorandums 和 memoranda 兩種。

以-um 結尾的拉丁語，原本的複數形是-a，但也有像這樣有兩種複數形存在的情況。其他的例子有 symposiums, symposia（座談會），referendums, referenda（公民投票）等等。

有不少外來語在被英語吸收之後，常常只以 -a 的複數形出現，像是 agenda（議程）、data（資料）、media（媒體）、strata（層）等，都是複數形。而他們原本接 um 的單數形式反而不常見，有些在英語中甚至已完全不使用了。

▶Exercises

請利用括弧內的詞語改寫下列例句，並盡量保持原來的語意。

(解答見250頁)

1. Be sure to include the name of the other party.
   (mention, who you had the business lunch with, don't forget)

2. No need to apologize.
   (don't, have to)

3. I want to commend you on the promptness of your report.
   (promptly, you should be congratulated, turning in)

◆◆◆◆◆◆◆◆◆◆◆◆◆◆◆◆ 簡短對話 ◆◆◆◆◆◆◆◆◆◆◆◆◆◆◆◆

Sawasaki: One problem with billing the company for actual meal costs is that the receipts don't show the tip.

Schumann: Don't you use a credit card?

Sawasaki: Often I do, but what difference does that make?

Schumann: Instead of tipping in cash, write in the tip on the credit card slip and submit it with your receipt. Oh, and don't forget to write the total charge on the line provided.

What difference does that make? 那又有甚麼差別?　**submit** 提交；呈遞

Lesson 9 Expense Report—總結

新人在進入新公司一段時間之後，當初的緊張感變淡了，工作也比較順利了。但就像澤崎一樣，也會開始陷入一種事情不問公司規定，只憑自己感覺行事的情緒之中。這是從商人士最危險的時期。

費用報銷報告的寫法，會因公司而有所不同。但大致說來，在較有體制的國外企業中，每份報銷報告都要受到嚴格的審查。以ABC食品公司為例，他們在員工出差時並不支付每日津貼，而多半採用實報實銷的方式。而且，像那種捏造「偽出差」，向公司請領計程車費的事情，是絕對禁止的。

若沒有在旅館住宿，就不能請領旅館費。但如果有替代支出的情形，還是可以在其他項目之下提出申請，這是有彈性的。

每日津貼通常不包含住宿費，只有膳食費而已（比方說早餐 10 dollars，晚餐午餐 15 dollers，25 dollars。此外，如果員工沒有在餐點上花費（像是在飛機上用餐或有人請客等的），公司也會把這些錢扣掉。有的公司甚至會不允許員工將一元、五角這種小費也予以報銷。

如果有偽造費用報銷報告的情形，最嚴厲的懲罰是解雇。即使公司不這麼做，個人在公司內的信用也將一落千丈。為了一點小錢而把工作砸了，這是很划不來的。

總之，對於公司報銷費用的種種規定，最好是先弄清楚，不要隨己意判斷，以免造成不必要的誤解。

Lesson 10

Smoking Etiquette

（抽菸的禮儀）

Lesson 10 的內容

這次到美國出差，澤崎最感驚奇的是吸菸者驟減的事實。即使是搭飛機，國內線亦全面禁菸。餐廳內的吸菸區僅有幾個座席，飯店裡有禁菸樓梯，菸灰缸開始從辦公室及會議廳消失，會議中則絕對禁止吸菸。不僅如此，老菸槍今後說不定還會丟掉飯碗呢！澤崎利用此次出差的機會，二度立誓不再吸菸。他的祕書山本很驚訝澤崎的改變，但並不打算向他看齊。澤崎摻雜著玩笑，從容地與山本談話。

Lesson 10

Smoking Etiquette (1)（抽菸的禮儀）

預習—*Sentences*

- You haven't given up smoking, have you?
- It's so easy to stop smoking.
- I'm totally addicted to nicotine.
- What made you quit?
- Each cigarette you smoke shortens your life.

Vignette

Yamamoto: I noticed, Shoichi, that you haven't picked up a cigarette ever since you returned from the U.S. trip. You haven't given up smoking by any chance, have you?

Sawasaki: Matter of fact, I have. And you should too, Nancy. It's so easy to stop smoking. I've done it a thousand times— but this time it's for good.

Yamamoto: I started smoking to reduce my weight and now I'm totally addicted to nicotine. But it's my only vice, so . . .

Sawasaki: You really ought to try. The only way to stop smoking is to just stop — no ifs, ands, or butts, if you'll excuse the pun.

Yamamoto: [*Sarcastically*] Ha-ha. Very funny. But I am trying. I've decided to cut down to only one cigarette —

Sawasaki: A day?

Yamamoto: No. At a time. But what made you quit?

Sawasaki: After 20 years of smoking, I finally realized how much harm I was doing to myself. Did you know, Nancy, that each cigarette you smoke shortens your life by five and a half minutes? And that a 25-year-old person who smokes two packs a day — which is probably what you are — has only a 50 percent chance of living to be 65?

狀況

自澤崎從美國出差回來後，就沒有再看過他抽菸。山本以為，「說不定澤崎已開始戒菸了」，若是這樣，山本將益發地成為公司的少數派。

山本：昭一，我發現你從美國出差回來後，不曾抽過一根菸耶。你是絕不會戒菸的，不是嗎？

澤崎：事實上，我是戒了。南西，妳也應該戒菸。戒菸是相當容易的哪。我曾戒過上千次，但這可是最後一次了。

山本：我開始抽菸時是為了減肥，而現在則是完全上癮了。但我就只這麼一個毛病，所以…

澤崎：妳真的該試試。戒菸的不二法門就是不抽，沒有if, and或是butt。原諒我用這種雙關語。

山本：[挖苦地] 哈－哈，很好笑。但我也正在試啊，我決定要把量減少到一根——

澤崎：一天？

山本：不是！是一次。是甚麼使你戒菸的？

澤崎：抽了二十年的菸，我終於了解到這給自己的傷害有多大。南西，妳知道嗎？妳所抽的每一根菸會縮短妳五分半鐘的生命。若一個二十五歲的人，每天抽上兩包香菸——也許你就是這樣——那他活到六十五歲的可能就只有百分之五十了。

Words and Phrases

give up 放棄	butt 〔美〕菸蒂
be addicted 上癮的	quit 放棄；停止
nicotine [ˋnɪkə͵tin] 尼古丁	shorten 縮短
vice 惡癖；惡習	pack （香菸的）一包

Vocabulary Building

● **by any chance** 萬一；或許

You look familiar. Is your last name Streisand, by any chance?

(妳看起來很面熟。妳該不會是姓史翠珊吧?)

● **matter of fact** 事實上；實際上

cf. The clerk said matter-of-factly that you have to affix your personal seal to consummate the deal.

(那職員說，事實上你還必須蓋上私章才算完成這個交易。)

● **for good** 最後一次地

Please don't cry. I won't be gone for good.

(請不要哭，我不會一去不回的。)

重點文法・語法

The only way to stop smoking is to just stop — no ifs, ands, butts, if you'll excuse the pun.

上句的意思是「戒菸的不二法門是，不講任何的理由，說不抽就不抽」。接在後面的 if, and, but 都當名詞用。但要注意的是，句中所用的是 butt，而不是 but 。在美式英語中，butt 指的是「香菸的菸蒂」。澤崎故意用這個同音異義字，只是在表示一個雙關語。在歐美，開玩笑時還會有「請別人允許」的習慣。這是澤崎之所以在句尾加上“if you'll excuse the pun”的原因。

▶ *Exercises*

請利用括弧內的詞語改寫下列例句，並盡量保持原來的語意。

(解答見250頁)

1. You haven't picked up a cigarette ever since you returned from the U.S.
   (smoked, your return)

2. The only way to stop smoking is to just stop.
   (be, a non-smoker, just not to smoke)

3. I finally realized how much harm I was doing to myself.
   (damage, causing to, figured out)

◆◆◆◆◆◆◆◆◆◆◆◆◆◆◆◆ 簡短對話 ◆◆◆◆◆◆◆◆◆◆◆◆◆◆◆◆

Yamamoto: If I'm deprived of the pleasure of smoking, I don't want to live to be 65.

Sawasaki: I understand how you feel. But there's one thing I'm sure about now. My wife can't nag me anymore. Every time there was something wrong with me, she used to say that I should stop smoking. She said just that when I broke my leg last year.

Yamamoto: Even though we're doing something perfectly legal, we smokers are often discriminated against. In the U.S. drug abuse is a much more serious problem in the workplace.

---

be deprived of 被剝奪… **nag** 嘮叨抱怨 **legal** 合法的 **discriminate against** 歧視 **drug abuse** 藥物濫用 **workplace** 工作場所

Lesson 10

Smoking Etiquette (2) (抽菸的禮儀)

預習—*Sentences*

· I've thrown away my ashtrays and lighters.
· Smokers are a dying breed.
· And now there are anti-smoking laws.
· Smoking is a matter of personal choice.
· What gives you the right to order me around?

Vignette

Yamamoto: So you are serious this time.

Sawasaki: Yes, sir. I've thrown away my ashtrays and lighters and I'm going to put up one of those " Thank you for not smoking" signs in my office.

Yamamoto: Then I'll have to find my "Vice is nice" sign. I guess I'm in the minority, though. Smoking is down considerably everywhere.

Sawasaki: You said it. Smokers are a dying breed. And I discovered during my trip to the States that smokers are really discriminated against in restaurants, airplanes, hotels, offices, and everywhere. You're literally abused if you smoke in public places. And now there are anti-smoking laws.

Yamamoto: I don't understand those laws. Smoking is really a matter of personal choice. It shouldn't be regulated by law. Law-enforcement officers should be after the guys who took your bag, not after me.

Sawasaki: At the convention I attended in New York, I saw a man light up a cigarette and immediately the woman sitting next to him screamed, "For Christ's sake, put out that cigarette. The smoke will kill me." The man gave her a dirty look and said, "What gives you the right to order me around? It doesn't say 'No smoking' anywhere."

■狀況

澤崎在美國時親身經歷到，人們那種輕視吸菸者的傾向。禁菸條例在各州間開始蔚為風氣。澤崎自己還在紐約的會議當中，親眼目睹了吸菸與不吸菸者之間彼此的仇視景象。或許，是這些事情堅定了他戒菸的決心。

山本：看來你這次是認真的了。

澤崎：沒錯。我已把我的菸灰缸和打火機全丟了，我還打算在我辦公室內貼上「請勿吸菸」的標誌呢！

山本：那我得找個「惡癖乃是魅力」的標誌。不過，我想我會是少數民族吧。現在不論在哪兒，抽菸的人比以前都少得多了。

澤崎：你說的沒錯，抽菸的人口愈來愈少了。我在美國時也發現，不管是在餐廳、機場、旅館、辦公室，或是其他任何地方，抽菸者都會受到差別待遇。如果你在公共場所抽菸，那些掛起來的字句標語，句句都在罵你。現在甚至有禁菸條例呢！

山本：我真不懂那些法律條文。抽菸不過就是個人意願的事嘛，不應該由法律來規範呀。警察應該抓的是那些偷了你包包的傢伙，而不是我。

澤崎：我在紐約參加會議時，就看見一個男的才點起了香菸，坐在他旁邊的一位女士立刻大喊：「天哪！把那根菸熄了！那煙會要我的命。」那個男的憎惡地看了她一眼，說：「你憑什麼這樣命令我？這裡又沒有甚麼「禁止吸菸」的標誌。」

Words and Phrases

Vice is nice. 惡癖乃是魅力。
minority 少數派
literally 完全地；實在地
abuse 破口大罵；詆毀
regulate 立法規定
law-enforcement officer 警官
be after 追著…不放
for Christ's sake 看在老天的份上；天哪！
order around 命令（人）做東做西

Vocabulary Building

- **You said it.** 你說的沒錯。

  "This morning's keynote speaker didn't know what he was talking about."
  —"You said it!"
  (「今天早上的主講人根本不知道他自己在說些甚麼。」「你說的沒錯。」)

- **dying breed** 瀕臨滅絕的人種

  Tom is one of the dying breed of executives who still have three-martini lunches.
  (湯姆至今還是拿三杯馬丁尼當午餐，像這樣的主管目前已瀕臨絕種了。)

- **put out** 消掉；熄滅；發布

  The public relations man's job is to put out press releases, as well as corporate fires.
  (公關的職責不僅是要調解公司內部的紛爭，還得負責對外發布新聞稿。)

重點文法・語法

Yes, sir.

澤崎在此乃是把山本視作對立的一方，因而用了Yes, sir.一詞。這個 sir 是美國的口語用法，跟對方的性別無關，使用於對肯定或否定的強調。

▶*Exercises* 請利用括弧內的詞語改寫下列例句，並盡量保持原來的語意。 （解答見250頁）

1. Smoking is down considerably everywhere.
   (in, a sharp drop, the number of smokers)

2. Law-enforcement officers should be after the guys who took your bag, not after me.
   (more concerned about, police department, than about)

3. What gives you the right to order me around?
   (push me, who do you think)

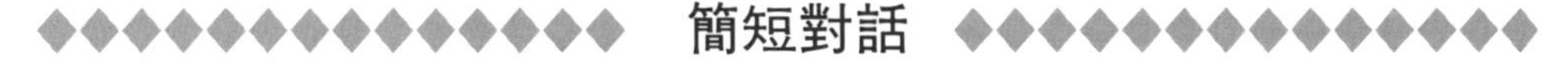

簡短對話

Yamamoto: Does cigarette smoke really endanger non-smokers?

Sawasaki: I've read the report that non-smoking wives of smokers have a higher risk of lung cancer, but I haven't seen any conclusive evidence. Why don't you like laws against public smoking?

Yamamoto: It's a waste of law-enforcement time. Laws may be appropriate to regulate smoking in dangerous situations, like at filling stations, but they're unnecessary when good judgment and common courtesy prevail. Most smokers can determine how, when and where they may smoke.

---

endanger 危害 **risk** 危險；傷害 **lung cancer** 肺癌 **conclusive evidence** 決定性的證據 **law-enforcement** 執法（者）的；警察的 **filling station** 加油站 **good judgment** 正確的認知 **courtesy** 禮儀 **prevail** 獲勝；佔優勢

Lesson 10

Smoking Etiquette (3) (吸菸的禮儀)

預習—*Sentences*

- Put that thing out or get out of here.
- They both made such a spectacle of themselves.
- Do you mind terribly waiting to smoke until later?
- Several heavy smokers were fired recently.
- I intend to continue smoking.

Vignette

Sawasaki: Then the lady went, "Don't you know passive smoke is a cause of serious diseases among non-smokers? Put that thing out or get out of here." But the man suggested in a nasty tone that she ought to be the one to leave if she was so concerned. She did but they both made such a spectacle of themselves. The moral of this story is that, these days, where there's smoke there's ire.

Yamamoto: As long as you're on a self-improvement kick, you might want to consider cutting down on your jokes. But seriously, it's mostly a matter of etiquette. If smoking really disturbed her, she should have turned to the man and asked in a polite and pleasant tone, "Do you mind terribly waiting to smoke until later?" He most likely would have obliged. Incidentally, Shoichi, I've heard on the grapevine that several heavy smokers in the New York head office were fired recently. Is that true?

Sawasaki: Yes, I've heard that rumor too. It probably is true. In a corporate culture like ours, everybody is supposed to be bright and healthy. Smoking is considered a sign of personal weakness and even low intelligence. Increasingly, they're being reprimanded, passed over for promotions and even dismissed in the U.S.

Yamamoto: No matter what you tell me, I intend to continue smoking.

Sawasaki: Sure, if that's your personal preference. But, Nancy, would you want your children to grow up to be smokers?

Yamamoto: You really got me. I guess my answer's "no."

■狀況

或許澤崎最在意的並不是吸菸影響健康，而是吸菸對日後的升遷可能會造成不良影響。以ABC食品公司的風氣而言，並不太能接受吸菸。今後，老菸槍或許都有可能被解雇。

澤崎：然後那女士又說：「你不知道二手菸是致使不吸菸者患重病的原因之一嗎？你把菸熄掉，不然就出去。」那男的用不高興的語調說，如果她真的這麼在意的話，她才是該出去的人。那女士真的出去了，但他們兩人也在眾人面前出了大糗。這故事的寓意就是說，這陣子，有香菸的地方，就有人會生氣。

山本：如果你還熱衷提升你個人修養的話，我想你最好還是別那麼愛開玩笑。不過說真的，這確實是禮貌的問題。如果那位女士真的頗受困擾，她應該和顏悅色地對那男的說「可不可以請你稍後再抽菸？」他應該是會答應的。對了，昭一，我聽到一些傳聞，說紐約總公司裡的幾位老菸槍最近被解雇了，是真的嗎？

澤崎：是啊，我也聽過這流言。或許是真的吧。在我們的公司文化中，每個人都應是健康有活力的。抽菸被看作是個人虛弱的象徵，甚至還會被認為智力不夠呢！在美國，有愈來愈多的吸菸族被上司叱責、取消升遷的機會，甚至還被解雇。

山本：不管你怎麼說，我還是會繼續抽菸的。

澤崎：當然啦，如果妳個人真的偏好此道的話。但是南西，妳會希望你的孩子長大後也成為吸菸族嗎？

山本：你真的問住我了。我想我會說「不希望」吧！

Words and Phrases

passive smoke 吸二手菸（吸進抽菸者所放出的煙味）
nasty 惡意的
make a spectacle of oneself 使自己出糗
moral 寓意
ire 怒氣
disturb 受到困擾
etiquette 禮儀
oblige 答應請求
incidentally 順便地；附帶一提地
rumor 流言
corporate culture 企業特質；企業文化
pass over 不理會；漠視
You got me. 你難倒我了；我服了你。

Vocabulary Building

● **on a kick** 熱衷…；為…著迷
Jill is on a crossword puzzle kick these days.
（吉兒最近迷上了填字遊戲。）

● **grapevine** 謠言
I've heard through the office grapevine, Anne, that you got an irresistible offer from a competitor.
（安，我聽到了辦公室謠傳說，我們一家對手公司向妳提出了相當令人心動的條件。）

● **reprimand** 譴責；叱責；申斥
The salesman was reprimanded for having a loose tongue.
（那個業務員因口風不緊而被申斥。）

重點文法・語法

Where there's smoke there's ire.

這又是一個比較俏皮的說法。本來這個諺語是 Where there's smoke there's fire「無火不生煙」，亦即「沒有火的地方就不起煙」。仿其音改為Where there's smoke there's ire.「有（香菸的）煙的地方就有怒火(ire)」一般稱這種改編的諺語為clipped proverb。

▶*Exercises*

請用括弧內的詞語改寫下列例句，並盡量保持原來的語意。

（解答見250頁）

1. Put that thing out or get out of here.
   (your cigarette, extinguish, leave)

2. I've heard on the grapevine that several heavy smokers were fired recently.
   (let go, in recent weeks, a rumor)

3. No matter what you tell me, I intend to continue smoking.
   (keep on, whatever)

◆◆◆◆◆◆◆◆◆◆◆◆◆◆◆◆ 簡短對話 ◆◆◆◆◆◆◆◆◆◆◆◆◆◆◆◆

Yamamoto: So you're saying that cigarette smoking is not only hazardous to your health but also to your career.

Sawasaki: You don't want your job prospects to go up in smoke, do you? Many companies in the United States seem to have the unwritten rule: If you want to advance, don't smoke.

Yamamoto: Is that right?

Sawasaki: Yes, smokers are sometimes considered to be mentally weak or not in control of themselves — or in some cases just plain slobs.

Yamamoto: I feel like I need a hole to crawl in.

---

hazardous 危害 **job prospects** 升遷機會 **go up in smoke** 泡湯，成泡影；如煙般消失 **unwritten rule** 不成文法 **advance** 晉升；升遷 **be in control of** 控制住… **slob** 懶人；笨蛋 **I need a hole to crawl in.** 我得找個地洞鑽進去了。〈無地自容之意〉

Lesson 10 Smoking Etiquette—總結

由於到美國出差，親眼見到了吸菸者銳減的事實，澤崎下定決心要戒菸。在此之前，他已不知發過多少誓要戒菸，但每次都不超過三天，不過他這次似乎是有點不一樣了。他與同是老菸槍的祕書山本，開始談論起抽菸的問題。山本雖然很清楚抽菸不是個好習慣，但恐怕一時也沒辦法切斷與尼古丁的緣分。當澤崎打算貼上「請勿吸菸，謝謝」(Thank you for not smoking)的 sign 時，山本嚴肅地說道，要以「惡癖乃是魅力」(Vice is nice) 來對抗。

現在在美國有一個傾向，即依據條例，嚴格規範在公共場所的吸菸問題。但是山本認為，「吸不吸菸是個人的嗜好問題，用法律來限制無法令人接受」。吸菸者認為，禁菸雖是禮儀、道德的問題，但禁菸條例卻壓抑了個人的喜好，有些人因吸菸心情變得舒坦，有些人則因此提高了思考能力。對此，不吸菸者反駁道，「香菸的煙造成他人的困擾，危害健康，也是空氣污染的元凶。自己生病也就罷了，但不要禍及他人。」

吸菸者與不吸菸者常是針鋒相對，而澤崎在美國經驗到的那種爭論則時有所見。他們彼此都不尊重對方的權利，也不稍作讓步。

若是真的不希望對方抽菸，只要溫和的說聲 Do you mind terribly waiting to smoke until later? 大部分的人都會停止抽菸的。但是，像澤崎那樣好不容易才下定決心戒菸的人，與其說是健康的緣故，倒不如說是考慮到了升遷的問題。抽菸者容易被視為意志薄弱的人。「想升遷，就戒菸」似乎已成為許多美國公司的不成文規定了。

Lesson 11

Wellness Challenge

（健康管理）

Lesson 11 的內容

戒菸中的澤崎，漸漸注意起自己的健康管理，聽說最近還和一些年輕女孩一起上有氧舞蹈課。

這是因為他去美國出差時，得知像紐約這樣的大都市，很多上班族在到公司前有做運動的習慣。於是回國後，澤崎便主動尋找這類機會，當他看到地鐵站前「早安有氧」的廣告之後，他馬上就加入了「有氧」的行列。

Lesson 11

Wellness Challenge (1) (健康管理)

預習—*Sentences*

· I hear that you've quit smoking.
· Three quarters of my class are middle-aged men.
· I've discovered this new lifestyle.
· It must be quite stimulating for you.
· I can do more work now with less fatigue.

Vignette

Noonan: I hear, Shoichi, that you've quite smoking.

Yamamoto: Not only that, Tom, but Shoichi has started taking aerobic classes.

Noonan: That's a very difficult language to master, I suppose.

Yamamoto: No, no. I'm talking about his physical fitness program, not Arabic.

Noonan: Oh, I beg your pardon. But I thought only young girls did that sort of thing. You know, in tights.

Sawasaki: Do you have to see my pink leotard to believe that I'm actually doing it? Joking aside, three quarters of my class are middle-aged men.

Noonan: Is that so? What time do you start?

Sawasaki: At 7:15 in the morning. We do aerobic dancing for 45 minutes. Three times a week. Then I can take a sauna, shave and still get to the office by 9. I've discovered this new lifestyle and I like it immensely.

Noonan: It must be quite stimulating for you.

Sawasaki: Yes, not only physically but also mentally. I can do more work now with less fatigue, and I sleep like a log every night.

* * *

■狀況

下面是一段辦公室裡的小插曲。當諾南問：「昭一，聽說你戒菸了!」，山本從旁插嘴道：「不僅如此，他還跳起有氧舞蹈來了呢!」但諾南一時沒有會意過來，冒出一句不對頭的話。

諾南：昭一，我聽說你已經戒菸了。

山本：湯姆，還不只那樣，昭一也開始上aerobic（[eə`robɪk]有氧舞蹈）。

諾南：我想這種語言大概很難學吧!

山本：不，不是，我說的是他要鍛鍊身體的計畫，不是Arabic（[`ærəbɪk] 阿拉伯文）。

諾南：哦，抱歉。可是我以為只有年輕女孩才會做那種事。你也知道的，要穿緊身衣那種。

澤崎：你是非得要看到我的粉紅色緊身衣，才會相信我真的在跳有氧舞蹈嗎?說正經的，我們班上有四分之三的人都是中年男子。

諾南：真的?那你們都幾點鐘開始?

澤崎：早上七點十五分開始，跳四十五分鐘的有氧舞蹈，一個禮拜三次。之後我還能洗個三溫暖，刮個臉，然後準九點到辦公室上班。我發現這是種新的生活方式，而我真的很喜歡這樣。

諾南：這一定相當能夠令你振奮起來。

澤崎：沒錯，而且不只是在身體上，連精神上都是。我現在可以做較多的工作，卻反而較不覺得累。而且我每天晚上都睡得像根木頭一樣。

* * *

Words and Phrases

aerobic [,eə`robɪk] 氧氣的
Arabic [`ærəbɪk] 阿拉伯文
I beg your pardon. 對不起。〈句尾降下語調〉
leotard [`liə,tɑrd] 緊身衣
three quarters 四分之三
middle-aged 中年的
sauna [`sɔnə, `saunə] 三溫暖（浴）
stimulating 刺激性的；鼓舞人的
fatigue [fə`tig] 疲勞
sleep like a log 睡得像根木頭；睡得很沈

Vocabulary Building

- **physical fitness** 身體狀況良好

  cf. You have to be physically fit if you want to be an astronaut.

  （要想成為一個太空人，你的身體狀況必須十分良好。）
- **joking aside** 不開玩笑；說正經的

  Joking aside, no one has ever published a scientific study on why people laugh.

  （說正經的，從來沒有人發表過研究報告，探討人類為甚麼會笑。）
- **lifestyle** 生活方式

  In today's lifestyle, "liquid lunches" aren't very popular.

  （就今日的生活方式來看，「喝酒午餐」並不普遍。）

重點文法・語法

Do you have to see my pink leotard?

大家所熟悉的 sandwich (>Earl of Sandwich), lynch (>Captain W. Lynch)（以私刑處死），其實都是從人名衍生而來，leotard 也是其中之一。Jules Léotard 為一名空中特技表演者。據說他表演時會穿一種上下相連的緊身運動衣，於是衍生出 leotard 這個詞。Léotard 在1870 年時死於天花，年僅二十八歲。

▶Exercises

請利用括弧內的詞語改寫下列例句，並盡量保持原來的語意。

(解答見251頁)

1. I'm talking about his physical fitness program, not Arabic.
   (mean, wellness, the Arabic)

2. Do you have to see my pink leotard to believe that I'm actually doing it?
   (convince you, show, do I have to)

3. Joking aside, three quarters of my class are middle-aged men.
   (75 percent, in their forties, seriously)

◆◆◆◆◆◆◆◆◆◆◆◆◆◆◆◆ 簡短對話 ◆◆◆◆◆◆◆◆◆◆◆◆◆◆◆◆

Sawasaki: You see, those who exercise regularly enjoy greater resistance to fatigue and illness. And they have a lower incidence of heart and arterial problems and lower levels of cholesterol and blood pressure. You should try too, Tom.

Noonan: But 7:15 is too early for me. Is that really the best time to do the workout?

Sawasaki: It really depends on your lifestyle. At my gym, many people exercise during the lunch hour, turning it into a time of very light snacking or simply avoiding food.

---

resistance to 對…有抵抗力 **fatigue** 疲勞 **incidence** 發生率 **arterial** 動脈的 **cholesterol** 膽固醇 **workout** 運動；練習 **gym** (=gymnasium) 體育館 **snacking** 簡餐

Lesson 11

Wellness Challenge (2) (健康管理)

預習—*Sentences*

· I couldn't agree with you more.
· Health is more than a personal matter.
· It's an organizational objective.
· Mike will give us the details.
· One unit is jogging 1,600 meters.

Vignette

Noonan: I've asked Shoichi to join us in discussing our anniversary project because I've just learned he's a health fiend.

Sawasaki: I can tell you that living a healthy lifestyle will become more and more important for businesspeople. Overweight, overanxious, chain-smoking executives will no longer be tolerated.

Noonan: I couldn't agree with you more. In many companies, health is more than a personal matter. It's an organizational objective and a management issue. Health-promotion programs are considered a long-term investment in human resources. In view of this, we've come to the conclusion that we want to inaugurate a health-related movement as part of our 50th anniversary celebration. Mike will give us the details.

Yamaguchi: Our idea is to kick off an incentive health-promotion program, tentatively called the "Wellness Challenge." Its main purpose is to encourage ongoing exercise, initially by our employees. The program will pay employees ¥ 100 for each "unit"of exercise they report. One unit is, for example, jogging 1,600 meters, swimming 400 meters, bicycling 6,400 meters or aerobic dancing for a quarter hour.

Sawasaki: Hmm, that means I can get nine units or ¥ 900 per week through aerobics.

Noonan: Right.

■狀況

一下子變成「健康迷」的澤崎，也加入ABC食品公司周年慶企畫的討論。「向健康挑戰」是他們的宣傳口號。在美國，像這類活動已在許多企業中展開，而這種想法能否在日本流行，且拭目以待。

諾南：我請了昭一來和我們一起討論周年慶計畫的事，因為我剛剛才得知他相當熱衷養生之道。

澤崎：我可以告訴你們，健康的生活方式對從商人士而言是愈來愈重要了。大家將不會再忍受那些過度肥胖、過度焦慮，菸又抽個不停的主管人員。

諾南：我非常同意你的話。在許多公司，健康不只是個人問題而已。健康乃是整個團體成員的目標，也是公司管理方面的一個課題。提升員工健康的計畫，被視作公司在人力資源上的長期投資。有鑑於此，我們達成結論，決定要開始進行一項與健康有關的活動，以作為公司五十週年慶的一部分。麥可會告訴我們細節。

山口：我們的想法是，要開始一個獎勵提升健康計畫，暫時定名為「向健康挑戰」。主要的目標是鼓勵持續性的運動，先由員工開始施行。公司會根據員工報上來的運動量，每個單位運動量給付一百日圓。而每個單位的標準是，慢跑一千六百公尺，游泳四百公尺，騎腳踏車六千四百公尺，或跳有氧舞蹈十五分鐘。

澤崎：嗯，那就是說，我每週這樣跳有氧舞蹈，就會有九個單位或是九百日圓囉！

諾南：沒錯。

Words and Phrases

anniversary 週年紀念	objective 目標；目的
fiend [find] …迷	inaugurate 開始
overweight 過重	tentatively 暫時的；試驗性的
chain-smoking *adj.* 不停抽菸的	exercise *n.* 運動
tolerate 容忍；容許	quarter hour 十五分鐘

Vocabulary Building

● **I couldn't agree with you more.** 你說的再正確不過了。

cf. I don't see how I can agree with you.

(我無法贊同你的見解。)

● **human resources** 人力資源

Our company takes pride in our excellent human resources.

(我們公司以擁有眾多優秀員工為榮。)

● **wellness** 健康

Exercise regularly. There's no substitute for wellness.

(要有規律的運動，個人健康是無可替代的。)

重點文法・語法

Its main purpose is to encourage ongoing exercise, initially by our employees.

ongoing 從 go on 引伸出「繼續的」、「正在進行中」的語意。像這類將「動詞＋介系詞」的順序對調，形成一個單字的詞彙，在英文中還有很多。以下是一些常見的例子：

oncoming (接近的)	inbuilt (內藏的)
onlooker (參觀者；旁觀者)	incoming (後繼的；進入的)
onset (開始)	intake (攝取量；吸收)
onrush (突擊)	outlook (展望；預測)
offset (抵銷物)	outgrow (變大)
off-putting (使不高興的)	outcome (結果)

▶Exercises

請利用括弧內的詞語改寫下列例句，並盡量保持原來的語意。

(解答見251頁)

1. Living a healthy lifestyle will become more and more important for businesspeople.
   (it's becoming, increasingly, to live)

2. We've come to the conclusion that we want to inaugurate a health-related movement.
   (our conclusion was, we'd, kick off)

3. Its main purpose is to encourage ongoing exercise, initially by our employees.
   (it aims at, regular, starting with)

◆◆◆◆◆◆◆◆◆◆◆◆◆◆◆◆ 簡短對話 ◆◆◆◆◆◆◆◆◆◆◆◆◆◆◆◆

Noonan: I don't mind doing exercise in the evening.

Sawasaki: They say that exercising after work often proves an effective way to relieve fatigue and give vent to built-up tension. But if you're going to exercise after a meal, you ought to eat lightly. Anyway you should find the time best suited to you.

Noonan: I hurt my ankle jogging a few months ago.

Sawasaki: My aerobics instructor says jogging is not for everyone and you shouldn't pursue it if it produces pain or injury. Walking vigorously is a good way to maintain your fitness.

---

prove 被發現是… **relieve fatigue** 消除疲勞 **give vent to** 發洩… **built-up tensions** 累積的緊張 **ankle** 足踝 **pursue** 繼續 **vigorously** 精力充沛的；強有力的 **fitness** 健康

Lesson 11

Wellness Challenge (3)（健康管理）

預習—*Sentences*

· How will you monitor what people do?
· It should be an honor system.
· That'll eliminate the weekend athletes.
· Where do you go from there?
· It sounds like a good image-builder.

Vignette

Noonan: How will you monitor what people actually do?
Yamaguchi: We won't. It should be an honor system. There'll be a monthly minimum. Participants will be paid only if they accumulate over 30 units per month. We also plan a cap of five units a day.
Sawasaki: I see. That'll eliminate the weekend athletes. But I'm not sure if I care for the idea of cash rewards. Personally, I'd prefer special gifts or company-paid trips.
Yamaguchi: The public relations department has carried out a quick internal survey. It seems that as many as four-fifths of our people are interested in taking part in such a program, and the majority would prefer cash incentives.
Noonan: That's fine with me. Where do you go from there?
Yamaguchi: Through the mass media, we'll communicate the message to other companies and encourage them to join the league. I'm fairly confident that we'll be able to generate a lot of publicity because of the uniqueness of the program. At the same time, we'll prepare literature on how to organize in-house wellness programs. Copies should be made available free of charge.
Sawasaki: Then we can position ABC Foods as the pioneer in corporate fitness programs while generating public goodwill.
Noonan: It sounds like a good image-builder. I like it.

■狀況

公司最後決定要以現金來獎勵持續運動的員工。而這個企畫案的另一主要目的，就是要替公司作宣傳。換言之，ABC食品公司經由這個公司內部的活動，透過媒體廣為報導，可藉以提升標榜「關懷健康」的企業形象。

諾南：那你要如何監督大家有沒有實際做到呢？

山口：我們不監督，而是採榮譽制度。我們會有一個最低月運動量。參加者每月必須累積到三十個運動單位才能得到獎金。此外，我們也計畫要訂一個每日運動量上限：五個單位。

澤崎：原來如此，這樣可以排除那些週末運動員。不過我覺得現金獎勵這個主意似乎不是很好。就我個人來說，我比較喜歡特別禮物或是公司招待的免費旅遊。

山口：公關部門曾簡單地進行過一次內部調查。似乎公司內近五分之四的人有興趣參與這樣一個計畫，其中大多數選擇要現金獎勵。

諾南：這點我沒意見，那之後你們計畫怎麼做？

山口：我們將透過大眾傳播媒體的宣傳，將這個訊息告知其他公司，並鼓勵他們共襄此舉。我確信我們會因這項獨特的計畫而吸引大眾廣泛的注意。同時，我們也會準備一些小冊子，說明如何籌畫這種公司內部的健康計畫。這些冊子將免費提供給需要的人。

澤崎：然後我們就可以把ABC 食品公司定位為公司健康計畫的先驅者，而吸引民眾的善意回應。

諾南：聽起來，這會相當有助於我們建立公司的形象。我喜歡這個計畫。

Words and Phrases

honor system 榮譽制度
accumulate 累積
cap 上限
eliminate 消除；排除
weekend athlete 週末運動者
incentive 誘因
join the league 加入聯盟
generate publicity 引起大眾注意
position *v.* 定位

Vocabulary Building

● **monitor** 監視

We will monitor the Chinese media on a regular basis and alert you of any articles that may have some bearing on your company.

（我們會定期監視中國媒體，若有任何與貴公司有關的報導定會警示你們。）

● **in-house** 公司內的

Does your company have an in-house translation capability or do you farm out translations?

（你們公司的翻譯工作是由內部負責，或交給外人呢?）

● **image-builder** 形象建立者

cf. It's time we started an image-building campaign in Japan.

（我們該在日本展開形象建立運動了。）

重點文法・語法

There'll be a monthly minimum.

雖然daily, weekly, monthly, bimonthly, semimonthly, yearly都是以ly結尾，但它們除用作副詞外，還有形容詞的用法。而像annually, biannually, biennially, semiannualy, triennially等，則皆為副詞；用作形容詞時，必須去掉ly。

而在語意上有微妙差異的，則為以bi開頭的字。如bimonthly為「隔月的」之意，但也有「每月二次」的語意（此意一般以semimonthly表示）。同樣地，biweekly也可解釋為「隔週的」或「一週二次」，biannually則可表「一年兩次」、「每半年」等。〈biennially只有「兩年一次」之意。〉

▶Exercises

請利用括弧內的詞語改寫下列例句，並盡量保持原來的語意。

(解答見251頁)

1. That'll eliminate the weekend athletes.
   (sometime, will be out, that way)

2. At the same time, we'll prepare literature on how to organize in-house wellness programs.
   (produce pamphlets, structure, simultaneously)

3. Copies should be made available free of charge.
   (free copies, distributed)

◆◆◆◆◆◆◆◆◆◆◆◆◆◆◆◆ 簡短對話 ◆◆◆◆◆◆◆◆◆◆◆◆◆◆◆◆

Noonan: Using part of the ¥80 million budget, we ought to buy a corporate membership in a major sports club.

Sawasaki: Good idea. Also, how about organizing a weight-loss competition among teams of ABC foods employees as part of the wellness program?

Noonan: How'd you do it?

Sawasaki: The combined weight of a team of, say, five employees would be measured at the outset. Then the competition is which team loses most weight in a given period of time.

Noonan: Weight loss implies eating less. I'm not sure if that's appropriate for a food company to sponsor.

---

corporate membership 法人會員權 **weight-loss competition** 減肥比賽 **at the outset** 最初 **in a given period of time** 在限期內 **imply** 意味；暗示

Lesson 11 Wellness Challenge—總結

曾經風靡一時的「慢跑」目前已逐漸退燒，取而代之的，該是wellness這個buzzword（專業流行語）。它搭上「健康風」的列車，一躍而為80年代美國企業界的新寵。

wellness原意為「健康」，就是藉由運動、攝取健康的飲食、不吸菸、飲酒適量等，而達到提升身體健康所做的努力。而本課所指的「健康」，是利用運動或workout讓自己有鍛鍊身體的「餘裕」，足以飲食及生活習慣控制意志（和體重）的力量。

也許很多人之所以會關心健康，與其說是為了長壽，不如說是為了趕時髦，或是不想被認為是意志薄弱的人等的理由。

現在，所謂附馬丁尼或威士忌的liquid lunch商業午餐，早已銷聲匿跡，有人認為breakfast meeting正逐漸成為business entertainment的主流。

如今lemon meringue pie等fattening而「不健康」的食品，也從員工餐廳撤離。公司的會議室，再也找不到菸灰缸，桌上只有芹菜、紅蘿蔔及diet drinks。而公司內設有jogging track、physical fitness center的企業也不在少數。

澤崎公司推出的Wellness Challenge企畫案，提供持續運動的員工cash award為獎勵，進而以此為增進全國上班族身體健康的宣傳活動。

諾南起勁地說道：「這會有助於我們建立公司的形象」。看來他已經是蓄勢待發了。

Lesson 12

Early Retirement

（提早退休）

Lesson 12 的內容

這真是個晴天霹靂，諾南突然要辭掉 ABC 食品公司的工作。在公司的精簡人事政策下，他決定接受這個早退方案，提前退休。這對向來視諾南為 mentor（良師）的澤崎來說，是極大的震撼。而關於諾南繼任者的消息更是大大令他震驚。

Lesson 12

Early Retirement (1) (提早退休)

預習—*Sentences*

· Can you spare a minute?
· There's something I wanted you to know.
· I thought you were still in your mid-50s.
· I've decided to take early retirement.
· My kids have all grown up.

Vignette

Noonan: It looks like everybody's keeping you busy. Can you spare a minute, Shoichi?

Sawasaki: Surely. Is it bad news?

Noonan: Well, there's something I wanted you to know before the official announcement is made. But please keep it within these four walls till then.

Sawasaki: All right, you can count on me.

Noonan: You may be surprised to know, Shoichi, but I'll be retiring from the company pretty soon.

Sawasaki: Retiring? No kidding. I thought you were still in your mid-50s.

Noonan: I am. But I've decided to take early retirement. The company has offered a special package to U.S. employees who are 55 or older with 21 or more years of service. I've done a great deal of soul-searching and it was a very difficult decision to make after 25 years. But the offer closes at the end of this month. Besides, my kids have all grown up. So I've decided to take up the option, or the "open window," as they sometimes call it.

Sawasaki: I'm just dumbfounded.

■狀況

諾南突然進到澤崎的辦公室，表情凝重。澤崎直覺地想到，「是壞消息吧！」結果居然是諾南要離職的事。澤崎十分失望，但諾南跟他說明了原因。

諾南：看起來好像每個人都把你忙得團團轉。昭一，你可以挪出一點時間來嗎？

澤崎：當然可以。有壞消息嗎？

諾南：嗯，在正式發布之前，有些事我想讓你知道一下。不過，你可得保密哦！

澤崎：沒問題，相信我吧！

諾南：昭一，你可能會很驚訝，我很快就要從公司退休了。

澤崎：退休？別開玩笑了。我以為你才五十五歲左右而已。

諾南：我是啊，不過，我已經決定提早退休了，公司方面對凡年滿五十五歲且任職服務滿二十一年的美籍主管人員，提供了一項特別的早退方案。對此，我已仔細地自我分析過，加上我在這邊工作都二十五年了，實在難以取捨。不過，因為這個方案的有效期限只到本月底，而我的孩子又都大了，所以我決定接受這個條件，或者說是他們所謂的「開窗政策」。

澤崎：我只是驚訝得不知該說甚麼才好。

Words and Phrases

count on 信賴；信託
mid-50s 五十五歲左右
early retirement 提早退休
service 服務
option 機會
be dumbfounded 吃驚；目瞪口呆

Vocabulary Building

- **keep something within these four walls** 把某物保留在屋子的四面牆中，意指保密；守口如瓶
  cf. Let's just keep the new project between you and me. OK?
  (這項新方案只有你和我知道，好嗎?)
- **No kidding.** 別開玩笑了。
  "I just bought a new car, Dad."—"No kidding. How are you going to pay for it, son?"
  (「爸，我剛買了一輛新車。」「別開玩笑了，兒子，你哪有錢買?」)
- **soul-searching** 自我省察；自我分析
  I asked myself a number of soul-searching questions before I decided to accept the job offer.
  (在決定接受這項工作之前，我問過自己一連串自我省察的問題。)

重點文法・語法

The company has offered a special package to U.S. employees who are 55 or older with 21 or more years of service.

more than 55原本不含55，不過因為很容易造成誤解，所以就採取55 or older和21 or more 這樣的說法。如此一來，到底包不包含 55 和 21 本身，意思就很清楚了。

▶Exercises

請利用括弧內的詞語改寫下列例句，並盡量保持原來的語意。

（解答見251頁）

1. It looks like everybody's keeping you busy.
   (appears, you are, as though)

2. Please keep it within these four walls.
   (you and me, between)

3. It was a very difficult decision to make after 25 years.
   (hard to make, the decision was, a quarter century)

◆◆◆◆◆◆◆◆◆◆◆◆◆◆◆ 簡短對話 ◆◆◆◆◆◆◆◆◆◆◆◆◆◆◆

Noonan: I want to tell you something, Shoichi, but you must promise you won't repeat it to anybody until the news is announced through the official channels. OK?

Sawasaki: OK, I promise, but judging from the expression on your face, it's probably bad news. How bad?

Noonan: Wait a minute. I didn't mean to suggest it was bad news. As a matter of fact, it's probably good news from my own personal viewpoint. I've decided to take early retirement.

Sawasaki: Did I hear you correctly? Did you say "retirement"?

---

repeat 重述 **judging from** 從…來判斷… **expression** 表情 **suggest** 意指；建議 **as a matter of fact** 實際上 **from one's own personal viewpoint** 就某人個人的觀點來看 **Did I hear you correctly?** 我沒聽錯（你的話）吧?

Lesson 12

Early Retirement (2) (提早退休)

預習—*Sentences*

- I've been looking to you as my mentor.
- I know that the company is keen on downsizing.
- It's not such a bad deal, though.
- Are you going to return to the States?
- I'm still pretty fit, you know.

Vignette

Sawasaki: I know for sure that we'll all miss you very much. I've been looking to you as my mentor, so I'll be especially sad to see you go. I've learned a great deal from your management style . . . I know that the company is keen on downsizing, but it never occurred to me that you'd be leaving.

Noonan: For me personally, it's not such a bad deal, though. On top of a generous lump-sum payment, I can get at least 55 percent of the pension I would have been eligible for at age 65. This is a way for ABC Foods to make our payroll lean without being mean.

Sawasaki: Are you going to return to the States and live in Florida or somewhere?

Noonan: Come on, Shoichi. I'll only be retiring from the company, not from life. A perpetual holiday is a good working definition of hell, as George Bernard Shaw said. I'm still pretty fit, you know.

Sawasaki: Oh, you mean you're going to leave the company but you'll remain in action? Is that it?

Noonan: Yes, I had an offer I couldn't refuse from the French foreign legion.

Sawasaki: You did, really?

Noonan: No, I was only kidding.

■狀況

諾南很欣賞澤崎，一直提拔有加。所以，知道諾南即將退休，澤崎最大的遺憾莫過於失去了諾南這樣一位良師(mentor)。可是公司的這項早退方案對諾南來說並沒那麼糟。聽到澤崎問他是否還會“in action”，諾南開玩笑說：「我精力旺盛得連法國外籍兵團都要來找我呢！」

澤崎：我深信大夥一定會非常想念你的。我一直把你看作是我的良師，所以我特別捨不得你離開。從你管理的風格中我學到了許多東西… 我曉得公司正在大量裁員，但是我從來也沒想到會是你要離職。

諾南：對我個人而言，這並不是那麼令人難過的事情哩！我現在走的話，公司會付給我一大筆錢，一次付清；更好的是，我可以拿到的退職金至少是正常六十五歲退休時的百分之五十五。這就是ABC食品公司要精簡人事，卻不使人覺得刻薄的方式。

澤崎：那你會回美國住在佛羅里達或其他地方嗎?

諾南：拜託，昭一，我只不過是從這家公司退休而已，我的人生可還不到退休年齡。就如蕭伯納說的，無止境的假期正是地獄的最佳寫照。你瞧，我還很健康呢！

澤崎：哦，你的意思是你離開公司後會仍舊保持活躍，是嗎?

諾南：沒錯，我在法國外籍志願兵團中還有份推不掉的差事呢！

澤崎：真的嗎?！

諾南：沒有啦！我只是在開玩笑。

Words and Phrases

miss 想念；思念
be keen on 熱衷於…
downsizing 裁員；人事縮減
deal 大量；許多
generous 慷慨大方的
eligible [ˋɛlɪdʒəbl̩] 有資格得到的
payroll 員工總數
lean without being mean （人事）精簡而不刻薄
perpetual [pɚˋpɛtʃuəl] 永久的；持續不斷的
definition 定義
foreign legion 外籍兵團

Vocabulary Building

- **mentor** 良師；導師；良師益友
  Your best potential mentor is your immediate supervisor.
  （你的直屬上司就是最有可能成為你良師的人。）
- **lump-sum payment** 一次總付的金額
  In lieu of a salary increase this year, you'll be receiving a lump-sum payment equivalent to five percent of your current salary.
  （今年公司不調薪了，替代方案是，一次給付各人目前薪資百分之五的金額。）
- **in action** 在活動中；在戰鬥中
  cf. My good friend's brother has been missing in action in Vietnam.
  （我好友的哥哥在越戰中失蹤。）

重點文法・語法

It never occurred to me that you'd be leaving.

occur, incur, recur 衍生自表示「跑」的cur，重音都在第二音節。所以接 -ed、-ing時，一定得重複最後的 r 而成為 occurred (occurring), incurred (incurring), recurred (recurring)。這是常會拼錯的字，請多加注意。

▶Exercises

請利用括弧內的詞語改寫下列例句，並盡量保持原來的語意。

(解答見251頁)

1. We'll all miss you very much.
   (missed, you'll)

2. It never occurred to me that you'd be leaving.
   (I, realized, might be)

3. This is a way for ABC Foods to make our payroll lean without being mean.
   (this way, can make)

◆◆◆◆◆◆◆◆◆◆◆◆◆◆◆ 簡短對話 ◆◆◆◆◆◆◆◆◆◆◆◆◆◆◆

Sawasaki: I guess the move is good for you even though we'll be very sorry to lose you. Our loss is someone else's gain. I wish I could get to know you much better.

Noonan: I'm quite ambivalent about leaving ABC Foods. But now that I've made the decision, there'll be no looking back. I'm enthusiastic about this new opportunity at a new company.

Sawasaki: I sincerely wish you good luck.

Noonan: Thank you. You know, Shoichi, I feel that one of the best decisions I made here was to hire you. I'll stay in the same industry and I'm sure our paths will cross.

---

loss 損失 **ambivalent about** 對於…感到心情矛盾 **looking back** 後悔；回頭看 **hire** 雇用 **our paths will cross** 我們會再碰面的

Lesson 12

Early Retirement (3)（提早退休）

預習—*Sentences*

· Several months ago, I met this guy.
· Our first encounter was rather brief.
· Then he offered you the job.
· My replacement is an extremely talented person.
· Is he somebody I know?

Vignette

Noonan: In fact, I'll remain in Japan and be the general manager of Crockett in Tokyo.

Sawasaki: Crockett? The pet food company?

Noonan: Yes. I'll tell you what happened. Several months ago, I met this guy, Doug Falcon, who was Crockett's international vice president at the time. They've been selling their products in Japan with brilliant success. Doug came here to see whether they should now manufacture in Japan on their own or work with local partners in a joint venture. Our first encounter was rather brief, but then he was made the president of the company just recently. I wrote to congratulate him on his appointment and he looked me up when he was here a few weeks ago.

Sawasaki: I see. Then he offered you the job. The pet food business seems to be doing fantastically well in Japan these days.

Noonan: That's right. And I'm sure that our paths will cross from time to time. By the way, my replacement coming from New York is an extremely talented person.

Sawasaki: They've already chosen your successor? Is he somebody I know?

Noonan: Er, actually it's a she. Her name is Julie Henry. She's probably about your age, has a Ph.D. in modern Japanese history, and she's got both beauty and brains. I'm sure you'll be able to work with her very well.

Sawasaki: Gee, I'm not so sure.

■狀況

諾南向澤崎說明了將去克洛基公司工作的原委。像是他幾個月前遇見當時身為國際副總裁的弗肯；而弗肯就任總裁時他也寄過賀函等等。對澤崎來說還有另一個震驚，那就是諾南的繼任者已選定，是個叫做茱莉 · 亨利的能幹女性。

諾南：事實上，我會繼續留在日本擔任克洛基在東京分公司的總經理。

澤崎：克洛基？那家寵物食品公司？

諾南：是的。告訴你這是怎麼一回事好了。幾個月前，我遇到道・弗肯這個人，他當時是克洛基國際公司的副總裁。他們公司在日本的銷售業績好極了，他來這裡是為視察他們公司到底是要在日本獨資生產呢，還是與當地人合作成立合資企業。我們第一次的見面很短暫，不過，他新近才升官，當了該公司的總裁；所以我寫了張賀卡恭賀他升遷。幾個星期前他來這裡時順道來看了我一下。

澤崎：我懂了，然後他就請你到他們公司工作。近來在日本，寵物食品的生意似乎好得很，如日中天哩！

諾南：沒錯。而且我相信我們日後不時還是會碰面的。順帶一提，將接替我職位的人是從紐約來的，十分精明能幹。

澤崎：公司已經選好你的繼任者了？他是我認識的人嗎？

諾南：呃，實際上她是女性，她的名字叫茱莉 · 亨利，年紀可能跟你差不多，是日本現代史博士，而且才貌雙全，我相信你一定可以跟她相處融洽的。

澤崎：老天，這我可不太確定。

Words and Phrases

brilliant 輝煌的；顯赫的
on one's own 獨自地；獨力
encounter 碰面；邂逅；遭遇
look someone up 探訪某人
fantastically 極好地
talented 有才能的
Ph.D. 博士學位；擁有博士學位的人；哲學博士
beauty and brains 才貌雙全；才色兼備

Vocabulary Building

- **joint venture** 合資企業
  ABC Foods has three joint ventures with blue-chip Japanese companies.
  (ABC食品公司與三家持有績優股票的日本廠商成立合資企業。)
- **paths will cross** （將來）會碰面的…
  I used to bump into Tom at cocktail parties, but he hasn't crossed my path recently.
  (我以前常會在雞尾酒會中不經意地碰到湯姆，但最近倒是沒看到他人。)
- **replacement** 接替者；繼任者
  cf. Tom Noonan will be replaced by Julie Henry, a young, attractive Ph.D. who's fluent in Japanese.
  (湯姆・諾南的職位將由茱莉・亨利繼任，她是一位年輕迷人、日語又講得很好的博士。)

重點文法・語法

I met this guy, Doug Falcon.

this 這個字是在國中一年級所學的基本單字。一般是在彼此都了解的情形下，用以指稱在時間、空間、或感覺上較為「靠近」的事物；但是在這篇文章當中的this guy（這個人），卻是澤崎沒有聽說過的 Doug Falcon 。

其實這是口語用法，在談及只存於說話者腦海，而聽者不知有其人（物）時，為了要使聽者有熟悉感而使用的一種說法。

▶*Exercises*

請利用括弧內的詞語改寫下列例句，並盡量保持原來的語意。

(解答見251頁)

1. They've been selling their products in Japan with brilliant success.
   (had brilliant success, marketing)

2. He was made the president of the company just recently.
   (not long ago, they made him)

3. My replacement coming from New York is an extremely talented person.
   (awfully, successor, able)

◆◆◆◆◆◆◆◆◆◆◆◆◆◆ 簡短對話 ◆◆◆◆◆◆◆◆◆◆◆◆◆◆

Noonan: Why do you feel that way?

Sawasaki: Well, I've never worked for a woman boss in my career. I just don't know how to relate to one.

Noonan: You relate to her just like any other human being. It's not that difficult. After all, you've worked for one of the most demanding bosses here at ABC Foods. I'll tell you, Shoichi, Julie is one of the most intelligent and sensitive businesspersons I've ever come across. You'll like her too.

Sawasaki: I guess that's another challenge. . . serving two female masters, at home and on the job.

---

relate to 與某人建立關係 **demanding** 嚴厲的 **sensitive** 敏銳的；敏感的 **come across** 碰見；遇見 **serve two masters** 同時服事或聽命於二個主人；侍候兩個主子

Lesson 12 Early Retirement — 總結

諾南說有祕密要告訴澤崎，但沒想到居然是他要離職一事。在聽到這個消息之後，澤崎相當沮喪。

不過，這對諾南而言並不是多麼糟糕的一件事。為使人事達到精簡，公司對於年滿五十五歲，且服務滿二十一年的美籍主管，特別提供了一個提早退休 (early retirement) 方案，他們若接受了的話，除可一次領清相當於一年收入的退職金(lump-sum bonus)外，每月還能領到養老年金，金額是六十五歲退休時的百分之五十五。

在一些美國企業中，lean and mean 已成了一句口號。也就是為了達到縮減編制 (downsizing) 的目的，得去除多餘的肥肉好成為 lean（無贅肉）；為此，即使是採用mean approach（卑鄙的手段）也得做。但諾南說 ABC 食品公司的 open-window plan 不會為了 lean 而變得 mean。

即使是這樣，離職以後的出路卻是個問題。諾南做夢也沒有想到，他這把年紀了還會轉到克洛基公司任職。

另一方面，知道諾南要離職，澤崎覺得頗為遺憾。諾南一向多方提攜澤崎，他這一走，也意味著澤崎將失去一位 mentor (良師)。而且，繼任者也許不會像諾南一樣地賞識他。

諾南還告訴澤崎，繼任者將是位擁有日本現代史博士學位的女性。這對澤崎來說簡直是雙重打擊。儘管諾南說這位女士相當優秀能幹，澤崎還是覺得，“Better the devil you know than the devil you don’t know.”（與其碰到一個不認識的惡魔，還寧可要一個自己認識的惡魔)。

Lesson 13

Working for a New Boss

（新上司）

Lesson 13 的內容

取代諾南成為澤崎新任上司的茱莉・亨利雖是才貌雙全、善於社交的女性，但澤崎最怕和外國女性說話；一遇上便有點手足無措、不知該說甚麼，再加上這位女性是自己上司，又比自己小了兩歲…。與亨利一起工作還算順利，只是澤崎總會有不自在的感覺。

Lesson 13

Working for a New Boss (1) (新上司)

預習—*Sentences*

· Let's start in on our drinks first.
· I'd like to know you better.
· I appreciate your thoughtfulness.
· What makes us so different?
· Level with me, by all means.

Vignette

Sawasaki: What is it that you wanted to talk to me about?
Henry: Let's start in on our drinks first. Here's to you.
Sawasaki: To you too.
Henry: I thought I'd like to know you better, Shoichi. You know, we've been working together just briefly but I have a feeling that you're trying to distance yourself from me. Tell me, is there anything about me that you have trouble relating to?
Sawasaki: I appreciate your thoughtfulness. The problem is I'm petrified to talk to Western women. I have no problem with Western men or Japanese women, but I . . . it's just uncomfortable.
Henry: Why? What makes us so different?
Sawasaki: I'll be perfectly honest with you, if I may.
Henry: Level with me, by all means.
Sawasaki: I think it's my cultural upbringing. I've been brought up in a society where the man holds the dominant position in everything and I've never questioned that. So it's difficult for me to accept a woman as an equal.
Henry: Much less a boss.
Sawasaki: Right! Sorry 'bout that.
Henry: It's all right.

■狀況

澤崎吃完午飯回來，便看到亨利所留的短箴：「假若今天下班後方便的話，希望和你談談」。下班後兩人便來到附近一家pub。亨利向澤崎說：「有甚麼話你儘管說。」

澤崎：妳想和我談甚麼？

亨利：我們先喝些飲料。敬你。

澤崎：我也敬妳。

亨利：昭一，我想多認識你。你知道，我們才一起工作沒多久，不過我覺得你在避著我。告訴我，是不是我有甚麼地方令你感到困擾？

澤崎：謝謝妳如此善體人意。問題在於我不知該怎麼跟西方女性講話。我可以毫無困難地跟西方男性或日本女性相處，可是我…就是覺得不自在。

亨利：為甚麼？我們有那麼不一樣嗎？

澤崎：如果可以，我會很坦誠地跟妳說。

亨利：當然，你就直說吧。

澤崎：我想是因為我的文化教養問題。我是在男性主導一切的社會長大，而我不曾質疑過那一點。所以我很難去接受一個女子跟我平起平坐。

亨利：更不用說是上司了。

澤崎：就是這個原因！很抱歉。

亨利：沒有關係的。

Words and Phrases

start in on 從…開始	thoughtfulness 設想周到
here's to 這杯敬…	by all means 無論怎麼一定要…
briefly 簡短地	upbringing 教養
distance from *v.* 與…疏遠	dominant 支配的；佔優勢的
relate to 使與…有關聯	Sorry 'bout that. 那件事我很抱歉。

Vocabulary Building

● **be petrified** 嚇呆；麻木

I was petrified to come across a live lion only about five meters away, but he just yawned and walked away from me.

（我碰到了一隻活生生的獅子，離我只有五公尺遠，我嚇得不知如何是好，而牠只是打個哈欠就走開了。）

● **level with** 對…開誠布公；對…說實話

Thank you for leveling with me. I like your candor.

（謝謝你告訴我實話。我喜歡你的坦誠。）

● **equal** 同等階級的人

The foreman was very popular because he treated everybody as his equal.

（這個領工人緣很好，因為他並不看低任何人。）

重點文法・語法

Much less a boss.

請試著將此理解為下面這個句子："It's difficult for me to accept a woman as an equal, much less a boss."

much less 通常會帶出一個否定句，用來表示「何況」的意思。在此表示「連將女性看作平等的一方都很困難了，何況是上司…」。

▶Exercises

請利用括弧內的詞語改寫下列例句，並盡量保持原來的語意。

(解答見251頁)

1. What is it that you wanted to talk to me about?
   (when you said, did you have, on your mind)

2. I appreciate your thoughtfulness.
   (being so thoughtful, thank)

3. I'll be perfectly honest with you, if I may.
   (allow me to be, will you)

◆◆◆◆◆◆◆◆◆◆◆◆◆◆◆ 簡短對話 ◆◆◆◆◆◆◆◆◆◆◆◆◆◆◆

Henry: I realized that we hardly know each other. Let's have a heart-to-heart talk. Is there anything about me that makes you keep your distance? I'm a big girl. I can take anything.

Sawasaki: No, it's not anything you've done. It just makes me a little uneasy to talk to you. You Western women seem to be so liberated. I guess it's my psychological attitude. It doesn't reflect on what you do on the job.

Henry: There should be no psychological barrier between us just because I'm a Western woman.

---

heart-to-heart 坦誠的；開誠布公的 **keep one's distance** 保持距離 **big girl** 成年的女性 **take** 承受 **uneasy** 不安的；侷促的 **liberated** 解放的 **psychological attitude** 心態 **reflect on** 反映在… **barrier** 障礙

Lesson 13

Working for a New Boss (2)（新上司）

預習—*Sentences*

· Mind if I have a refill?
· Think of what her folks would say.
· You have all the ingredients of success.
· If it's a man, he's a "born leader."
· The same old story.

Vignette

Sawasaki: I'm also part of a new minority—males reporting to female bosses. It's such a switch. Mind if I have a refill?

Henry: Go right ahead. Believe me, though, you're not unique in your reaction. Some men in the States threaten to quit at the news that they'll be reporting to a woman. Others demand a transfer. The relationships between male subordinates and female bosses are often strained. It's a hot issue.

Sawasaki: I've never mentioned to my wife that I now have a female boss. I probably never will. Think of what her folks would say. Sorry.

Henry: I understand your feelings perfectly well. But how do you think I got my present position?

Sawasaki: You have a good education, strong will, perseverance and an outgoing personality— all the ingredients of success.

Henry: Very frequently people say that when a woman succeeds it's due to luck or legislation. When a man succeeds, it's because he was capable. Articulate and strong-willed women are considered "bitchy." If it's a man, he's a " born leader." The same old story.

Sawasaki: But isn't it true that most women are too emotional to make rational decisions and that they don't have the capacity for scientific and technical skills? I don't allow my wife to drive.

■狀況

澤崎稍微喝了點酒後，在外國女性面前也逐漸放得開來。也許亨利早就想到這一點了。亨利說明男部屬和女上司的關係就算在美國也是很微妙的。

澤崎：我也是新少數派的一員了 —— 女上司的下屬。這轉變還真大。介意我再喝一杯嗎?

亨利：請。說真的，並不只是你有這種反應而已。在美國有些男性在得知會成為女上司的下屬時便威脅要辭職，其他的則要求調職。男下屬和女上司間的關係往往很緊張。這是個熱門的話題。

澤崎：我從沒跟我太太提過我現在有個女上司了。我可能永遠都不會告訴她。想想她的親友會怎麼說。別介意。

亨利：我很能體會你的心情。不過你認為我是怎麼升到現在的職位的?

澤崎：妳受過良好的教育、意志堅定、有毅力、個性外向 —— 所有成功的要素都有。

亨利：人們常說女人的成功是因為運氣好或是法律保障之故，而男人則是因其能力才成功的。能言善道、意志堅定的女性會被視為「有壞心眼」，但如果是男人，卻說他是個「天生的領導者」。從以前到現在，一點沒變。

澤崎：不過事實上大部分的女性都太情緒化，而無法做出理智的決定。而且她們在科學和技術方面也不太行，不是嗎? 我就不讓我太太開車。

Words and Phrases

minority 少數派
refill 再注滿（飲料）
threaten 威脅
transfer 調職
subordinate 屬下
strain 使緊張
hot issue 爭議頗大的課題；熱門話題
folks 雙親；親屬
perseverance 毅力
ingredient 要素；成分
legislation 立法；法律
bitchy 惡毒的；毒辣的
born leader 天生的領導者

Vocabulary Building

- **report to** 隸屬於…；是…的下屬

  Who do you report to in your organization?

  (公司中誰是你的上司?)

- **outgoing** 外向的；離開的；將卸任的

  cf. There will be a large farewell party at the embassy tomorrow for the outgoing ambassador.

  (明天在大使館會有個為即將卸任的大使所舉辦的大型歡送會。)

- **articulate** 說話清晰的；能清楚表達自己意見的

  cf. Be free to articulate your grievances, Anita. I need to know specifics about your case of sexual harassment.

  (安妮塔，清楚地說出你受到的委屈，我需要瞭解妳性騷擾案中的詳盡細節。)

重點文法・語法

The relationships between male subordinates and female bosses are often strained.

male 是表示「男性」、「雄性」，而female 是表示「女性」、「雌性」。這兩個字不止用於人，也用於其他動物或植物。以前，若用這個字來指人會帶有輕蔑的意思，但近來則因其 neutrality（中性）而逐漸變得普遍。

▶Exercises

請利用括弧內的詞語改寫下列例句，並盡量保持原來的語意。

(解答見252頁)

1. You're not unique in your reaction.
   (like that, not the only one, react)

2. The relationships between male subordinates and female bosses are often strained.
   (have strained relationships)

3. I've never mentioned to my wife that I now have a female boss.
   (doesn't know, I report to, woman)

◆◆◆◆◆◆◆◆◆◆◆◆◆◆◆ 簡短對話 ◆◆◆◆◆◆◆◆◆◆◆◆◆◆◆

Sawasaki: Don't women have much higher turnover than men?

Henry: The rate is only slightly higher for women. But statistics say that men tend to take longer and more frequent sick leaves than women, at least in America. There are a lot of these myths that need to be cleared up.

Sawasaki: How do you feel about being one of the few foreign women executives in Japan? Have you had any problems?

Henry: Yes, some Japanese men have asked me quite bluntly if I came to Japan to find a husband. Others ask if I'm at all interested in marrying, as though marriage is all there is for a woman to do. That really makes me mad. It's none of their business.

---

turnover 離職率 **tend to** 易於… **sick leave** 病假 **myth** 神話；不實的想法 **clear up** 澄清；解決 **bluntly** 率直地；唐突地 **mad** 憤怒的 **none of someone's business** 與某人不相干

Lesson 13

Working for a New Boss (3)（新上司）

預習—*Sentences*

· You're a real male chauvinist.
· Men would use swearwords in front of me.
· That stopped the apologies.
· You're stereotyping again.
· That sounds awful, doesn't it?

Vignette

Henry: You're a real male chauvinist, aren't you, Shoichi? Regardless of sex, some individuals just aren't fit to sit behind the wheel— or behind a manager's desk, as the case may be. When I was in the States, men would sometimes use swearwords in front of me. I didn't mind the language, but I did resent it when the man would turn to me and apologize. Finally, one day I said,"Look, I don't give a shit what words you use." That stopped the apologies.

Sawasaki: [*Laughs*]You even have a sense of humor, unlike a lot of women.

Henry: You're stereotyping again, Shoichi. You definitely have a gender bias. Do you feel that you wouldn't want to work for a supervisor because she's a woman?

Sawasaki: That sounds awful, doesn't it?

Henry: I think it's an injustice. It so happens that right now I have more responsibility in this company than you do. And it's only incidental that I'm a woman.

Sawasaki: You're right. Even though I may not be able to change my outlook on women overnight, it was good to have this conversation with you today. I think we understand each other a little better.

Henry: I do too. Let me get the check, OK?

■狀況

聽到澤崎「不讓老婆開車」這樣的大男人主義作風，亨利似乎有些意外。澤崎對女性是有點偏見。不過，澤崎自己也深知，這種想法不是一朝一夕就能改變的。

亨利：昭一，你真大男人主義耶，對不對。撇開性別不談，有些人就是不適合去操控方向盤──或在其他的情形中，像是擔任經理的職務。我在美國時，男人有時會當著我的面罵髒話。我不在意他們用甚麼字眼，可是我很受不了那個說話的人轉過來跟我道歉。終於，有一天我告訴他們：「聽好，我才不甩你用甚麼字眼呢！」他們也就不再道歉了。

澤崎：[笑] 妳還真有幽默感，不像大多數的女人。

亨利：昭一，你又來了。你真的有性別歧視。你覺得，你會因為上司是個女人就不願替她工作嗎？

澤崎：那聽來很糟，不是嗎？

亨利：我認為那並不公平。現在的情形是，我在公司中的職權比你大。只不巧，我是個女人罷了。

澤崎：妳說得不錯。即使我無法在一夜之間改變對女人的看法，但今天跟妳談了這些也頗有助益。我想我們都多認識了對方一些。

亨利：我也是。我來付帳，可以嗎？

Words and Phrases

male chauvinist [ˋʃovɪˌnɪst] 男性沙文主義者
regardless of 不分；不顧
wheel 車子的方向盤
swearword 咒詛；罵人的言語
resent 厭惡
apologize 道歉
sense of humor 幽默感
gender bias 性別歧視
injustice 不公平
incidental 附帶的；不重要的

Vocabulary Building

- **stereotype** *v.* 使成定型 *n.* 一成不變的觀念；刻板的觀念
  cf. Fujiyama and geisha are the old American stereotypes about Japan.
  (美國人提起日本就會想到富士山和藝伎。)
- **outlook** 前途；見解
  What's the economic outlook for next year?
  (明年經濟的前景如何?)
- **check** 帳單；存條
  I can't find my suitcase and it may have been lost. Here's my baggage check.
  (我找不到我的皮箱，有可能遺失了。這是我的行李存條。)

重點文法・語法

I don't give a shit what words you use.

這句話的意思是「我才不甩你用什麼字眼呢!」，shit 是「糞」的意思、典型的 four-letter word (粗話)。以前在女性面前絕對不能使用這個字，若是不小心說了便得向對方道歉；但最近也有女性使用的情況。亨利覺得男性可以在同性間稀鬆平常地使用粗話，但在女性面前使用時卻得一一致歉，這件事違反了「兩性平等」的原則，所以她感到很不滿意。

▶*Exercises*

請利用括弧內的詞語改寫下列例句，並盡量保持原來的語意。

(解答見252頁)

1. Regardless of sex, some individuals just aren't fit to sit behind the wheel.
   (drive, people, without regard to)

2. Men would sometimes use swearwords in front of me.
   (in my presence, swear)

3. You wouldn't want to work for a supervisor because she's a woman.
   (report to, female supervisor, on account of her sex)

◆◆◆◆◆◆◆◆◆◆◆◆◆◆◆ 簡短對話 ◆◆◆◆◆◆◆◆◆◆◆◆◆◆◆

Sawasaki: What about in the States? Is there complete equality of the sexes?

Henry: The federal government has passed laws against discrimination by sex, age, race, religion, and other factors. If a woman employee feels that she's being unfairly treated, she can bring the matter to court. Now, Shoichi, all I'm asking for is that you look at our working relationship with an open mind. Is that too much to ask?

Sawasaki: No. That's fair enough.

Henry: All right, let's have another round of drinks before I have to run.

---

equality of the sexes 性別平等 **federal government** 聯邦政府 **bring the matter to court** 訴諸法律途徑 **with an open mind** 不帶偏見地 **Is that too much to ask?** 這樣的要求過份嗎? **That's fair enough.** 很合理;很公平。**round of drinks** 在場者每人都喝個一杯

Lesson 13 Working for a New Boss—總結

雖然知道女性主管在美國有暴增的趨勢，但澤崎想都沒想過這件事會發生在自己身上。有個比自己年輕的女上司，老實說，澤崎覺得怪丟臉的。所以他也沒有跟太太說起這件事。

亨利為了和澤崎把問題說開來，決定在下班後邀他去附近的酒吧。她有效地運用了包含「時間」和「空間」的nonverbal communication（非言辭的傳達）。也就是因為有這樣的「時間」（非辦公的「個人」時間）和「空間」（pub 這樣的“neutral space”中立空間）要素，澤崎也才能無所顧忌地談話吧！如果時間是上午九點，地點是亨利的辦公室，那麼，真心話怕也說不出來。

甚至在最後，亨利也使用了屬於「物」的nonverbal communication。亨利 pick up了帳單，是為了給澤崎一個印象：這不是約會，所以身為上司的我付帳是理所當然的。

煩惱不知如何跟西方女性應對的還不只是澤崎一人。最近就連美國商業界中，道德觀和價值觀也開始有所轉變了。

其中最為複雜難懂的便是有關女性的事。70 年代初期的 women's liberation movement（婦女解放運動），使得女性所遭受的公然歧視消失了，而工作上的 unisex（無分男女）也有所進展，出現了男性總機和男護士。今後，也許像女上司和男祕書這樣的組合也不會太稀奇了。

亨利知道 “I'd like to know you better.” 是個讓對方開口的甜言蜜語，澤崎必定是受了影響，所以最後才會說：「即使我無法在一夜之間改變女性的看法，但今天跟妳談了這些也頗有助益。」可是澤崎在這位新上司手下真能 happy 地繼續工作下去嗎?

Lesson 14

Paper Chase Day

（文件清理日）

Lesson 14 的內容

最近 ABC 食品公司的抽屜和櫃子都有滿出來的狀況，桌上文件堆積如山，走廊也像是倉庫一般。這樣怎麼行！澤崎建議實施他以前公司實施過的「文件清理日」制度。

Lesson 14

Paper-Chase Day (1)（文件清理日）

預習—*Sentences*

· Sorry to bother you.
· He can't find it in any of his files.
· You *are* a well-organized person, aren't you?
· This report was filed under "Marketing."
· I wish everybody else did that.

Vignette

Yamamoto: Shoichi, sorry to bother you about such a trifling matter as this but Mike Yamaguchi is looking for a copy of the feasibility report on telemarketing conducted by our management consultants. Says he can't find it in any of his files. Actually I'm not surprised. You know the way he stacks up piles of paper all over his office. This is the third time he's come to me for a missing document.

Sawasaki: Don't be too upset, Nancy. Give him a copy of my report. I have it right here in my desk-side cabinet. Here you go.

Yamamoto: You *are* a well-organized person, aren't you? You always know which file to go to for any information. How do you manage to do that?

Sawasaki: Well, not always. But I learned my system from Tom Noonan. Remember he used to say, "If you don't know where a document is, it might as well not exist"? I use broad generic headings, the way he did, because overly specific labels are hard to remember. This report was filed under "Marketing."

Yamamoto: I see. But you also weed out documents from time to time as part of keeping your files updated, don't you? I wish everybody else did that. Our file cabinets are bursting with paper.

Sawasaki: I have an idea. Maybe we need a "paper-chase day."

狀況

麥可·山口好像又弄丟了文件，令山本也有些不知所措；最近辦公室到處同樣地也有文件滿溢的情形。澤崎想到了一個好主意。

山本：昭一，抱歉為了這麼瑣碎的事來麻煩你，但是麥可·山口在找關於電話行銷可行性的報告，就是我們管理顧問做的那份。他說他在所有檔案裡都找不到。事實上，我並不驚訝。你也知道他是怎麼把文件堆得整間辦公室都是。這是他第三次來找我要失蹤的文件。

澤崎：不要為此太過心煩了，南西。給他一份我的報告。我就放在桌上的檔案櫃裡。喏，在這兒。

山本：你真是個有組織的人耶，對不對？你總是知道哪些資料的檔案在哪，你是怎麼辦到的？

澤崎：這個嘛，也不是總是如此啦！不過，我這套系統是向湯姆·諾南學的。記得他常說的一句話嗎？「如果你不曉得某份文件在哪，那它跟不存在其實也沒甚麼兩樣。」就跟湯姆一樣，我的檔案櫃上所使用的標題都是一般廣泛性的，因為標籤若分類太細，要一一記住也很難。這份報告是歸檔在「行銷」下面。

山本：我明白了。但你也會不時地清掉過時的文件，使手邊保持最新資料，對不對？我希望每個人都能那樣做，因為我們的檔案櫃已經塞滿文件了。

澤崎：我有個主意。也許我們需要一個「文件清理日」。

Words and Phrases

bother 打擾
trifling [ˋtraɪflɪŋ] 微小的；瑣碎的
stack up 堆積
missing 不見了；失蹤的
be upset 煩亂
desk-side cabinet 桌上型檔案櫃
manage to 設法…
generic 一般的
weed out 從…除去無用的部分
updated 最新的
file cabinet 檔案櫃
burst 幾乎脹破

Vocabulary Building

● **feasibility report** 可行性報告

cf. This feasibility study is incomplete because it doesn't include the investment returns likely to be produced.

(這份可行性報告由於沒有將可能的投資收益算進去，所以還不完全。)

● **telemarketing** 電話行銷〈利用電話來推廣產品〉

You can sell many types of goods and services by telephone, but I never thought of using a telemarketing agency in promoting investment opportunities in Cambodia.

(你是可以藉由電話來達成許多貨品或服務的交易，不過，我可從來沒有想過要在柬埔寨利用電話行銷代理來推廣投資機會。)

● **management consultant** 管理顧問

Management consultants usually work on a time-input fee basis.

(管理顧問通常是計時索費。)

重點文法・語法

I use broad generic headings.

generic 是指「一般的」，但也有「未受商標保護」或「一般名稱的」之意。若是說 generic brand，是指完全不加品牌名，標籤上只標示此商品的一般名稱（香菸、威士忌、洗滌劑）、 容量以及法律規定事項；而多餘的裝飾、包裝則一概沒有，機能性和實用性為其重點，也就是所謂的無品牌商品。

▶Exercises

請利用括弧內的詞語改寫下列例句，並盡量保持原來的語意。

(解答見252頁)

1. Actually I'm not surprised.
   (to tell the truth, he doesn't)

2. This is the third time he's come to me for a missing document.
   (twice before, to inquire about)

3. If you don't know where a document is, it might as well not exist.
   (in which file, filed, have been lost)

◆◆◆◆◆◆◆◆◆◆◆◆◆◆◆◆ 簡短對話 ◆◆◆◆◆◆◆◆◆◆◆◆◆◆◆◆

Yamamoto: You know, it really burns me up the way he'll come rushing in here and say, " Nancy, I need this, ""Nancy, I want that."

Sawasaki: Believe me, I know exactly how you feel. After a couple of years at my old job I was always getting phone calls from people other than my boss asking for help on one thing or another.

Yamamoto: Did you do what they wanted?

Sawasaki: Often I didn't feel I could say no. But I consoled myself that the reason they were calling me was because they knew they could depend on me.

---

burn up 〔口語〕令人發怒 **rush in** 衝進 **one thing or another** 各種事情 **console** 安慰 **depend on** 依賴…

Lesson 14

Paper-Chase Day (2) (文件清理日)

預習—*Sentences*

· My door's always open.
· Everybody should come in on a weekend.
· That's not a bad suggestion.
· Where did you get the idea?
· It was something of a fun event.

Vignette

Sawasaki: May I come in?
Henry: Of course, Shoichi. My door's always open. So tell me, what's up?
Sawasaki: I was wondering if you've taken a good look around our offices lately. This place is a mess. Paper's flowing out of everybody's drawers and cabinets.
Henry: I know. Mike Yamaguchi has just requested the purchase of additional file cabinets.
Sawasaki: That's just the point. We don't need more file space to store more paper. What we need is a paper-chase day.
Henry: Paper-chase day?
Sawasaki: Yes, everybody should come in on a weekend and throw out old and unnecessary documents, manila folders and files. Reorganize our cabinets and make the place look tidy.
Henry: Hmm, that's not a bad suggestion. I hate to think how much time we all waste looking for missing files. Where did you get the idea?
Sawasaki: From International Foods, where I used to work.
Henry: Didn't the employees complain about having to come to work on a weekend?
Sawasaki: We got an extra day off in the summer. And it was something of a fun event.

狀況

澤崎馬上到上司亨利那兒去，說明「文件清理日」的構想。這個構想的重點在於丟掉不必要的文件，而不是增加收放文件的空間。

澤崎：我可以進來嗎？

亨利：當然，昭一。我的門永遠敞開。告訴我，發生甚麼事了？

澤崎：我在想，不知妳最近有沒有好好地環視一下我們的辦公室。這地方現在是一團糟，大家的抽屜和櫃子都有文件滿溢的現象。

亨利：我知道。麥可・山口剛剛才要求再購買一些檔案櫃。

澤崎：這就是問題所在。我們需要的不是更多的檔案空間來存放愈來愈多的文件。我們需要的是一個文件清理日。

亨利：文件清理日？

澤崎：是呀，每個人都應該找個週末到辦公室來，清掉那些老舊無用的資料、舊文件夾以及過時的檔案。重新整理我們的櫃子，好使這地方看來整齊一點。

亨利：嗯，這是個不錯的建議。我實在不願去想我們總共花了多少時間在尋找那些失蹤的檔案。你從哪裡得到這個點子的？

澤崎：從國際食品公司，我以前的東家。

亨利：員工們不會抱怨週末來上班嗎？

澤崎：我們夏天會多放一天假。而且這件事還蠻好玩的。

Words and Phrases

mess 一團糟
drawers 抽屜；櫥櫃
request *v.* 要求；請求
purchase [ˋpɝtʃəs] *n.* 購買
store *n.* 儲存；存放
throw out 丟掉
manila folder 馬尼拉紙製的文件夾
reorganize 重新整理
tidy *adj.* 整齊的
hmm 嗯
complain 抱怨
extra 額外的
day off 休假

Vocabulary Building

● **What's up?** 〔口語〕怎麼了?

"Hi, Bill. What's up?"—"Hi. Oh, nothing going on around here, Joe."

(「嗨，比爾。有甚麼事嗎?」「嗨。喬，沒甚麼事。」

● **additional** 額外的；外加的

There will be additional charges for assignments outside the main contract.

(主契約以外的工作指派須另外付費。)

● **That's just the point.** 那就是問題所在。

"I don't know if I can trust Chuck."—"That's just the point. Chuck has let us down before."

(「我不知道我是否可以信任查克。」「那就是問題所在。查克以前讓我們失望過。」)

重點文法・語法

From International Foods, where I used to work.

used to是一種慣用法，意指「過去常…、過去習慣於…」，通常只使用於過去直述句。字典上雖有否定型的 use(d)n't 和 didn't use(d) to、疑問句的 Did you use(d) to . . .? 等，但一般不太常用。

尤其是在書面語上，最好還是避免使用過去直述句以外的形式。

▶Exercises

請利用括弧內的詞語改寫下列例句，並盡量保持原來的語意。 (解答見252頁)

1. I was wondering if you've taken a good look around our offices lately.
   (take, did you ever)

2. I hate to think how much time we all waste looking for missing files.
   (it bothers me, is lost, trying to locate)

3. Didn't the employees complain about having to come to work on a weekend?
   (any complaints, report, were there)

◆◆◆◆◆◆◆◆◆◆◆◆◆◆◆◆ 簡短對話 ◆◆◆◆◆◆◆◆◆◆◆◆◆◆◆◆

Henry: Back at corporate headquarters we had a rule that you were to leave nothing on your desk when you went home, except for your telephone.

Sawasaki: That's exactly what I was told to do when I started working here. But it was already pretty much of a dead letter then, and the situation has been deteriorating rapidly ever since.

Henry: Obviously we can't go on like this. More file cabinets is one thing, but before you know it they'll be saying we need a bigger office. And with the way rents are in Tokyo . . .

---

corporate headquarters 公司總部 **pretty much of** 無異是… **dead letter** 不被執行的規定 **deteriorate** 惡化

Lesson 14

Paper-Chase Day (3)（文件清理日）

預習—*Sentences*

· We even gave a special prize.
· Let's make a copy of everything.
· You must be joking.
· We should also clean out our computer files.
· Can I make you the project manager?

Vignette

Sawasaki: At the end of the day, we celebrated the demise of old files with pizza and beer. We even gave a special prize to the person who tossed out the most paper.

Henry: That should encourage him to hoard even more paper for the next time. I'd give an award to someone who can come up with a better central filing system.

Sawasaki: Filing isn't just a clerical function. The managers should also understand how the system works. If it's set up properly, we should be able to retrieve any piece of paper from the office files within three minutes.

Henry: You're right. File retrieval shouldn't be a guessing game. That reminds me, somewhere I read that there's a close correlation between promotability and neat desks.

Sawasaki: Yes, but there's always someone who hates to get rid of paper. When we had a paper-chase day at International Foods, one of my colleagues said, "Just in case we need any of this information in the future, let's make a copy of everything we throw out."

Henry: [*Laughing*] You must be joking.

Sawasaki: I guess he's still there, unless he got buried in a paper avalanche.

Henry: While we're at it, we should also clean out our computer files. Can I make you the project manager, Shoichi, to work on the details?

Sawasaki: Uh, sure.

■狀況

「你要能在三分鐘內從一堆檔案中取出你要的資料」「你能否升遷跟你桌面的整齊與否密切相關」——對於那些不懂如何整理檔案而搞得辦公室一團亂的人來說，這些話可能會有些刺耳。不過澤崎已被任命為文件清理日的計畫執行人了。

澤崎：一天結束時，我們用披薩和啤酒慶祝舊檔案的終結。我們甚至頒獎給文件丟得最多的人。

亨利：那會鼓勵他囤積更多文件，以備下次清理之用。倒是如果有人能想出一套更好的中央檔案管理系統，我要頒個獎給他。

澤崎：檔案管理不只是事務性的工作而已。主管們也得明白這系統是如何運作的。如果系統建立得當，我們就可以在三分鐘內從辦公室的檔案中取出任何文件。

亨利：你說的對，檔案檢索不應是猜謎遊戲。這使我想起，我曾在某處讀到一些東西，它說你能否得到升遷，與你的桌面整齊與否有密切的關係。

澤崎：是呀，但總是有人不喜歡把文件扔掉。以前在國際食品公司時，有一次遇到文件清理日，我一個同事就說，「搞不好以後會需要這些資料，所以我們來把所有要丟的東西都做個影本吧!」

亨利：[笑著]你一定在開玩笑。

澤崎：我猜他仍在那裡，除非他那些堆積如山的文件倒下來把他埋起來了。

亨利：我們在清理文件時，也應該要清理一下電腦檔案。昭一，我可以任命你為計畫執行人來處理一些細節嗎?

澤崎：噢，當然。

Words and Phrases

celebrate 慶祝
demise [dɪˋmaɪz]〔文〕死亡
pizza [ˋpitsə] 披薩
toss out 丟棄
hoard 囤積
come up with 想出…
guessing game 猜謎遊戲
correlation 相互關聯
neat 整齊的
colleague [ˋkɑlig] 同事
just in case 以防萬一
avalanche [ˋævl̩ˌæntʃ] 雪崩
detail 細節

Vocabulary Building

● **clerical** 事務性的

cf. As part of your secretarial function, you must serve coffee or tea to visitors.

（祕書的工作之一，就是要為訪客端茶倒咖啡。）

● **retrieve** 取出（文件）；檢索

With this personal computer, you can instantly retrieve any stock market data.

（有了這臺個人電腦，你可以馬上叫出股市的任何資料。）

● **promotability** 升遷的可能性

cf. Indicate if the employee is promotable to the next layer in the company within the next 18 months.

（這指明了在未來十八個月內，員工在公司內是否能得到升遷，更上一層樓的可能性。）

重點文法・語法

We celebrated the demise of old files with pizza and beer.

在歐美辦公室等場合的簡便餐會中，「披薩和啤酒」是典型的食物。稍加高級的則有葡萄酒和乳酪，因此也有pizza and beer party或wine and cheese party的說法。

▶Exercises

請利用括弧內的詞語改寫下列例句，並盡量保持原來的語意。

（解答見252頁）

1. We even gave a special prize to the person who tossed out the most paper.
   (presented, discarded, award)

2. I'd give an award to someone who can come up with a better central filing system.
   (more efficient, think up, should be given)

3. There's always someone who hates to get rid of paper.
   (somebody, abhors, dumping)

◆◆◆◆◆◆◆◆◆◆◆◆◆◆◆◆ 簡短對話 ◆◆◆◆◆◆◆◆◆◆◆◆◆◆◆◆

Henry: But you know something, Shoichi? Most of the Japanese company offices I've been to are even worse. Not only are there stacks of paper everywhere, but there seems to be no attention paid to attractive office design.

Sawasaki: You're quite right. It would never occur to most traditional managers here that they should spend money to make their offices look nice. They'd probably think it was wasteful.

Henry: It really comes as a shock to someone like me, who always thought that the Japanese valued neatness and beauty, when I see the state of people's workplaces here.

You know something? 你知道嗎？ **stacks of** 一堆一堆的 **pay no attention to** 沒注意… **traditional** 傳統的 **wasteful** 浪費的 **value** *v.* 重視 **neatness** 整齊 **workplace** 工作場所

Lesson 14 Paper-Chase Day — 總結

■ ■ ■

英語之中常說 A cluttered desk is a sign of a cluttered mind.「雜亂無章的桌子象徵紊亂不清的思考。」淩亂的辦公室不只在心理和思考上會產生紊亂，而且在尋找文件時更會造成時間上的浪費。

有些公司每年都會有幾次 paper-chase day，將舊檔案或文件丟掉以提高業務效率。

但只要一不留神，文件馬上又會堆積起來。歸檔的首要原則就是不留無用之物；此外，如果有查看檔案的機會，也得隨時將過時的文件丟棄。

在做檔案分類的標籤時，切忌過度細分，否則有時連建檔人都會搞不清楚要如何檢索。也請記得檔案分類上要用 broad generic heading，也要避免以形容詞或數字等做開頭。

而縱使將新的報告收存在稱做 New Report 或 1995 Report 的檔案裏，過了幾個月，也可能全然忘掉歸到哪個檔裏去了。為防止這樣的情況，也可將 heading 做成 Report-New, Report-1995 等。

Lesson 15

Workaholic

（工作狂）

Lesson 15 的內容

最近，澤崎整個人簡直成了「工作機器」。早上比誰都早到，而晚上卻要待到九點、十點才回家。每天晚餐都吃泡麵。這一次，他在晚上十一點時，差點撞到回來拿家門鑰匙的茱莉・亨利。澤崎是不是成了所謂的「工作狂」呢？

Lesson 15

Workaholic (1)（工作狂）

預習—*Sentences*

· I can't believe you're still here.
· There's so much to do around here.
· Work gets piled up while I'm away.
· I can't make head or tail of it.
· You certainly exhibit the symptoms.

Vignette

Henry: Shoichi! You scared the daylights out of me. I can't believe you're still here. Do you realize it's 11 o'clock? Time to go home and get some sleep.

Sawasaki: Sorry to surprise you. I heard a noise over here and thought I should check it out. But tell me, what's a nice lady like you doing in a place like this? Still a bit early for a power breakfast meeting, isn't it?

Henry: [*Sarcastically*] Very funny. No, actually I was at a party and discovered that I left the key to my apartment in my office. So I stopped by to pick it up. I had no idea you were still at work.

Sawasaki: Well, there's so much to do around here. And I still haven't caught up from my last business trip. Work gets piled up while I'm away and after I'm back there seems to be a never-ending stream of paper crossing my desk. I was just working on a status report turned in by a brand manager. I wish he had done a better job of organizing the material and putting it in perspective. I can't make head or tail of it.

Henry: You know, Shoichi, I'm afraid you're turning into an incurable workaholic. You certainly exhibit the symptoms.

Sawasaki: What symptoms?

Henry: Recently your whole life seems to be just work and instant noodles. Don't let work become an end in itself or a way of fooling yourself and others into believing that you're indispensable. I'm really worried about you, Shoichi.

Sawasaki: Are you trying to tell me that I'm dispensable?

Henry: We're all dispensable. You, me, everybody.

■狀況

澤崎今天又是工作到十一點。他聽到茱莉・亨利的辦公室有奇怪的聲響，所以跑去察看，結果撞見了亨利。亨利幾乎嚇破了膽，而澤崎的回答卻是：「工作做不完。」

亨利：昭一！我讓你給嚇死了。真不敢相信你還在這兒。你知道現在十一點了嗎？該回家睡覺了。

澤崎：抱歉嚇到你了。我聽到這裡有聲音，就過來察看。不過，告訴我，像你這麼可愛的小姐在這種地方做甚麼？開早餐會報還有點早吧，不是嗎？

亨利：[譏諷地]很有趣。事實上，我是去參加一個晚宴，然後發現我把公寓鑰匙放在辦公室裡了。所以我回來拿鑰匙，沒想到你居然還在工作。

澤崎：這裡有很多事情要做。上次出差回來後，我一直沒能把落後的進度補回來。我不在時工作都堆積如山了，我回來後，桌上文件更是像潮水一樣湧進來，沒完沒了。我剛剛在看一位品牌經理所做的現況報告。我真希望他在處理這些資料時多費點心，把事情依其相互關係來陳述。我簡直搞不清整個來龍去脈。

亨利：昭一，我怕你快變成無可救藥的工作狂了。你確實有那些徵兆。

澤崎：甚麼徵兆？

亨利：最近，你整個生活中似乎只有工作和速食麵。別讓工作本身成為一種目的或是讓工作愚弄了自己，也愚弄了別人，以為自己是個不可或缺的重要角色。昭一，我真的很擔心你。

澤崎：你是要告訴我，我的存在可有可無？

亨利：我們都是可有可無，不只你我，每個人都是。

Words and Phrases

scare the daylights out of someone 把…嚇壞了
power breakfast meeting 早餐會報
stop by 路過暫時拜訪（逗留）
catch up 趕上
never-ending 永無休止的
turn in 呈交；提出
in perspective 正確而平衡地
incurable 無可救藥的
exhibit 顯示
symptom [ˋsɪmptəm] 症狀；徵兆
indispensable 不可或缺的

Vocabulary Building

- **status report** 現況報告
  The day-to-day work I don't mind, but writing my monthly status reports is deadly.
  （我不在意每天的工作，可是寫每月的現況報告實在是要了我的命。）
- **brand manager** 品牌經理（專門負責某一品牌的經理）
  The sales of the product picked up after a new brand manager took over.
  （這個產品在一位新品牌經理接管後，銷售額便增加了。）
- **can't make head or tail of [something]** 〔口語〕一點也不瞭解；搞不清楚
  I just couldn't make head or tail of what the angry customer was saying.
  （我就是一點都不了解那生氣的顧客在說些甚麼。）

重點文法・語法

What's a nice lady like you doing in a place like this?

澤崎雖是和上司亨利開玩笑地這麼說，但這句臺詞（如 What's a nice girl like you doing in a crummy joint like this?）一定得小心使用，因為這原本是男性向妓女搭訕、詢問身世境遇時所常用的技倆。現代主要用於男性對女性（或女性故意對男性）幽默或故意誇大地搭話等情況。

可是若說的時候沒把語氣掌握好，也有可能聽來陳腐或令對方不快。

▶*Exercises*

請利用括弧內的詞語改寫下列例句，並盡量保持原來的語意。

(解答見252頁)

1. I had no idea you were still at work.
   (working, never knew)

2. I was just working on a status report turned in by a brand manager.
   (have been busy, reviewing, product manager)

3. Are you trying to tell me that I'm dispensable?
   (suggest, can be dispensed with, do you mean)

◆◆◆◆◆◆◆◆◆◆◆◆◆◆ 簡短對話 ◆◆◆◆◆◆◆◆◆◆◆◆◆◆

Sawasaki: I really don't mind traveling on business. It gives me a chance to meet new people and go to new places. But I hate coming back to a desk loaded with a couple of weeks' worth of work to catch up on.

Henry: How about Etsuko? I don't suppose she likes being left on her own while you're gone.

Sawasaki: She's never complained. Since I'm practically never home in the evening, breakfast is the only time she sees me anyway. And when I'm not there she can sleep late and let the kids look after themselves.

Henry: Oh, I'm sure she misses you. She probably just doesn't think you'd respond if she said so.

---

travel on business 商務旅行 **loaded with** 裝滿；擺滿 **worth of** 相當於某分量的… **catch up on** 趕上（落後的工作） **on one's own** 獨自 **practically** 實際上 **look after** 照顧 **respond** 回應；回答

Lesson 15

Workaholic (2) （工作狂）

預習—*Sentences*

· You can get addicted to either.
· I've been raised in the Japanese tradition.
· Idleness is considered a sin.
· Hard workers get their jobs done.
· See what I mean?

Vignette

Henry: The way we used to put it in the States is that you should dispense with somebody as soon as they start getting indispensable. It's not healthy to have a situation where the absence of a single person can make the whole office fall apart.

Sawasaki: Even so, I'd rather be a workaholic than an alcoholic.

Henry: Both work and alcohol can be fine in moderation. But you can get addicted to either, and it's dangerous for you if you do.

Sawasaki: Well, I've been raised in the Japanese tradition, which values diligence and frugality. Hard work is the highest virtue of all and idleness is considered a sin.

Henry: Yes, I understand that. But hard work is one thing; being a workaholic is another.

Sawasaki: I'm sorry?

Henry: Don't get me wrong, Shoichi. I'm not saying I don't appreciate your work. But hard workers get their jobs done; workaholics get done in by their jobs. When's the last time you took a vacation?

Sawasaki: I haven't had time to since I started here.

Henry: See what I mean? In English we have a proverb, "All work and no play makes Jack a dull boy." You have a fine personality, with lots of drive and energy, but you're going to burn yourself outunless you let up a little bit.

Sawasaki: But I've seen executives in this company who take their jobs even more seriously than I do. It's all they seem to think about even when they're socializing.

Henry: Oh, I know those types. I used to have a boss like that.

■狀況

澤崎說，就算是「工作狂」也勝過酒精中毒，因為已往所受的教育都說「勤勞」是最崇高的美德。可是亨利說「工作和酒精一樣，都得有所節制，而且工作狂和勤勞是不同的」。

亨利：在美國，我們習慣的說法是，當某人開始變得重要、不可或缺時，你應該立即解雇他。因為如果事情演變到少一個人，就可使公司解體了，那是很不正常的。

澤崎：就算是這樣，我也寧願當個工作狂而不願成為酒鬼。

亨利：其實，只要適度的話，工作和酒精都是好的。但不管是哪一個，你都不能過度沈迷，否則就很危險了。

澤崎：我是在日本這個重視勤勞與節儉的傳統中長大的。努力工作是最崇高的美德，無所事事則是一種罪惡。

亨利：沒錯，我能了解。不過，努力工作是一回事；工作狂可又是另一回事。

澤崎：這話怎麼說？

亨利：昭一，別誤解。我並不是說我不賞識你的工作。不過，認真工作的人能夠駕馭他的工作，把工作作好；可是工作狂卻被工作牽著鼻子走，把自己搞得精疲力竭。你上次度假是甚麼時候的事了？

澤崎：自從我到這兒來之後，還沒有功夫去度假呢！

亨利：你懂我的意思了吧？我們英文有句諺語：「一味工作而沒有娛樂的人是很乏味的。」你是一個個性很好的人，而且充滿幹勁，但如果你不稍微鬆懈一下，你會把自己的精力給耗光的。

澤崎：可是我看到這個公司的主管們，個個都比我把工作看得嚴重。就算在社交場合，他們心裡所想的，似乎也盡是工作。

亨利：噢，我很清楚這種類型的人，我以前的老闆就是這種人。

Words and Phrases

put 表達
dispense with 摒棄
fall apart （體制的）瓦解；崩潰
alcoholic [ˌælkəˋhɔlɪk] 酒鬼；酗酒者
get addicted to 迷於…；上癮
diligence [ˋdɪlədʒəns] 勤勞
frugality [fruˋgælətɪ] 節儉
idleness 閒混
sin 罪惡
I'm sorry? 我不了解；怎麼說?〈請對方把話講清楚〉
let up 放鬆
those types 那些類型的人
socialize 〔口語〕交際

Vocabulary Building

- **in moderation** 適度地

  cf. You need to moderate your spending habits.
  （你在花錢的習慣上必須有所節制。）

- **get done in by** 被…搞得精疲力竭

  cf. Benny's constant lack of sleep finally did him in.
  （邦尼因為經常缺乏睡眠，終於累垮了。）

- **burn oneself out** 耗盡某人的全副精力

  People in high-stress jobs have to be careful not to burn themselves out.
  （工作壓力大的人必須小心，不要耗盡自己全部精力。）

重點文法・語法

Both work and alcohol can be fine in moderation.

名詞分可數與不可數，這是以能否使用複數形來區分。但有時候同一個名詞可能在某些情況下是可數，在某些情況下卻是不可數。

work 若是指「工作」，屬於不可數名詞，不能用複數。但若寫成works，就成了「作品」的意思。

同樣的，表示「顏色」的 color 雖然是不可數名詞，但若作「顏料」、「性格」、「國旗」等意時，則作可數名詞，可寫成複數形的colors 。此外，water 平常雖是不可數名詞，但寫成複數就成了「洪水」、「海水」、「河水」的意思。

▶Exercises

請利用括弧內的詞語改寫下列例句，並盡量保持原來的語意。

(解答見252頁)

1. I'd rather be a workaholic than an alcoholic.
   (prefer being, to being)

2. Hard work is one thing; being a workaholic is another.
   (working hard, not the same as)

3. I haven't had time to since I started here.
   (too busy, joined this company)

◆◆◆◆◆◆◆◆◆◆◆◆◆◆◆ 簡短對話 ◆◆◆◆◆◆◆◆◆◆◆◆◆◆◆

Sawasaki: Besides, even if I took a vacation, what would I do? My kids are busy studying, and when they're not, they'd rather be with their friends than go somewhere with me.

Henry: Couldn't just you and Etsuko take a trip by yourselves? I should think it would be a nice change of pace for both of you.

Sawasaki: I suppose we could, but traveling is so expensive.

Henry: Oh, Shoichi, you're impossible! I'm sure you can afford it. If not, you could save the money by cutting back a bit on your after-hours bar-crawling.

Sawasaki: Well, I suppose so.

---

take a trip 旅行 **change of pace** 改變步調 **impossible** 棘手的；難辦的 **cut back on** 減少 **after-hours** 下班後的 **bar-crawling** 流連於酒吧的

Lesson 15

Workaholic (3)（工作狂）

預習—*Sentences*

· I walked over to his table.
· Who was that, anybody I know?
· I'd say you are.
· You should also delegate more.
· Anyway, let's get out of here.

Vignette

Henry: I remember the time we were attending the annual management meeting at a hotel in Florida a few years ago. The last evening there was a party for the whole group in the hotel ballroom. I had been trying for days to get my boss to give me some time to talk about my business plans for the following year, but he was always too busy. So I walked over to his table, apologized for interrupting, and asked if I could ride back on the plane with him the next day so we could discuss my plans then. He said he already had an in-flight meeting set up and told me to pull up a chair and talk to him right then and there. So there I was in my party gear giving him an impromptu presentation without so much as a flipchart. And all the while his wife was giving me these hostile looks. Believe me, it was murder.

Sawasaki: Who was that, anybody I know?

Henry: No, he left the company a couple of years ago, but I'm sure he's still spreading stress wherever he goes.

Sawasaki: Am I "spreading stress" too?

Henry: Whether you care to admit it or not, I'd say you are. You're probably also breeding some resentment if you want others to work like you. You ought to learn how to manage your energy to pace yourself and maintain a good psychological balance. You should also delegate more.

Sawasaki: I guess you may be right.

Henry: Anyway, let's get out of here. And tomorrow I want you to promise to spend the evening with your family for a change.

Sawasaki: Yes, ma'am.

■狀況

不過，每個國家都有「工作狂」，亨利以前的上司也是如此。正因為對這樣的狀況有過經驗，所以亨利似乎對澤崎近來的情形很掛心。

亨利：我記得幾年前我們到佛羅里達一家飯店參加年度管理會議。會議的最後一晚，在飯店的舞廳有個為全體與會人員所舉行的宴會。那幾天，我一直想找機會跟我的老闆好好談談我對於來年的事業計畫。可是他一直都很忙。所以，在宴會上，我就走到他那桌，道個歉打岔，並問他隔天我能不能跟他搭同一班飛機回去，好在機上談談我的計畫。結果他說他已經排了個機上會議了，還叫我拉張椅子坐下來，就地跟他談好了。所以，我就一身宴會裝扮，跟他作即席報告，甚至連個解說用的掛圖都沒有。還有，在我報告的過程中，她太太一直用充滿敵意的眼光看著我。說真的，那簡直是謀殺。

澤崎：你說的這個人是誰，我認識嗎？

亨利：你不認識。他幾年前就離開公司了，但我相信，他走到哪兒，就把壓力散播到哪兒。

澤崎：我也會「散播壓力」嗎？

亨利：不管你承不承認，我都得說你會。如果你要別人也像你一樣的工作法，那你可能會引起別人的反感。你應該學著如何調適自己的精力，找出一個合宜的步調，並在心理上維持良好的平衡狀態。你也該多把工作委派出去，不要甚麼都自己來。

澤崎：我想你可能是對的。

亨利：好啦，我們離開這裡吧！而且，我要你答應，明天晚上改變一下，陪陪你的家人。

澤崎：遵命，夫人。

Words and Phrases

interrupt 打斷
in-flight 在飛機內進行的
set up 安排
pull up 拉
gear 〔口語〕服裝
hostile [ˋhɑst(ɪ)l] 帶有敵意的
spread 散播
breed 引起
resentment 憎惡；反感
pace *v.* 為…調整步調
psychological 心理上的
delegate （任務的）委派
for a change 改變一下

Vocabulary Building

● **impromptu** [ɪmˋprɑmptu] 即席的
Before I knew it, I was giving an impromptu speech to the assembled group.
(我甚至還不清楚是怎麼一回事，就發現自己在對一群人發表即席演說了。)

● **without so much as** 甚至連…都沒有
He found himself without so much as a penny to his name.
(他發現他自己一文不名。)

● **It's murder.** 〈用以比喻非常困難，不愉快，或麻煩的事〉簡直是變相的謀殺。
cf. If my boss wants me to work overtime on my wedding anniversary, I'm entitled to yell bloody murder.
(如果我老闆要我在我結婚週年紀念那天加班的話，我有權大喊那是殘忍的謀殺。)

重點文法・語法

I remember the time we were attending the annual management meeting.

attend 這個動詞在表示「出席」的意思時不需要介系詞，但表示「照料」、「照顧」、「工作」時，則要像 attend on the sick (照料病人)、attend to business 等加上 on 或 to 等介系詞。

▶*Exercises*

請利用括弧內的詞語改寫下列例句，並盡量保持原來的語意。

(解答見253頁)

1. His wife was giving me these hostile looks.
   (looking at, angry expression)

2. He left the company a couple of years ago.
   (stopped working for, two or three)

3. Whether you care to admit it or not, I'd say you are.
   (like it, the truth is)

◆◆◆◆◆◆◆◆◆◆◆◆◆◆◆ 簡短對話 ◆◆◆◆◆◆◆◆◆◆◆◆◆◆◆

Henry: What really burned me up about that man was the way he would make you feel lazy if you didn't work as hard as he did.

Sawasaki: I suppose he didn't take vacations either.

Henry: No, actually he took at least three weeks every summer. He had a place on the coast in Maine, and he used to go down there.

Sawasaki: That must have been a sort of vacation for you too.

Henry: It would have been, except that he would call in once, sometimes twice, a day.

---

burn up 〔口語〕使人發怒（生氣） **a sort of** 一種 **except that** 除了 **call in** 打電話進來

Lesson 15 Workaholic — 總結

workaholic 是由 alcoholic 衍生而來。有可能是源自美國牧師 Wayne Cates 所著的 *Confessions of a Workaholic* (1971)一書。

workaholic 指的是「沒有工作就活不下去的人」。工作和酒精都算是人生的一些要素，有人可以在「量」上取得平衡，但也有人會「濫用」。這二者都有可能令人上癮中毒。

不過，工作和酒精確實是兩個不同的東西。工作是必要的，酒精則不必然。工作是勞心，酒精卻是娛樂；工作會產生壓力，而(適量的）酒精則有助紓解壓力。

茱莉・亨利似乎認為，「工作是為了享受人生，但絕不能成為人生的目的」。她也說，對公司而言，沒有甚麼人是真正不可或缺的。

澤崎所受的教育告訴他，「勤勞乃最崇高的美德，懶惰則是罪惡」，但亨利以為，事情並不是這麼簡單。她覺得「認真玩，認真學」的精神比較實際，像"All work and no play makes Jack a dull boy."中的 Jack 則不可取。energy level 高的人（英語稱作 powerhouse, fireball, live wire 等）也必須控制自己的精力，在心理上取得一個平衡點。

可是，聽說真正的工作狂在休假時也不改其精神——他們可以專心地休假，而且投入相當的精力與熱情。所以，像澤崎這樣，平時整天工作，但週末卻在家裡閒得發慌的上班族，恐怕也不是真正的 workaholic，而只是個工作繁忙的人吧！

Lesson 16

Employee Dishonesty

（員工的欺騙行為）

Lesson 16 的內容

財務部那邊又有事要找澤崎了，不過，這次跟澤崎本身無關，而是營業部經理麥可・山口所惹的麻煩。山口上個月才服務屆滿十五週年，但卻涉嫌非法開支。這件事相當令人震驚。而令山口行跡敗露的則是那些令人懷疑的奠儀。

Lesson 16

Employee Dishonesty (1)（員工的欺騙行為）

預習—*Sentences*

- Give me a break, will you?
- May as well get it over with.
- I'll give you a quick recap.
- Only the three of us are to know about it.
- Excuse me just a second, Juergen.

Vignette

Yamamoto: Juergen Schumann wants to see you, Shoichi.
Sawasaki: Oh no, not again. Give me a break, will you?
Yamamoto: He asked you to meet him in Julie's office.
Sawasaki: What? In Julie's office? What the hell have I done this time, I wonder?
Yamamoto: He didn't tell me what it was about, but he sounded pretty grim ,I'm afraid to say.
Sawasaki: May as well get it over with, I guess.

* * *

Schumann: Shoichi, thank you for joining us. I've just started explaining to Julie about the situation with Mike Yamaguchi. I'll give you a quick recap, but first let me mention that this is in strict confidence. Only the three of us are to know about it at this stage. All right?
Sawasaki: Sure. What's the story?
Schumann: I've been doing the yearly check of inordinate payments, as required by company policy. In the past I understand that the traditional mid-year and year-end gifts to customers created slight problems at Corporate Finance in New York but now they fully appreciate the local customs on that score. In the course of the financial review this time, though, I've discovered that Mike has paid large sums in condolence money—what they call *koden*—to customers or their relatives without any proof of actual payment.
Sawasaki: Excuse me just a second, Juergen, but there's no way you can get a receipt at a funeral.

■狀況

得知優根·舒曼要求自己在茱莉·亨利的辦公室見他，令澤崎相當不安，因為上次的費用報銷報告曾出過問題。不過，這次所發生的事顯然要嚴重得多了。

山本：昭一，優根·舒曼想要見你。

澤崎：哦，別又是那回事了吧！可以饒了我嗎？

山本：他要你到茱莉的辦公室去，他在那裏。

澤崎：甚麼？在茱莉的辦公室，我這回到底又做了甚麼了？

山本：他沒有說是為了甚麼事，不過他聽起來很嚴肅。

澤崎：我猜他是想作個了結吧！

＊　＊　＊

舒曼：昭一，謝謝你來參與我們的討論。我剛剛才開始跟茱莉解釋麥可·山口的情況。我會很快地給你作個摘要，不過，我首先要提的是，這件事要絕對保密。在目前這個階段，就只有我們三人知道，可以嗎？

澤崎：那當然。是怎麼一回事？

舒曼：基於公司政策的需要，我在查對今年度一些開支太兇的帳目。就我瞭解，公司過去在傳統中元和歲暮送禮物給客戶的事上，曾給紐約總公司的財務部造成一些困擾，不過在這一點上，他們現在已經完全能夠理解本地的風俗了。只是，在這次的財務審查中，我發現麥可在喪弔上支出了大筆的金錢——就是他們所說的奠儀——支付對象都是客戶和他們的親戚，不過，他甚麼開支證明都沒有。

澤崎：優根，抱歉稍等一下，在葬禮中是沒有辦法拿到收據的。

Words and Phrases

Give me a break. 饒了我吧！
what the hell 到底是甚麼
grim 冷酷的
recap (<recapitulation) 摘要
inordinate [ɪn`ɔrdənɪt] 過度的；沒有節制的
mid-year and year-end gifts 年中及歲暮時的饋贈
appreciate 感激；瞭解
on that score 在那一點上
in the course of 在…當中
condolence [kən`doləns] 弔慰
funeral 葬禮

Vocabulary Building

- **not again** 別又是那回事了吧
  cf. Don't tell me you've lost your keys again!
  (別告訴我你又把鑰匙搞丟了！)
- **get it over with** 結束；完畢
  If you have to do something you don't want to, you should get it over with quickly.
  (假如有些事是你必須做卻又不想做的，那你應該快快將之結束掉。)
- **in strict confidence** 極機密地
  cf. Clyde took me into his confidence about his plan to retire.
  (克萊德很機密地把他要退休的計畫告訴我。)

重點文法・語法

I'll give you a quick recap.

recap是recapitulate的縮略，意指「重點重複」或「歸納」。英語中有不少字是像這樣省去字尾的，請參考下例：

lab <laboratory（實驗室）
high-tech <high-technology（高科技）
op ed <opposite editorial（與社論相對的其它版面）
math <mathematics（數學）
condo <condominium（分戶出售的公寓）
perks <perquisites（超額收益）
sci-fi <science fiction（SF、科幻小說）

▶Exercises

請利用括弧內的詞語改寫下列例句，並盡量保持原來的語意。

（解答見253頁）

1. He asked you to meet him in Julie's office.
   (he said he wanted, to come to, for a meeting)

2. He didn't tell me what it was about, but he sounded pretty grim.
   (the subject, didn't say, awfully)

3. Only the three of us are to know about it at this stage.
   (I don't want anyone else, at this point in time, share the knowledge)

◆◆◆◆◆◆◆◆◆◆◆◆◆◆◆ 簡短對話 ◆◆◆◆◆◆◆◆◆◆◆◆◆◆◆

Sawasaki: I wonder why we have to meet in Julie's office. If I've violated one of his myriad rules again, I wish he'd just tell about it instead of calling me on the carpet in front of the boss.

Yamamoto: Shoichi, aren't you forgetting one possibility?

Sawasaki: What's that?

Yamamoto: If your conscience is clear, maybe it's not about anything you've done. It could be about some other problem, don't you think?

Sawasaki: Well, let's hope so.

---

violate 違反 **myriad** 無數的 **call someone on the carpet** 訓叱某人 **conscience is clear** 問心無愧

Lesson 16

Employee Dishonesty (2)（員工的欺騙行為）

預習—*Sentences*

- I looked into the other payments.
- Unfortunately, this company is also phony.
- There's no office at the address given.
- How could Mike be so stupid?
- It was difficult for me to accept at first.

Vignette

Sawasaki: How are you supposed to verify a payment like that? Don't you just have to trust people?

Schumann: I quite understand the difficulty.What alerted me to Mike's case was the fact that he's been to eight funerals during the past year and paid up to ¥150,000 each time. I also found out that at least five of the people were either still alive or never existed.

Sawasaki: Oh?

Schumann: I became curious and looked into the other payments related to Mike. One thing I discovered is that he has approved six invoices in the last nine months from a company called Adrian Design. The total amount billed to us is about ¥ 4 million. Unfortunately, this company is also phony.

Henry: How did you find that out?

Schumann: The telephone number listed on the invoice is out of service. And there's no office at the address given. I actually went there myself. It was a condominium registered under the name of none other than Mike's wife.

Henry: Oh, but Juergen . . . How could Mike be so stupid? But isn't all of this only circumstantial evidence so far? It's hard for me to convince myself that he's really involved in any wrongdoing.

Schumann: Believe me, it was difficult for me to accept at first too. But to top all that, I got a call this morning from a finance company.

■狀況

奠儀的事已令人充滿疑惑，而請款四百萬圓要支付設計公司一事更足以令人嗅出，這是一件有計畫的罪行。亨利在得知此事後的第一個反應是，麥可怎麼會這麼傻?

澤崎：像那樣的支出，要叫人如何提出證明？你信任他們不就好了嗎？

舒曼：我十分瞭解這個困難性。不過，我之所以對麥可的事產生警覺，是因為他去年一年內參加了八次葬禮，每次的支出都高達十五萬日幣。我也發現到，那些所謂的故去者中，至少有五人不是還活著，就是根本不存在。

澤崎：哦？

舒曼：我開始好奇並調查了其它跟麥可有關的支出。結果我發現了一件事，他在過去九個月以來，核准過六張發票，是一家叫做阿得雷恩設計公司開的。發票總額是四百萬日幣。不幸的是，這家公司也是虛假的。

亨利：你怎麼發現的？

舒曼：發票上印的電話號碼已經停止使用。而發票上的地址則根本沒有辦公室。實際上，我還親自去了一趟。那是一間分戶出售的公寓，登記的所有者不是別人，正是麥可的太太。

亨利：噢，可是優根…麥可怎麼會這麼笨？不過，目前我們所有的不都只是情況（間接）證據而已嗎？我實在很難說服自己，麥可居然會跟這種罪行有牽扯！

舒曼：老實說，我一開始也很難接受。不過，最嚴重的是，我今天早上接到一通金融公司打來的電話。

Words and Phrases

alert 使…開始注意
approve 批准
invoice *n.* 發票
bill *v.* 送帳單給…
phony *adj.* 假的；虛設的
condominium 一整棟公寓建築中分戶出售的一個單位
circumstantial 情況的；根據情況判定的；間接的
convince 使…相信
wrongdoing 罪行
to top all that 尤有甚者；最嚴重的是
finance company 金融公司

Vocabulary Building

● **verify** 證明
Do you have anything to verify you are older than 18?
(你有沒有甚麼東西可以證明你已經滿十八歲了?)

● **out of service** 沒有在使用的；沒有營業的
All the phones in the area were knocked out of service by the cable fire.
(因為電纜走火，這地區附近所有的電話線路全部停止使用。)

● **none other than** 不是別人，正是…
My new secretary turned out to be none other than my wife's best friend.
(我的新祕書居然就是我太太最好的朋友。)

重點文法・語法

Believe me, it was difficult for me to accept at first.

Believe me 照文字直譯是「相信我」，但是英語之中並沒有那麼強烈的意思，一般多用在「真的」、「事實上」、「老實說」這類較輕微的語氣。若要強調「這是真的喔！請相信我」時，可說 Believe you me!

▶ Exercises

請利用括弧內的詞語改寫下列例句，並盡量保持原來的語意。

(解答見253頁)

1. How are you supposed to verify a payment like that?
   (substantiate, can you possibly)

2. How did you find that out?
   (able, determine)

3. It was difficult for me to accept at first.
   (found it, believe)

◆◆◆◆◆◆◆◆◆◆◆◆◆◆ 簡短對話 ◆◆◆◆◆◆◆◆◆◆◆◆◆◆

Henry: Was the design work actually done?

Schumann: Some of it seems to have been completed, but it's hard to tell because there's so little information in the file. One thing that's for sure is that the charges are way out of line.

Henry: I can't believe it. Mike just celebrated his 15th anniversary with the company last month.

Schumann: Computerization and electronic money transfer systems make it easier to succumb to temptation. No one's there to see the look of guilt on your face when you're doing the evil act.

Henry: Often, money is the yardstick by which people measure success and it's a very corrupting gauge.

---

for sure 確定的；肯定的 **way** 〔口語〕太過；非常地 **out of line** 不合常情的；不合理的 **anniversary** 紀念日 **electronic money transfer** 電子匯款 **succumb to temptation** 向誘惑屈服 **look of guilt** 有罪惡感的表情 **yardstick** 標準；尺度 **corrupting** 使人墮落的 **gauge** 尺度；度量標準

Lesson 16

Employee Dishonesty (3)（員工的欺騙行為）

預習—*Sentences*

- I really hope he has some good explanation.
- How did it go?
- He admitted it was a front for his wife.
- He claimed he had done nothing really wrong.
- I think he realized the game was up.

Vignette

Schumann: They're asking for a court injunction to seize Mike's salary for a ¥5 million loan on which he hasn't been making the repayments.

Henry: Juergen, you ought to talk to Mike and get his side of the story, if he has any. I really hope he has some good explanation for all this.

* * *

Henry: How did it go?

Schumann: When I faced Mike with what I knew about Adrian Design, he admitted it was a front for his wife—soon to be his ex-wife, since apparently they're in the process of getting divorced. Anyway, his story was that she actually did what he called "design consultation" for the company but that he was afraid to have her bill the company using her own name, so he had her make up this fictitious corporation, open a bank account in its name, and use her place as its mailing address. But he claimed he had done nothing really wrong.

Sawasaki: How about those fishy condolence money payments?

Schumann: When I hit him with those, together with the phone call from the loan outfit, I think he realized the game was up. He said that he would tender his resignation immediately and use his severance allowance to pay off the loan.

Henry: A case like this probably warrants a disciplinary dismissal, but I think I'll let Mike collect his voluntary severance package. Lord knows, he can certainly use the money. I only wish this hadn't happened.

Sawasaki: Don't we all!

■狀況

山口甚至還借了許多高利貸。西洋鏡被拆穿後，他打算提出辭呈，用公司給他的退職金來償清借款。公司本來是有理由立刻開除他的，但是…

舒曼：他們請求法院簽發強制令來扣押麥可的薪資，因為他跟他們借貸了五百萬日幣卻沒有償還。

亨利：優根，你應該跟麥可談談，聽聽他怎麼說，如果他有話要說的話。我真希望他對這一切能有個合理的解釋。

* * *

亨利：事情怎麼樣了?

舒曼：我把我所知關於阿得雷恩設計公司的事當面跟他提了，他承認，這是他太太的一個幌子。他太太很快就要變成他的前妻了，因為他們似乎正在辦離婚手續。不管怎樣，他的說法是，他太太真的有替公司作了一些他所謂的設計顧問工作，只是他不敢讓她用她自己的名字把帳單寄給公司。所以要她假造了這家公司，用這個公司的名義在銀行開了個戶頭，然後拿她住的地方當作通訊處。不過，他堅稱自己沒有做甚麼真正的錯事。

澤崎：還有那些虛構的喪弔金呢?

舒曼：當我質問到有關那些奠儀，還有那通借貸公司來的電話時，我想他也瞭解到遊戲結束了。他說他會立刻遞上辭呈，拿他的退職金來付清這筆借款。

亨利：在這種情況下，應該可以適用懲罰性開除了。不過，我想我會讓他使用他的自願退職方案。他當然可以用這筆錢。我只是希望這件事沒發生就好了。

澤崎：我們不都是這樣嗎!

Words and Phrases

injunction 強制令
seize [siz] 扣押
repayment 應償還的款項
face v. 使面對
front 幌子
fictitious [fɪk`tɪʃəs] 虛設的；徒有空殼的
fishy 可疑的
Game is up. 遊戲結束了；把戲被揭穿了。
tender 提出
pay off 償清
warrant [`wɔrənt] 使…成為合理
voluntary 自發的；自願的
severance package 資遣方案

Vocabulary Building

- **severance allowance** 退職金

  The company pays a generous severance allowance, but there's no pension plan for retirees.

  (對於接受資遣方案的員工，公司的給付十分優渥，可是正常退休的人員卻反而沒有退休金可拿。)

- **disciplinary dismissal** 開除以資懲戒；懲罰性開除

  The grounds for disciplinary dismissal are stated clearly in the work rules.

  (有關懲罰性開除的處罰根據，在工作守則中都說得很詳盡。)

- **Lord knows . . .** 的確

  Lord knows he's going to have a hard time finding another job.

  (對他而言，要再找份工作的確會相當困難。)

重點文法・語法

Don't we all!

感嘆句並非僅限於以 what 或 how 為首的句子。直述句、疑問句、命令句亦可作感嘆句。譬如：

I goofed! (直述句) (我敗得很慘!)

What's that! (疑問句) (那究竟是怎麼回事!)

Try harder! (命令句) (再努力點!)

"Don't we all!" 是接在 "I only wish this hadn't happened." 之後的感嘆句。像 "Don't we all (wish this hadn't happened)?" 這種型態的疑問句常被用作感嘆句。

▶*Exercises*

請利用括弧內的詞語改寫下列例句，並盡量保持原來的語意。

(解答見253頁)

1. You ought to talk to Mike and get his side of the story.
   (for, why don't, ask Mike)

2. Apparently they're in the process of getting divorced.
   (seem to be, splitting up)

3. He can certainly use the money.
   (I'm sure, needs)

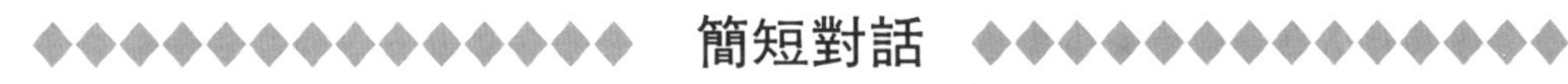

簡短對話

Henry: Juergen, I certainly owe you a big thank-you for getting to the bottom of this so efficiently.

Schumann: Oh, it's nothing. I was just doing my job.

Henry: Maybe so, but doing it very well. I realize that being an accountant isn't the best way to win friends in the company under any circumstances, and on top of that you have to cope with being a third-country national, a German working for an American company in Japan. It must really be rough at times.

Schumann: But I truly enjoy my profession. That makes it a lot easier.

---

owe 欠 **get to the bottom of** 查明…的真相 **win friends** 獲得友誼 **under any circumstances** 在任何情況下 **on top of that** 再加上 **cope with** 處理… **third-country national** 居住在第三國的國民（既非母國，又非所屬公司的本國） **rough** 不愉快的 **at times** 有時

Lesson 16 Employee Dishonesty — 總結

企業不論表面看起來多麼平穩,多少總會潛藏一些違法的事情。像 ABC 食品公司這種擁有數萬員工的企業，就相當於一個有數十萬人口的都市。在這樣的都市，當然會有犯罪，也因此才有消防隊及警察的成立。

但企業裏沒有警力，所以也無法取締員工的不法行為，因此只能跟心術不正的人鬥智。

有些人會使用公司的信封、信紙，將私人信件和公司信件一起寄出，或是用公司的影印機來影印自己的東西，如果公司對這些事情等閒視之，有些員工可能就會得寸進尺，開始把公司的文具帶回家裡，把跟女朋友吃飯的花費報在公司的交際費裡，或是把坐電車的費用虛報成坐計程車的費用。

如果這些都能安然過關，接下來就是把包給朋友的奠儀假報成是包給客戶的親友，因為奠儀不需要收據。若這也沒有引起懷疑的話，下一步就是捏造一個假葬禮，奠儀五萬元。然後，再過一段時間，葬禮的奠儀就要漲到十五萬元了！山口恐怕就是受錢財的誘惑而掉入這樣的陷阱裡吧！美國許多跨國企業會定期查核一些超額的支出項目,優根・舒曼就是在做這件事。ABC 食品公司嚴禁員工「利用回扣、賄賂或個人優待等方式，來誘使客戶下採購單、使公司在政府的法令政策中取得優惠，或用以回報對方這些利己的動作」。(all kickbacks, bribes or "personal favors" intended to induce or reward favorable buying decisions and governmental actions)。不過，一些年節時候的饋贈當然不在此限。

Lesson 17

Career Planning

（生涯規劃）

Lesson 17 的內容

澤崎昭一自從進入ABC食品公司之後，一直是兢兢業業，而且，每天都面臨不同的挑戰。可是他還是有種隱憂，覺得一直這樣下去，遲早會達到這份事業的極限。所以，他開始考慮換份工作。當他正有此念時，卻從茱莉・亨利那兒得知，紐約總公司決定要他過去。澤崎高興得難以形容。

Lesson 17

Career Planning (1)（生涯規劃）

預習—*Sentences*

- I owe you an apology, Shoichi.
- I certainly appreciate your concern.
- You know, I really have to commend you.
- You've accomplished everything expected of you.
- I think you're being too generous.

Vignette

Henry: I owe you an apology, Shoichi, for not getting around to your performance evaluation sooner. It's not that I had forgotten about it. On the contrary, your future career path with us has been one of the matters uppermost on my mind these past couple of months.

Sawasaki: Honestly, Julie, I haven't minded waiting, and I certainly appreciate your concern.

Henry: As you can see on your appraisal form, I've given you a rating of "outstanding" in all three major areas of accomplishment: customer relations, sales effectiveness, and business development. You know, I really have to commend you on an all-around excellent performance. The only problem I had in doing your appraisal is that I couldn't think of anything to put down under "evaluation of results not achieved." You've accomplished everything expected of you, and more.

Sawasaki: I must say that I think you're being too generous, especially on the last score. I've committed a blunder or two in the business development area, if you recall.

Henry: Oh, you mean that deal you initiated with the Taiwanese trading company that turned out to be a hoax? Listen, Shoichi, my philosophy is that it's far better to try many times and accept some failures along the way than only to go for the sure things. It's like baseball, where the batters with the best home-run records also strike out more than the other players. As far as I'm concerned, that Taiwan flap isn't even worth mentioning on an appraisal sheet.

Sawasaki: But aside from specific cases like that, I also feel inadequate about myself in a number of respects, especially my ability to communicate in English.

■狀況

澤崎的上司亨利終於開始考核他的工作績效了。在亨利的觀察中，澤崎簡直無懈可擊，所以她所給的評分也相當之高。

亨利：昭一,我得向你說聲抱歉，因為我沒有早點抽空做你的考績。我可不是忘了。相反地，過去幾個月來，我最常在想的事情之一就是，你在ABC食品公司日後的發展。

澤崎：茱莉，老實說，我不在乎等待，但我很感激妳的關心。

亨利：就如你在你的考核表上所看到的，在顧客關係、銷售績效，以及業務拓展三大項成績中，我給你評的都是「傑出」。你知道，我真的得誇獎你這樣全方位的優秀表現。我在做你的考核表時唯一的問題就是，在「未完成任務評量」這一欄下，我不知道可以寫些甚麼。每一件你份內的工作，你都能一一完成，甚至還超出公司的要求。

澤崎：我得說，我覺得妳太寬大了，特別是在最後一項。如果妳回想一下就會記得，在業務拓展上，我曾經犯過一兩個錯。

亨利：哦，你是指上回你主導跟臺商作生意，後來卻發現是個騙局那次嗎？聽著，昭一，我的哲學是，與其只做有把握的事，還不如多方嘗試，過程中或許有失敗，但仍是值得的。這就像棒球一樣，全壘打次數最多的打者，他遭三振的機會也比別人多得多。就我而言，那次在臺灣的失敗在這張考核表上根本不值一提。

澤崎：可是，除了像這種比較具體的事例之外，我覺得自己在好些方面也有些不足，特別是我的英文溝通能力。

Words and Phrases

apology 道歉	generous 寬大的
uppermost 最高的；最先想到的	blunder 過錯；失敗
appraisal form 考核（績）表	initiate 開始；發起
sales effectiveness 銷售績效	hoax 騙局
business development 業務拓展	flap 失敗
commend 稱讚	respect 方面

Vocabulary Building

- **get around to** 找時間做…

  It was a week before I finally got around to answering the letter.

  （等我終於有空來回那封信時，距離我收到那信已過了一星期了。）

- **it's not that** 並不是…

  It's not that I can't do that job; it's just that I don't think it's worth doing.

  （並不是我無法做那份工作，我只是認為不值得做罷了。）

- **on the contrary** 相反地

  cf. Why do you always have to be so contrary about other people's suggestions?

  （對於別人的提議，為何你老是得這樣唱反調?）

重點文法・語法

I really have to commend you on an all-around excellent performance.

all-around 是「多才多藝的」、「萬能的」、「總括性的」之意，但在英國則使用 all-round。而「多才多藝的人」、「全能選手」則是 all-arounder (all-rounder《英》）。

另外，around-the-clock 是指「持續二十四小時不斷」，有「全天候」之意，但在英國也多半使用round-the-clock。

如 around 500 years ago（約五百年前）一般，美式英語的特徵就是用around來代替about。

▶*Exercises*

請利用括弧內的詞語改寫下列例句，並盡量保持原來的語意。

(解答見253頁)

1. I owe you an apology.
   (apologize, must)

2. You've accomplished everything expected of you, and more.
   (delivered the goods, more than)

3. I've committed a blunder or two in the business development area, if you recall.
   (made a couple of errors, I may remind you)

◆◆◆◆◆◆◆◆◆◆◆◆◆◆◆ 簡短對話 ◆◆◆◆◆◆◆◆◆◆◆◆◆◆◆

Sawasaki: All these years I've been studying and using English, and I still have a hard time writing a simple business report.

Henry: Listen, there are plenty of businessmen and -women in the United States who can't even write a decent letter. You do a lot better than some people I could name at headquarters.

Sawasaki: It's nice of you to say that, but . . .

Henry: Sure, Shoichi, you still have some room for improvement in that area. But given your diligence and the present level of your skills, I'm sure you can make good progress in your writing ability if you set your mind to it.

Sawasaki: Maybe I should get myself some formal training.

Henry: That might not be a bad idea.

---

have a hard time ...ing 做…時有困難 **decent** 夠水準的；相當好的；不錯的 **room for** …的餘地 **given** 把…考量進去的話 **diligence** 勤勉 **set one's mind to** 專心做…

Lesson 17

Career Planning (2)（生涯規劃）

預習—*Sentences*

· You have a good command of English.
· I see no reason for you to feel "inadequate."
· I really felt I was learning fast.
· The easiest gains always come first.
· I enjoy hard work and responsibility.

Vignette

Henry: Now we're getting into the area of professional skills. I've rated you "outstanding" in analytical skills, planning and organization, technical expertise, and assertiveness and initiative. For verbal and written communication skills and for flexibility, my rating is "excellent" or "fully satisfactory." What I'm saying basically is that you have a good command of English but you may need to learn how to write more concisely and effectively. You might want to look into training programs in that area. Otherwise, though, I see no reason for you to feel "inadequate" in any way.

Sawasaki: Well, the first year I was with ABC Foods, I really felt I was learning fast, absorbing knowledge <u>like a dry sponge</u>, and that I was applying my new knowledge to my work pretty successfully. But now I feel that my <u>learning curve</u> is rising much slower.

Henry: That's only natural. The easiest gains always come first. You shouldn't let yourself get discouraged on that account.There's an old proverb that says, "Be not afraid of going slowly, be afraid only of standing still." I'd suggest that you might take it a little bit easier. Having said that, I should also admit that I realize you may be frustrated by the lack of attractive career opportunities for you at ABC Foods in Japan.

Sawasaki: Actually, you're right. I enjoy hard work and responsibility, and I feel a sort of obsession for excellence, if I may say so. But looking at the operation here, I realize that my career will probably <u>plateau</u> in, say, three to five years' time. In all honesty, I may want to look for new challenges at that point.

■狀況

在溝通能力和適應性方面，亨利的評分稍微低了一點。但她仍然認為澤崎的英語能力很好，不過她也建議澤崎在書寫方面能更簡潔有效率一些。

亨利：現在我們來看專業技能這一部分。在分析技巧、計畫、組織、技術性專業知識，以及做事的果斷和創造力上，我都給你打了「傑出」。至於口頭和書面上的溝通技巧，以及適應性方面，我給的是「優秀」或「十分滿意」。基本上，我要說的是，你的英文能力不錯；不過，在書寫上，你可能需要學習如何才會更簡潔、更有效率。也許你會想找一些這方面的訓練課程。不過，除了這點以外，我看不出來你有甚麼理由覺得自己還「有所不足」的。

澤崎：是這樣的，在ABC食品公司的第一年中，我真的覺得自己學得很快，吸收知識的速度像塊乾海綿。而且，我還能很成功地把新學來的東西運用到工作上。可是，我覺得現在學習曲線上升的速度慢多了。

亨利：這是很自然的啊！先到的總是最好學的東西。你不應該因為這樣就提不起勁來。有句老話說，「不怕走得慢，就怕不前進。」我建議你別把這事看得太嚴重。不過，既然都說了這些，我也該承認，我知道你可能會因為ABC食品公司日本分公司無法給你甚麼吸引人的事業機會而覺得沮喪。

澤崎：事實上，妳說對了。我很喜歡艱難的工作和身上肩負責任的感覺，而且我覺得自己對於「優秀」有點著迷，如果可以這麼說的話。可是，看到這裡的運作情形，我心裡明白，未來的三到五年間我的事業可能會就這樣停滯不前。很坦白地說，就基於這個原因，我會想要另尋挑戰。

Words and Phrases

expertise [ˌɛkspɚˋtiz] 專業知識
assertiveness 果斷
initiative 創造力；進取心
flexibility 適應性
concisely and effectively 簡潔且有效率的
absorb 吸收
having said that 既然這麼說
obsession for 對…著迷
excellence 優秀

Vocabulary Building

- **like a dry sponge** 像一塊乾海綿一樣〈比喻吸收能力強〉
  The new employee soaked up everything I taught him like a dry sponge.
  (這位新進員工吸收能力很強，我所教他的事，他像塊乾海綿一樣全都吸收進去了。)
- **learning curve** 學習曲線
  The learning curve always tends to be steeper near the beginning.
  (學習曲線在一開始的階段總是會比較陡。)
- **plateau** [plæˋto] (達到某階段後) 停滯不前
  I'm afraid that I've plateaued in my current position and can't expect any promotion.
  (我怕我會一直停留在目前的職位上，無法升遷。)

重點文法・語法

I realize you may be frustrated by the lack of attractive career opportunities.

使用字尾-ize (英式拼法是-ise) 的動詞，除了realize之外，尚有formalize (形式化)、criticize (批評)、jeopardize (使陷入危險)、hospitalize (使入院) 等已確立的字，但有部分較新的-ize 造字用法，還未獲得一般大眾的認可。

譬如 prioritize (決定先後順序)、finalize (使成最後)、normalize (正常化)、incentivize (給與獎金)、privatize (民營化) 等傳播界的流行用語，由於這些字的正誤與否尚未成定議，有些人會覺得這些不是正統英語而不予接受，所以在使用時需多考慮一下。

▶Exercises

請利用括弧內的詞語改寫下列例句，並盡量保持原來的語意。

(解答見253頁)

1. I see no reason for you to feel "inadequate."
   (there's, "not capable")

2. You shouldn't let yourself get discouraged on that account.
   (don't let, discourage you)

3. In all honesty, I may want to look for new challenges at that point.
   (to be honest with you, change in my career)

◆◆◆◆◆◆◆◆◆◆◆◆◆◆◆◆ 簡短對話 ◆◆◆◆◆◆◆◆◆◆◆◆◆◆◆◆

Henry: All in all, Shoichi, I'd say you're a real quick study. You seem to pick up new information so fast that it doesn't surprise me that you find your pace of absorption slowing down after a while.

Sawasaki: Well, I guess if you took at it that way . . .

Henry: Another area where I have to rate you highly is your ability to respond to criticism in a constructive manner.

Sawasaki: Actually, I hate being criticized, but I hate even more letting myself get irritated by it. So I try my best to accept it if it's valid and modify my options or behavior accordingly.

Henry: If only everybody in the office would take that approach!

---

all in all 總之 **quick study** 學習能力強的人 **absorption** 吸收 **after a while** 不久 **rate highly** 給予很高評價 **constructive** 建設性的 **get irritated** 變得急躁 **valid** 合理的

Lesson 17

Career Planning (3)（生涯規劃）

預習—*Sentences*

· I don't think I'm ready for a change.
· I think that's a highly realistic assessment.
· The assignment will be for a period of at least three years.
· I'm sure you'll get a lot out of it.
· Don't thank me, thank yourself.

Vignette

Henry: I'm sure that a highly marketable young individual like you will have no trouble finding job offers, if you haven't received some already.

Sawasaki: I'd be lying if I said I hadn't. Right now I don't think I'm ready for a change. There's still so much I want to learn about this business. But I also recognize that sooner or later I'm likely to run into a career block within ABC Foods.

Henry: Shoichi, I think that's a highly realistic assessment of your own prospects with this company—if you stay in Japan, that is.

Sawasaki: Could you explain what you mean by that?

Henry: Sure. What I mean is that you should experience an overseas assignment to keep from falling into a rut here. It would broaden your horizons, and it should also unblock your path to further advancement within the organization. Based on some earlier conversations we've had, I've recommended you for a transfer to Corporate Marketing in New York. The official approval just came in this morning. Congratulations, Shoichi.

Sawasaki: I, er . . . Thanks, Julie.

Henry: The assignment will be for a period of at least three years. You'll be exposed to various phases of our business in the States, and eventually you can expect to return here as a key member of our management team. I'm sure you'll get a lot out of it, and I'm confident that you'll enjoy it too.

Sawasaki: This is so sudden, I don't know exactly what to say. But I really appreciate your support, and I'll do my best to live up to your expectations. Anyway, thank you.

Henry: Don't thank me, thank yourself. You earned it.

■狀況

最後，亨利告訴澤崎一個大消息：要轉任紐約公司行銷部門的人選已正式決定，兩個月後，澤崎將調到紐約總公司。

亨利：我確信，像你這樣一位如此有潛力的年輕人，要找到新工作絕非難事，搞不好已經有人向你接頭了。

澤崎：假如我說沒有的話，那就是在說謊了。不過，我覺得自己現在還沒有準備好要換工作。在這個行業中，我要學的還有很多。不過，我也很清楚，繼續待在ABC食品公司的話，我遲早要碰到生涯瓶頸的。

亨利：昭一，我想你這樣子評估你在這家公司的前景，是相當實際的，——也就是說，如果你還一直待在日本的話。

澤崎：妳可以解釋一下這是甚麼意思嗎？

亨利：當然。我的意思是，為了不使你因為一直待在這裏而陷入一種公式化的狀態，你應該嘗試點不同的歷練，像是調派到海外去。這會擴大你的視野，而且也能突破你前面的事業道路，使你在這個組織內有晉升的可能。根據我們早先的一些談話，我已經向上級推薦，把你調到紐約的公司行銷部門。我今天早上剛收到正式的批准。恭喜了，昭一。

澤崎：我，呃…謝謝，茱莉。

亨利：這個職務至少有三年。你在美國，會接觸到我們這個事業的各個層面。結束之後，你可能會回到這裏，成為我們管理階層的重要份子。我確定，你會有很大的收穫，而且，我也相信你會很喜歡的。

澤崎：這件事太突然了，我不知道該說甚麼。不過，我真的很感激妳的支持，我也會盡力達到妳的期望。無論如何，謝謝妳。

亨利：別謝我，謝你自己吧！這是你應得的。

Words and Phrases

marketable 可開發的；有潛能的
individual 個人
assignment 任務
unblock *v.* 掃除障礙
advancement 晉升；升遷
transfer 調職
be exposed to 置身於…的情況下；有機會接觸到…
phase 階段
live up to 使自己達到…（別人的期望）
You earned it. 這是你應得的。

Vocabulary Building

- **career block** 事業（生涯）的瓶頸

  cf. Jack found his career path blocked by the large number of senior employees in the company.

  （傑克發現到，公司裡為數眾多的資深員工阻礙了他事業往前的道路。）

- **rut** 一成不變（的狀態）；常規

  Don't let yourself get into a rut, either personally or professionally.

  （不管你是在個人或事業上，都不要讓自己落入一成不變的狀態中。）

- **horizons** 視野

  It is often said that travel broadens one's horizons.

  （常言道，旅行能拓展人的視野。）

重點文法・語法

It should also unblock your path to further advancement within the organization.

形容詞、副詞的比較級、最高級，一般是在原來的詞後面加上-er, -est, 或以more、most 修飾。但是也有像 good / better / best, bad / worse / worst 的不規則變化。

這裡的 further 也是不規則變化的一種，原形為 far。far 的比較級有 farther 和 further 兩種，使用方法各不相同，前者指「距離」，後者指「程度或量」，但現代英語（特別是口語）中，兩種情況都使用further，幾乎見不到 farther 這個字了。

▶Exercises

請利用括弧內的詞語改寫下列例句，並盡量保持原來的語意。

(解答見253頁)

1. I'd be lying if I said I hadn't.
   (have to admit, have)

2. You can expect to return here as a key member of our management team.
   (be a key player on, after you)

3. I'll do my best to live up to your expectations.
   (all I can, disappoint you)

◆◆◆◆◆◆◆◆◆◆◆◆◆◆◆ 簡短對話 ◆◆◆◆◆◆◆◆◆◆◆◆◆◆◆

Henry: Oh, one more thing, Shoichi.

Sawasaki: Yeah?

Henry: I do hope you won't have to leave your family behind when you go to the States, the way so many Japanese businessmen seem to these days.

Sawasaki: Well, as you realize, the children's education tends to be a paramount concern for a lot of people. They're afraid that their kids won't be able to get into good schools if they spend too long abroad.

Henry: That strikes me as rather sad.

Sawasaki: I agree. Personally, I think it's good chance for children to be exposed to a different culture. I'll have to discuss this with Etsuko, but I'm almost positive she'll want us all to go together.

---

leave one's family behind 把家人留下，隻身前往 **paramount** 最重要的；優先的 **concern** 關心的事 **strike** 給某人留下深刻印象 **positive** 確信的

Lesson 17 Career Planning — 總結

適值第一冊的末了，請讀者記得本課茱莉・亨利所說過的話。

“It's far better to try many times and accept some failures along the way than only to go for the sure things.”「與其只做有把握的事，還不如多方嘗試，過程中或有失敗，也是值得。」

然後亨利更以棒球為比方 ，“The batters with the best home-run records also strike out more than the other players.”「全壘打次數最多的打者，他遭三振的機會也比別人來得多。」

美國的棒球大聯盟中，曾經有位名叫 Ty Cobb的著名外野手。保持三點六七的打擊紀錄，盜壘134次，成功了96次，成功率約百分之七十二。Cobb 也被稱作 the greatest player in baseball history, 1936年進入 Baseball Hall of Fame（棒球名人堂）。

還有一位名叫Max Carey的選手。盜壘53次，成功51次，成功率約達百分之九十六。

喜歡棒球的美國人都知道 Ty Cobb, 但是Max Carey 甚至沒有被列入The World Almanac Book of Who 的紀錄。

如果凡事都要等到有十足把握才下手去做，那恐怕不知道要等到何年何月了。我們不應害怕犯錯。我想這個道理不僅適用於商業界，語言的學習也是一樣的。要勇於嘗試，說出來，不要怕，語言能力的進步就決定於此！

Answers to Exercises

Lesson 1

(1)

1. You were more qualified than anyone to get the job.
2. I feel embarrassed addressing you as Tom.
3. You'll return to normal before long.

(2)

1. Show Shoichi how to do his expense sheets.
2. There's nothing Nancy doesn't know about the company.
3. I can give you some tips about fine restaurants near here.

(3)

1. You were with International Foods, I understand.
2. Also they're less aggressive than we are.
3. You'll soon get used to our corporate style.

Lesson 2

(1)

1. I'd really like you to help me figure out how this company runs.
2. I'd like to offer to you as much help as you need.
3. Let me know if there's anything unclear to you.

(2)

1. I was told the office was open from 9 to 5:30.
2. Managers are allowed to choose their own work schedules.
3. You're supposed to work minimum of 37½ hours a week.

(3)

1. It's against employee rules to eat in the conference room.
2. It's possible you may receive presents from vendors.
3. Semi–yealy gifts and occasional dinner invitations are all right.

Lesson 3

(1)

1. Pardon me. I didn't recognize your name.
2. Do you mind spelling your name for me, sir?
3. Does Mr. Noonan understand what this is all about?

(2)

1. I'm afaid Mr. Noonan is occupied at the moment.
2. When's the most convenient time of the day to call him?
3. He's busy with out-of-town visitors this week.

(3)

1. It's been a long time since I last heard from you.
2. It sounds like you're calling from a far-off country.
3. I'll leave Hong Kong next week to visit Tokyo.

Lesson 4

(1)

1. I'd like to know what business you have in Tokyo this time.
2. I'm being transferred to Tokyo shortly.
3. I'm positive your employer will help you locate a nice place.

(2)

1. I can't help but feel it'll be an unproductive meeting.
2. Would you like to give him a tour before bringing him in?
3. Is he expecting you?

(3)

1. The findings of the market research are quite reassuring.
2. Take a look at our detailed quantitative study presented in this report.
3. According to our research, your company has a strong quality image.

Lesson 5

(1)

1. The computer center just opened, so I haven't visited it either.
2. I'm worried about this presentation I have to give in New York.
3. I intend to spend the last weekend in Hawaii en route to Tokyo.

(2)

1. Could you give them a ring and advise them I will be absent?
2. You were good enough to catch my grammatical mistakes and correct them.
3. I'd be helpess without your assistance.

(3)

1. You know how to reach me.
2. I guess you can hold all invoices until I come back.
3. You are a sweet person, Shoichi. But that's all right.

Lesson 6

(1)

1. The flight was very pleasant but I had a most bizarre encounter.
2. Professional thieves need just a few seconds to do the job.
3. Police said that I was the sixth visitor from Japan to get into trouble.

(2)

1. Some speakers were so boring they put me to sleep.
2. Your card says you're with ABC Foods.
3. Farmers are greatly dependent on feed grains from overseas.

(3)

1. Soaring land costs are forcing people to commute to work over increasingly long distances.
2. You've already spent a great deal of energy by the time you get to the office.
3. Are housing costs high in Japan?

Lesson 7

(1)

1. That was the most splendid dinner I've enjoyed in many years.
2. The least expensive steak dinner would cost 200 percent more in Tokyo.
3. Now that strikes me as a decent institution.

(2)

1. I object to that kind of aggressive style.
2. It's so troublesome for us to calculate how much to give the waiter.
3. That's not a good answer to my dilemma.

(3)

1. What if the service was below par?
2. In my opinion, you'd better leave something all the time.
3. You can always choose not to return to the same place.

Lesson 8

(1)

1. I wish to have dinner with you tonight.
2. I appreciated his thoughtfulness, but I didn't like the place.
3. Is there any problem with raw fish?

(2)

1. You need a native to hit a restaurant like this.
2. I wonder how your first visit to headquarters went.
3. Knowing the key people on the other end is a necessity.

(3)

1. It'll adversely affect our cash flow.
2. Japanese corporations sometimes use promissory notes in paying their suppliers.
3. Don't they understand that you don't provide banking services ?

Lesson 9

(1)

1. Those accountants are always in a hurry to get something done.
2. I want to talk to you about the statement you turned in for the NewYork visit.
3. Perhaps you misunderstand a few things.

(2)

1. Honestly speaking, my friend in New Jersey put me up.
2. In that case, you can't charge the company for accommodations.
3. I take it that you ate breakfast and some other meals at your friend's house.

(3)

1. Don't forget to mention who you had the business lunch with.
2. You don't have to apologize.
3. You should be congratulated for turning in your report promptly.

Lesson 10

(1)

1. You haven't smoked a cigarette ever since your return from the U.S.
2. The only way to be a non-smoker is just not to smoke.
3. I finally figured out how much damage I was causing to myself.

(2)

1. There is a sharp drop in the number of smokers everywhere.
2. The police department should be more concerned about the guy who took your bag than about me.
3. Who do you think you are to push me around?

(3)

1. Extinguish your cigarette, or leave.
2. I've heard a rumor that several heavy smokers were let go in recent weeks.

3. whatever you tell me, I intend to keep on smoking.

Lesson 11

(1)

1. I mean his wellness program, not the Arabic language.
2. Do I have to show you my pink leotard to convince you that I'm actually doing it?
3. Seriously, 75 percent of my class are men in their forties.

(2)

1. It's becoming increasingly important for businesspeople to live a healthy lifestyle.
2. Our conclusion was we'd kick off a health-related movment.
3. It aims at encouraging regular exercise, starting with our employees.

(3)

1. That way, the sometime athletes will be out.
2. Simultaneously, we'll produce pamphlets on how to structure in–house wellness programs.
3. Free copies should be distributed.

Lesson 12

(1)

1. It appears as though you are keeping busy.
2. Please keep it between you and me.
3. The decision was a very hard to make after a quarter century.

(2)

1. You'll be missed very much.
2. I never realized that you might be leaving.
3. This way ABC Foods can make our payroll lean without being mean.

(3)

1. They've had brilliant success in marketing their products in Japan.
2. They made him the president of the company not long ago.
3. My successor coming from New York is an awfully able person.

Lesson 13

(1)

1. What did you hae on your mind when you said you wanted to talk to me?

2. Thank you for being so thoughtful.
3. Allow me to be perfectly honest with you, will you?

(2)

1. You're not the only one to react like that.
2. Male subordinates and female bosses often have strained relationships.
3. My wife doesn't know that I now report to a woman.

(3)

1. Without regard to sex, some people just aren't fit to drive.
2. Men would sometimes swear in my presence.
3. You wouldn't want to report to a female supervisor on account of her sex.

Lesson 14

(1)

1. To tell the truth, he doesn't surprise me.
2. He's come to me twice before to inquire about a missing document.
3. If you don't know in which file a document is filed, it might as well have been lost.

(2)

1. Did you ever take a good look around our offices lately?
2. It bothers me to think how much time is lost trying to locate missing files.
3. Were there any complaints about having to report to work on a weekend?

(3)

1. We even presented a special award to the person who discarded the most paper.
2. An award should be given to someone who can think up a more efficient central filing system.
3. There's always somebody who abhors dumping paper.

Lesson 15

(1)

1. I never knew you were still working.
2. I have been busy reviewing a status report turned in by a product manager.
3. Do you mean to suggest that I can be dispensed with?

(2)

1. I prefer being a workaholic to being an alcoholic.
2. Working hard is not the same as being a workaholic.
3. I've been too busy to since I joined this company.

(3)

1. His wife was looking at me with an angry expression.
2. He stopped working for the company two or three years ago.
3. Whether you like it or not, the truth is you are.

Lesson 16

(1)

1. He said he wanted you to come to Jule's office for a meeting.
2. He didn't say what the subject was, but he sounded awfully grim.
3. I don't want anyone else to share the knowledge at this point in time.

(2)

1. How can you possibly substantiate a payment like that?
2. How were you able to determine that?
3. It found it diffcult to believe at first.

(3)

1. Why don't you ask Mike for his side of the story?
2. They seem to be in the process of splitting up.
3. I'm sure he needs the money.

Lesson 17

(1)

1. I must apologize to you.
2. You've more than delivered the goods.
3. I've made a couple of errors in the business development area, if I may remind you.

(2)

1. There's no reason for you to feel "not capable."
2. Don't let that discourage you.
3. To be honest with you, I may want to look for a change in my career.

(3)

1. I have to admit I have.
2. After you return here, you can expect to be a key player on our management team.
3. I'll do all I can not to disappoint you.

Key Words and Idioms

單字片語一覽表

課文中出現的主要單字及片語依字母順序檢索如下。
括孤內的數字表示該單字出現的頁數

exorbitant （價格、要求等）過高的；過分的 (84)
expect 預期；期待 (52)
expense account 開支帳 (130)
expense report 開支報告(122)
expense sheet 費用傳票 (14)
expertise 專業知識 (238)
extra 額外的 (196)
extremely 極度地；極端地 (18)

F

face 使面對 (228)
Fair enough. 好吧；可以啊！〈消極地同意對方所說之事〉 (122)
fall apart （體制的）瓦解；破裂 (210)
fantastic 極好的 (70)
fantastically 極好地 (172)
fare 費用 (98)
fatigue 疲勞 (150)
favorite 最喜歡的人或物 (112)
feasibility report 可行性報告 (192)
feed grains 穀物飼料 (84)
feel at home 感覺像在自己本國內 (94)
fictitious 虛設的；只有空殼的 (228)
fiend （耽於某事的）迷；狂 (154)
file cabinet 檔案櫃 (192)
fill out 填寫 (14)
finance company 金融公司 (224)
fishy 可疑的 (228)
fistful 一把之量（的） (98)
fit 強健的；身體狀況佳的 (52)
flap 失敗 (234)
flexibility 適應性 (238)
flexible 有彈性的 (32)
flextime (flexitime) 彈性工時〈員工可以彈性調整上下班時間，只要上班時數達到公司要求即可〉 (28)
flight 航空旅行 (80)
folk etymology 通俗語源〈像是 tulip 解釋成 two lips〉 (98)
folks 雙親；親屬 (182)
food additive 食品添加物 (42)
for a change 改變一下 (214)
for a second 一下子；瞬間 (94)
for Christ's sake 看在老天的分上 (140)
for good 永遠 (136)
foreign legion 外籍兵團 (168)
free lunch 不要錢的午餐 (32)
freezing 極冷的 (84)
front 幌子 (228)
frugality 節儉 (210)
function 職責；功用；集會 (14)
funeral 葬禮 (220)

G

Game is up 遊戲結束了。〈把戲被拆穿了〉 (228)
garner 獲得 (60)

H

I

(196)

marketable 可開發的；有潛能的 (242)

marvelous 奇妙的；難以置信的 (52)

mass transit system 大眾運輸系統 (88)

matter of fact 實際上 (136)

meat-packing 〔美〕精肉業的 (84)

mentor 良師；導師 (168)

mess 一團糟 (196)

mid-50s 五十五歲左右 (164)

middle-aged 中年的 (150)

mid-year and year-end gifts 年中及歲暮時的饋贈 (220)

minority 少數派 (140)、(182)

miscellaneous 雜費 (130)

miss 想念 (168)

missing 不見了；失蹤的 (192)

misunderstanding 誤會 (122)

monitor 監督 (158)

moral 教訓；寓意 (144)

Mr. Noonan's office. 諾南先生辦公室。(38)

Ms. 女士〈用於稱呼未婚或不明其婚姻狀況的女性〉 (10)

N

nasty 惡意的 (144)

neat 整齊的 (200)

never-ending 永無休止的 (206)

newsstand 書報攤 (80)

nicotine 尼古丁 (136)

night on the town （遊逛）夜晚的街道 (126)

No kidding. 不是開玩笑的吧！(164)

none other than 不是別人，正是… (224)

nonexistent 不存在的 (102)

not again 別又是那回事了吧 (220)

not that it matters 也不是甚麼要緊的事 (28)

O

objective 目標 (154)

oblige 答應請求 (144)

obsession for 對…的著迷 (238)

on a kick 熱衷於某事 (144)

on occasion 有時；偶而 (102)

on one's own 獨自地；獨力 (172)

on that score 在那一點上 (220)

on the contrary 相反地 (234)

on the line 在線上 (42)

One moment, please 請稍等。(38)

one or the other 兩者其中之一 (130)

open 敞開心胸的；沒有隱瞞的；率直的 (18)

opt for 選擇… (130)

option 選擇 (164)

order around 把人差來差去 (140)

orient 使適應環境；使熟悉狀況 (18)

out of service 沒有在使用的；沒有營

業的 (224)

out of this world 不同凡響的；舉世無雙的 (52)

out of town （因出差到外地而）不在〈out-of-town *adj.* 從外地來的〉(46)

outgoing 外向的；離開的；卸任的 (182)

outlook 前途；見解 (186)

out-of-pocket expenses 實際開支 (126)

outsider 局外人；非本公司的人 (10)

overweight 肥胖的；過重的 (154)

P

pace 為…調整步調 (214)

pack 一包（香菸）(136)

pass over 略過；忽視 (144)

passive smoke 抽二手菸〈因旁邊有人吸菸使然〉(144)

pasture 牧場 (84)

path will cross 會再碰面 (172)

pay off 償清 (228)

payable 到期應付的 (116)

payroll 員工總數 (168)

per diem 每日的零用金 (126)

perfect 完美的；熟練的 (10)

performance 工作表現；業績 (28)

perpetual 永久的；無終止的 (168)

perseverance 毅力 (182)

personal 親展〈也可用 Personal and Confidential〉(74)

Ph.D. 博士學位；擁有博士學位的人 (172)

phase 階段 (242)

phony 假的；虛設的 (224)

physical fitness 身體狀況良好 (150)

pitch 〔俗〕發表；宣傳 (66)

pizza 披薩 (200)

plateau （到達某一階段後）停滯不前 (238)

porter 腳夫；侍者 (94)

porterage 運費 (130)

position 為…定位 (158)

positive 確信的 (66)

power breakfast meeting 早餐會報〈邊用早餐邊開會〉(206)

prefer 偏好… (32)

preprinted 事先印好的 (102)

presume 認為；推想 (126)

pro (〈professional) 專家；熟諳此道者 (80)

procedure 程序 (130)

projection 預測 (60)

prominently 突出的；醒目的 (98)

promissory note 期票 (112)

promotability 升遷的可能性 (200)

promptness 迅速；敏捷 (98)

proof 校樣 (70)

Q

R

S

T

take something personally 把某事當作人身攻擊 (130)

talented 有才能的 (172)

telemarketing 電話行銷〈利用電話來推廣產品〉 (192)

tend to 傾向於… (94)

tender 提出 (228)

tentatively 暫時的；試驗性的 (154)

That's just the point. 那就是問題所在。(196)

That's not a bad deal. 這個交易不壞。(94)

theory 理論；學理 (98)

things 事情；事態 (46)

those types 那些類型的人 (210)

thoughtful 體貼的；設想周到的 (108)

thoughtfulness 設想周到 (178)

threaten 威脅 (182)

three quarters 四分之三 (150)

throw out 丟掉 (196)

tidy 整齊的 (196)

to be honest with you 坦白跟你說 (126)

to say the least 至少 (18)

to top all that 尤有甚者；最嚴重的是 (224)

tolerate 認可；容忍 (154)

toss out 丟棄 (200)

tour （工廠等的）參觀；巡禮 (56)

transfer 調職 (182)、(242)

traveler's check 旅行支票 (70)

trifling 微小的；瑣碎的 (192)

turn away 不理睬 (46)

turn in 呈交；提出 (206)

U

unacceptable 無法接受的 (24)

unblock 掃除障礙 (242)

uneasy 不安的 (52)

up to par 達到標準的 (102)

upbringing 教養 (178)

updated 最新的 (192)

up-market 高檔市場的 (60)

uppermost 最高的；最先想到的 (234)

ups and downs 起伏；變動 (46)

urgent 緊急的 (70)、(122)

V

verification 證明 (126)

verify 証明 (224)

vice 惡習 (136)

Vice is nice. 惡癖乃是魅力。(140)

voluntary 自發的；自願的 (228)

W

want something done yesterday 很急地要某件事盡速完成〈今天才命令下去，卻希望早在昨天就已做好〉 (122)

Y

三民新英漢辭典

—— (增訂完美版) ——

⊙收錄詞目增至67,500項　（詞條增至46,000項）。

⊙新增搭配欄，羅列常用詞語間的組合關係，讓讀者掌握英語的慣用搭配，說出道地的英語。

⊙詳列原義、引申義，確實掌握字詞釋義，加強英語字彙的活用能力。

⊙附有精美插圖千餘幅，輔助詞義理解。

⊙附錄包括詳盡的「英文文法總整理」、「發音要領解說」，提昇學習效率。

⊙雙色印刷，並附彩色簡明英、美及世界地圖。

在學及進修者　適用

三民袖珍英漢辭典

- 收錄字數最多，詞條達58,000字。
- 從最新的商業用語、時事用詞到日常生活用語等詞彙全數網羅。
- 字義解釋廣泛，爲輔助上班族和大學生學習的最佳利器。
- 雙色套印，查閱更便捷。
- 輕巧便利的口袋型設計，最適於外出攜帶。

上班族・大專生 適用